Libby Purves is a writer and also a broadcaster who has presented the talk programme *Midweek* on Radio 4 since 1984 and formerly presented *Today*. She is a main columnist on *The Times* and in 1999 was named the Granada 'What the Papers Say' Columnist of the Year, and awarded an O.B.E for services to journalism.

This is her ninth novel. Her previous novels include *Casting Off*, *A Long Walk in Wintertime*, *Home Leave*, *More Lives Than One*, *Regatta*, *Passing Go*, *A Free Woman* and *Mother Country*. She has also written an account of her thirty-year broadcasting career, *Radio: A True Love Story*.

She lives in Suffolk with her husband the broadcaster and writer Paul Heiney, and their son and daughter.

CONTINENTAL DRIFT

Henry is a radio DJ: young, hip and single, but fretting about his little son. Philip is an ex-MP, ruined by scandal and disowned by his party; Diana, his long-suffering wife, is struggling to find a life of her own. Marianne is three stone overweight after glumly replacing her husband with chocolate eclairs and gin. Lizzie is battling with illness and trying not to think about it. Into their lives, by accident, comes Eva: a naïve and happy Polish backpacker working her way round Europe. As the values of their comfortable world clash with those of emerging Eastern Europe, the five English characters find comedy, tragedy and romance unfolding with bewildering speed.

Books by Libby Purves
Published by The House of Ulverscroft:

CASTING OFF
A LONG WALK IN WINTERTIME
HOME LEAVE
MORE LIVES THAN ONE
REGATTA
PASSING GO
A FREE WOMAN
MOTHER COUNTRY
RADIO: A TRUE LOVE STORY

LIBBY PURVES

◆

CONTINENTAL DRIFT

Complete and Unabridged

CHARNWOOD
Leicester

First published in Great Britain in 2003 by
Hodder and Stoughton
London

First Charnwood Edition
published 2004
by arrangement with
Hodder and Stoughton
a division of Hodder Headline
London

British Library CIP Data

Purves, Libby
    Continental drift.—Large print ed.—
Charnwood library series
    1. Poles—Great Britain—Fiction
    2. England—Social life and customs—Fiction
    3. Large type books
    I. Title
    823.9′14 [F]

    ISBN 1–84395–244–0

Published by
F. A. Thorpe (Publishing)
Anstey, Leicestershire

Set by Words & Graphics Ltd.
Anstey, Leicestershire
Printed and bound in Great Britain by
T. J. International Ltd., Padstow, Cornwall

This book is printed on acid-free paper

To young Peggy Tinsley who once crossed
the Continent in the other direction

1

'Okayyyy!' called the young man, throwing his head back and blinking a little in the bright spring sunshine. 'Let's get mooo-ving!' He reached for the sunglasses which lay on the loudspeaker beside him, and which were already beginning to vibrate and jump to the rising beat of the music. Clapping them on to his face with one practised movement, he gave a fluid little shimmy, stabbed heavenwards with the microphone, and — returning it to the level of his chin — completed the sentence with, 'Bee-cause — here come — da Village People! Whoo, boys!'

The music swung on, exhorting young men to Go West. Apart from the one with the microphone, however, and a balding technician sitting in a white van with a vast roof aerial, there were few men under sixty in sight. The Market Square at this hour was the preserve of women shoppers, pensioners and lunch-hour schoolchildren perching on the stone horse-trough with bags of chips from McDonald's. Smaller children, shopping reluctantly with their mothers, began to bounce to the music, slowing down their burdened parents still further and threatening the stability of overladen baby-buggies. Shopkeepers looked on, mildly diverted. A small dog lifted its leg against the placard bearing a snaky logo and the legend RADIO 2C ROADSHOW — COMING 2 C YOU!

'Whooo!' yelled the disc jockey, over a bridge in the music. 'Coming next — the Where Am I? quiz! And later, our very own Madam Mayor, live and kickin'!' He nodded to the technician cramped in the front seat of the white van, who flipped the fader shut. Once he had seen its red light fade the young man stuffed the microphone into the pocket of his khaki combat trousers. Next to the platform, a blonde woman in a blue quilted vest and striped blouse, who had been scribbling on a clipboard, looked up at him. She pointed to the watch hanging round her neck on a rather folksy embroidered strap.

'Henry!' she said, with faint maternal exasperation in her tone.

'What?' said the man, still jigging to the music. His tone was far from irritable: he fixed her with a beaming grin.

'There isn't time for the Where Am I? quiz,' said the woman, pointing now at her board. 'Now that you've started another record, you'll have to go straight to the news and weather.'

'There's three minutes!' Henry brandished his own watch, which swung on a leather bootlace against his exuberantly garish palm-tree-patterned shirt.

'Yeah, but Roger said we had to do the trailer. For the Silver Band Concert. It's' — she glanced down at her board — 'a minute-fifteen.'

'I hate silver bands,' said Henry, with the grand simplicity of a spoiled child who expects no contradiction. 'And Roger's gone off somewhere, so how he expects — '

'Bog,' said the hitherto silent technician from

2

the car. He had a loud, rasping voice, and on the pavement a white-haired lady with a wicker shopping trolley jumped nervously. 'Roger went to the Gents under the Town Hall. Got the squitters, I reckon. Moanin' about how you shouldn't eat mussels this far from the sea. Third time since we got here.'

'It's not my job to tell you what to do, Henry,' said the blonde woman, with amiable calm. 'But Roger will be furious if you don't do the Silver Band trail. And so will Steve. It's costing a lot of money.' She glanced to the left along the handsome Georgian frontages of the square, towards a discreet stone sign saying WC. A familiar figure was emerging, trudging towards them with the despondent air of a man still preoccupied with his digestive system. She jerked her head warningly. 'He's coming back. Do something.'

'Voiceover,' said the young man. He pulled out the microphone and made a swooping sign with his hand at the technician, who obediently flipped the microphone to LIVE and faded the music as the next chorus began. Two schoolgirls, hanging around outside Top Shop, began to wander towards his podium. He grinned at them, pushed a button on the grimy cartridge machine at his side, and abruptly the Village People were overlaid by an echoing, sepulchral version of Henry's voice saying 'Where Am I Now?' and a tape of birdsong, sawing noises and a child's voice singing a snatch of folk-song. 'I'm looking at larches, and chimneys with a history,' said Henry, live and unechoing this time, which

3

caused a couple of mothers with pushchairs to appear slightly baffled as they glanced around the treeless, birdless square. 'The clue is in the beat of a dark bird's wing. Oh, yeah!' He signalled for the music to fade up again and began singing along: '*Go We-eest, life is peaceful there, go West, lots of open air* . . . ' Then he tired of this, made a snapping-shut gesture at the man in the van, and twirled his microphone between his fingers as the two schoolgirls, giggling, approached the podium.

'We know!'

'We did it in Environmental Studies!'

'It's Ravenbrook, innit? Where the old sawmill was and the house wiv three chimneys?'

The producer was nearly with them now, and the woman in the blue quilted vest cast a glance of wary amusement at the two men's meeting.

'What you doing the quiz for?' hissed Roger, ignoring the schoolgirls. He was a pale, dumpy man in his late-thirties, almost a full foot shorter than the rangy disc jockey. He moved out of earshot of the listening girls and jabbed his finger at the DJ. 'God, I just go to the bog for five minutes and you start sodding around . . . we used the last prize of the week yesterday, remember? Because we were holding over the quiz till Monday?'

The presenter clapped his hand to his brow and said, 'Su-gar! Never mind. Winners must have prizes or society collapses! Mic, please.' As his microphone went live and the music faded again he said smoothly: 'And we've even got winners, in record time — two lurrrvly girls

4

— what's your name, sweetheart?'

'Janine,' said the taller of the two, dark-haired and heavyset. Her friend nudged her sharply.

'Shurrup! We're s'posed to be in a study period. Dickhead!'

'Like, who's going to be listening in school?' said Janine.

'Your mum listens!'

Henry's smoothness did not desert him. 'Ja-ja-gorgeous-Janine!' he said. 'Lovely golden hair there.' He winked, and the two girls convulsed with giggles. 'Bet you're glad you're too old for school now!'

The blonde woman and the producer exchanged despairing glances. Roger made a gesture with his hands to indicate that Henry was laying it on rather too thick. Henry saw it, grinned, and laid it on thicker. 'And I like the tattoo, Janine — great idea having your Uni crest on your collarbone — I always hadda weakness for students.'

Janine exploded into giggles. Her friend, after a moment of slow-witted shock, followed her. 'Anyhow — you guessed the quiz right, you said Ravenbrook, so you deserve a prize,' said Henry. 'And here it is! A unique prize! Listeners at home, just imagine the thrill as Hezza W. loses his shirt to two beautiful tattooed chicks . . .'

Listeners at home would have heard his voice grow muffled for a moment, becoming indistinct against the jaunty bounce of the faded music. To the intense amusement of the woman with the clipboard, and the alarm of the pallid producer,

5

in one swift movement the young man peeled off his Hawaiian shirt, revealing a muscular torso and a glimpse of boxer shorts above the waistband of his trousers.

'And what a prize, to kick off Two C-Comes-To-See-You week! A Hezza Hawaii-Five-O shirt, all for you. Or your boyfriend, 'cos my shirts iz too *macho* for babes.' He threw the shirt at the giggling girls, and added in suddenly severe tones: 'But now — to take us into the two o'clock news from Claudie back in the studio — hear about the weekend's high spot: Silver Band Sunday goes live! Maeve McCutcheon's got news of that!' He held his nose and pulled an imaginary lavatory chain as a blare of trumpets filled the square from the loudspeakers, drowning the last words of the song. A woman's amplified voice began to talk excitedly about the concert. Then Henry nodded to the technician, mouthed 'Straight to news!' and stepped down, laying the microphone on the loudspeaker with the complacent air of having completed a job with credit.

'You're a bloody liability,' said Roger crossly. 'Get some clothes on or we'll have the police round.'

'I've got another two shirts in the back of the van,' said the bare-chested Henry cheerfully, taking off his sunglasses and polishing them on the back of his trousers.

'Two spares, yet! So much for spontaneous gestures,' jeered the blonde woman, laying her clipboard down on the edge of his little stage. 'I don't suppose Sir Walter Raleigh had a couple of

6

spare cloaks standing by. How long've you been planning that little stunt?'

'I've been waiting,' he said sententiously, 'for a chance to show my hard-earned abs and pecs to a woman of the world like yourself, who appreciates the finer things of life.' Off the air, the young man's manner was quieter, crisper, even cultivated. The manager of Two Counties Radio, who had never quite conquered his own Brummie vowels, was once provoked to describe him as 'a black Bertie Wooster'.

'Cover up, for God's sake,' said the producer. 'Diana, is there any chance — '

'I was just going to ask,' said the woman affably. 'Who wants coffee? I can nip to Starbucks and be back by the one-ten handover.'

'Do that,' said Roger wearily. 'Gimme the board, I'll be OK if you don't make it in time. But not coffee, Tazo tea for me. Coffee sets my stomach off.'

'Dave?'

'Milky one for me,' said the technician, easing out of the car and stretching his limbs. 'No sugar. Can I have a muffin?' He fumbled for change in his pockets.

'Hez?' said the woman.

'Cappuccino. I'll come and give you a hand,' said Henry. 'Might have a pastry.' He sucked in his smooth dark stomach and patted his chest complacently.

'You bloody well will not!' exploded the producer. 'You'll put your bloody shirt on and sit right here, going through the running order for the second hour. The Mayor is coming to talk

7

about the Jubilee Appeal.'

Henry winked, and sat on the edge of the platform shaking out his spare shirt. Diana Hunton-Hall, laughing to herself, walked quickly across the sunlit square towards the coffee-shop. She was a woman who liked her job, very much indeed.

★ ★ ★

A thousand miles away another broadcast was under way in a far more gorgeous square. Tall Flemish gables in orange, red and yellow and a pricklingly ornate Town Hall loomed over elegant paved and patterned spaces. In that city, gay umbrellas and the railings and awnings of cafés spoke of a far older tradition of *kaffeeklatsch* than Starbucks'. Wroclaw, shabby at the edges, flyposted with election posters which hung tattered and smeared like visible grunts of disillusion, nonetheless bore a triumphant air of self-conscious cosmopolitanism. If the English market square was a peaceful backwater, this city had existed for centuries in the full confusion of history's torrent.

She had seen armies come and go, languages change, suicidal sieges and backdoor betrayals; she had served emperors and kings and a Führer, commissars and priests and popes. She had been flooded and starved and looted and wrecked and restored. Like a world-weary serial divorcee she had changed her name without changing her nature: she had been Vratsao, Wratislavia, Wroclaw, Breslau, and Wroclaw again. Her very instability lent her history a kind of grace, like a rhythmically weaving drunkard: although her repose had nothing of the sleepiness of the English market town, this was a strangely restful city. Everything had happened to her already, so there was little to fear.

Spring had brought pale green leaves to the dusty trees, and grass forced its way through the rubble of the building-sites around the university. Here in the great square of Rynek were plenty of young men, who might well have heeded the bouncy invocation to Go West: knots of busy students wandering from lecture halls together or wooing bright-haired girls, idlers watching the daily life of the city centre for want of jobs to do, waiters tapping their feet boredly beneath awnings, hoping for the year's first tourists and wishing that the world's wealthy would show enough originality to divert from the honeypot of Krakow 200 kilometres to the south-east.

A number of them, however, had an unusual spectacle to enliven the ennui of the moment. On the same day that Two Counties Radio hauled itself out of its 1960s concrete office-block to play Village People tracks in a dozy English market square, Wroclaw had its own visitation of microphone-bearing hucksters. A yellow tent, with open sides, surrounded a platform close to the incongruously modernist glass fountain behind the Ratusz. The letters RGKZ-FM surmounted a curious scene. Two presenters in denim jackets, one ponytailed and one bald, presided over an outsized set of old-fashioned scales almost allegorically medi-eval in style. To complete the impression of fourteenth-century justice a death-like figure in a black monastic habit and cowl stood to one side. With portentous electronic echo over their voices, the DJs were chanting, as they had been doing for most of the morning, a singsong rhyme:

> *'Oi, city people! High and Low!*
> *Win or lose? You'll never know!'*

With every repetition of the couplet a figure from a long, patient queue moved forward, bearing some handbag, grip or briefcase. Each of them in turn put something on the scale, paused, and took it off again, before filing off past the hooded monk and being given a promotional card.

The dark, big-eyed girl who came around the corner and saw this charade seemed unsur-prised, but something about the set of her shoulders in their skimpy cotton vest conveyed that she was more than a little put out. She sat on the edge of the fountain ignoring the cool spray at her back and watched for a few minutes, tapping one toe on the cobbles. Next to her a German tourist, identifiable as such by his tightly gripped guidebook, shuffled closer and cleared his throat.

'Was ist das?' he asked, pointing at the swaying disc jockeys in the tent. When she did not respond, in halting English he repeated, 'Vot is happening here?'

The girl, Eva Danuta Krystyna Borkowska, Polish to her fingertips and thus always reluctant to answer questions posed in German or Russian, replied readily enough to the English enquiry.

'It is a competition. For the radio. For ten thousand zloty! The scales are very delicate, they say.' She made a balancing motion with her pretty white hands. 'And the prize goes to the person whose bag weighs *exactly* the same as the secret weight on the other side. You see?' She glanced at the man with sharp, teacherly exactness.

'Perhaps,' said the German, frowning with the effort of translation, 'people will come back many times and make their bag a bit lighter or heavier each time?'

'No,' said the girl scornfully. 'It is very clever. The scale does not say if you were too light or too heavy. So it is difficult, I think.'

Silence fell, and the two strangers watched the hypnotic scene, bizarre yet oddly dreary with the shuffling queue, the chanted monotonous rhyme and the unvarying anticlimax as disappointed contestants picked up their bags, backpacks, baskets and cases from the plate and wandered away. Since there was never any indication of a near miss, there was little tension. The watching knots of passers-by showed no sign of excitement, only a mild bovine curiosity followed by an eyeing-up of the queue to decide whether they had time to try their luck.

It was not, reflected Eva, a terribly happy scene. She was by nature given to analysis, and after a few moments decided what the problem was. To be fun, a competition or a Lotto should have two things: near misses, and a prize which everybody wanted but nobody urgently needed. The truth was that despite the gay new municipal splendours of the city's heart, too many of this crowd on Rynek were just that bit too desperate for an extra ten thousand zloty. Even now, in the eleventh year of democracy and freedom, with Poland on the very threshold of the European Union, life was so hard that money on this scale was a mirage of delirium. A discontented little *moue* flickered on the girl's lips. No, she thought, for all they had been told, life for them still was not markedly better. Not enough to count. Not like on Western TV.

That thin old woman coming up now, with the strong worn face and the old-fashioned wool flowers embroidered on her peasant basket: what would she do with so much money? More than two thousand dollars US? Eva shook her head. The woman just wanted to live without fear, eat properly, or maybe afford to get out of her cracking concrete apartment and cleaning job and go back to the mountains. But in the mountains she would still be poor. The boy behind her? Well, for him it could mean university full-time, not working all hours to live. Perhaps the man with the briefcase, self-conscious in this queue of scruffier citizens, dreamed of a decent car so that his business clients would take him more seriously. Everyone was broke, here. Everybody scratched a living.

That was the boring part of everybody's life. It never changed.

And Eva herself? Ah, she would have no trouble using such money, and because she was young her use of it would be more glorious. She knew by heart the bus fares out of Poland: 260 zloty to Antwerp, 300 to Calais, 400 all the way to London, England. With a prize like that she would have money to travel, perhaps find Manda or some new friends, perhaps go to Holland to see where Hania was working as an au pair. Or go to Scotland, where they sang the beautiful ballads she had done in school, and where (so Tadeusz said) his brother Adam had a job in the university laboratory. But Jesu, with ten thousand you could probably get to America or Canada, on a plane!

If they would give you a visa. Obviously. Not easy if you were Polish, an East European outsider, excluded from all the world's fun. But if you proved you had money . . .

She gave herself a little shake. No point in self-pity, she was fine. But yes, *psiakrew cholera!* she should have brought a bag with her, at least to try her luck. Wouldn't have won, but you had to try. Usually she would have had a bag — university books until this year, then the working girl's bag containing walking shoes for the long haul home, lunch, and a book or two to read in the endless, dull hours behind the dark reception desk in the hotel. But, bah! This was her day off, after a late night checking in three dozen Russians for some conference, so the spring sunshine had tempted her to take the long

13

walk in, through the suburbs to Rynek with her arms swinging free and only a few coins in her pocket.

She watched the people climb on to the platform, place their bags on the scale with care (as if care could make any difference!) and trudge down again past the death-monk with that deadly air of resignation. She wondered whether it was fixed so nobody won. Her father would say so: he thought everything was fixed — by the government, the church, the capitalists, the Mafia, the police, whoever. This was, Eva understood, a legacy of the years under Communism, his detestable twisted education, and the disappointments of his working life at the library. He had been neither a party member nor a rebel, poor Tatusiu! Just a middling, head-down, permanently disgruntled pawn in their game. You could not expect idealism of him now. Yes, he would definitely think the bag game was fixed.

Into her thoughts, like a bursting bubble, broke a hubbub of exuberant friendship. Familiar faces surrounded her.

'Eva!' shouted Tadeusz, jumping up and down in front of her, waving his arms like wings. 'Speak to me!' He turned to Staj and Halina, who were giggling behind him. 'She is hypnotized by these idiots! Come on, before it's too late — shake her!' They had all, as students the year before, watched a stage hypnotist in a university hall, and continued the joke about the man's portentous warnings on the risk of hypnosis for the weak-minded who might never come out of their trance.

'Shut up!' said Eva, amused. 'I was just watching because I forgot to bring my bag out. For the competition.'

'We'll try mine,' said the young man. He moved closer to her, and put an arm round her narrow shoulders. Eva glanced sideways, with the faint flicker of desire that always troubled her in his vicinity. It was all the more troubling because she knew that for him, for Tadek, it was more than a flicker. But for her — 'No, not enough,' she said to herself. 'Not enough for marriage, not enough for the other thing. The big risk.' Halina was watching them closely, her left hand on her hip, her right seductively twisting her long hennaed hair: Halina, thought Eva ruefully, would have said yes, to either marriage or the big risk. Tadek could have snapped his fingers and got her. He was tall, and clever, and his fine crinkled eyes were always laughing, and his hair was soft and fair over his collar, just shaggy enough to annoy his old-fashioned parents and earn him nicknames at university. He had a job promised, too: a government job which his parents were far happier about, working for the police. Not outside: at a desk, in an office. These were his last days of freedom, his last chance to drift around Rynek laughing and broke like a student.

She shrugged off his arm. 'Go and do it, then,' she said. 'Join the fools in the queue!'

'Bring me luck!' said Tadek, staying close to her. 'Put something in the bag to make it ex-act-ly right.'

'I haven't got ... ' began Eva, but then glancing down she saw that the German had left his guidebook on the rim of the fountain. She looked around the bright square, but there was no sign of him; quickly she picked it up and jammed it into the top of the young man's untidy canvas bag. 'Go! Before he comes back.'

'You're on ten per cent, OK?' he called over his shoulder, as he loped off to the end of the queue.

'Twenty!' shouted Eva, and he grinned and stuck his thumb up. There was a brief, indefinably awkward silence between the group left behind, and after a moment Eva broke it by turning to Halina and dumpy little Staj. 'Hi, anyway,' she said. And to the red-haired girl: 'Did you get the job at the ticket place?'

'No,' said the girl, tension had relaxed as her friend shrugged off Tadek's arm. 'They say there aren't enough tourists. Perhaps in the summer.'

'Too bad. Shall I tell you if any jobs come up at the hotel? They have lots of conferences, business is OK.'

'If you like. But no cleaning,' said Halina. Eva grimaced. They had cleaned hotel rooms together every summer of their university life, tidying the detritus of newspapers, softporn paperbacks, empty minibar bottles and opulent Western underwear. In Eva it had bred a restless desire to travel and see this careless wealthy world for herself. In Halina it had created the opposite feeling, a prudish xenophobia.

16

Foreigners, she would say, were obviously all pigs.

'Well, her father was a big Communist Party member,' said mischievous Adam. 'It's genetically programmed in her. She doesn't get capitalism at all.'

Now, Eva just nodded. 'No cleaning!' she echoed. 'Like the professors used to say, a diploma deserves a desk.'

'Maria is working for a diplomat. Swedish,' said Staj proudly. 'She is a nanny. She earns more than she would at any desk in this city. They have no idea about Polish wages, and why should she tell them?'

They discussed jobs desultorily, with half an eye on the tall youth's progress up the queue with his canvas bag. All the time, the radio men's chanting continued, a monotonous sing-song underpinning every conversation or train of thought in the vast space between the tall buildings. It was fifteen minutes before their friend stepped up, and the lounging group were almost too bored to watch, so rhythmic and inevitable was the pattern of each person's ascent to the platform, ceremonial bag-placing, and defeated downward slouch.

'Go, Tadi!' said little Staj half-heartedly, and the girls shrugged and turned deliberately away.

Before they could complete the movement, though, an extraordinary sound rent the air: a blaring electronic chime, followed by dead silence, then a roar led by the disc jockeys on the platform.

17

'The prize is won!' they chanted in unison. 'Not by a kilo, not by a gramme, not by a milli but a microgramme!' They let off hand-held fireworks, blew whistles, stamped and roared, egging the crowd on to cheers. Tadeusz stood on the platform, blinking slightly, clutching his satchel. The monk had flung off his dark habit and revealed himself to be a pretty blonde girl in a very short skirt and low blouse. She was kissing him on the cheek.

'What's your name, lad?' A microphone was thrust under his nose by one of the DJs:

'Tadeusz Voronski.'

'Student?'

'I have graduated. I am starting work next week for' — Eva held her breath, but he remembered not to mention the police. Always wiser not to, even now — 'in an office.'

'So what do you need with the money, huh? You give it to me?' The interviewer, high on his own wit, did a little jig. 'All for me?'

'No. I need it because I will get married.'

A roar of approval, led by the other presenter, rippled through the crowd. 'Where's the girl?'

There was a stir in the little knot of young people, but before Staj and Halina could notice, Eva had moved smartly behind the flowing glass screen of the fountain. Tadek lifted his finger to point, but not seeing her he dropped it again. Halina flashed her eyes, then hooded them angrily.

'Never mind the girl,' said Tadek's voice, echoing round the square on the loudspeakers.

He had rallied from his shock. 'Where's the money?'

The crowd cheered him again. Eva stood behind the wall of green glass and pouring water, her legs unaccountably shaking, until her friends came to find her.

2

Diana Hunton-Hall drove slowly home after the broadcast, easing her dusty Renault from the marketplace car park, around the golden stone Town Hall and out through the Victorian brick suburb to the open countryside beyond. The little car went slower with every half-mile, as if playing out in visible form the reluctance of its mistress. Diana, at the wheel, was unaware of this and thought her pace normal and steady; only a sharp hoot from a van behind her in the lane made her glance at the speedometer and realize with mortification that she was dawdling along at under twenty miles an hour.

Even so, she pulled in to let him pass, rather than speeding up for the final mile home. When Garton Manor sprawled at last before her, golden and gracious in the spring afternoon sun, she looked at it with rueful, constrained affection. It was such a pretty little manor house: idyllic, finely chimneyed, with generous windows and twin pillars holding up the portico. It was hard to look at it, even when you had lived there on and off for twenty years, without falling into estate-agent language. 'Spacious hallway, four recep, mature gardens, rural outlook . . . '

Twenty years! Was it really? It must have been. They had bought the house for weekends just after the 1982 election, when Manda was tiny and Philip was full of hope for his future in government. When they moved there full-time a few years later, giving up the big London flat, he even resigned from a couple of awkward directorships in full expectation of public office, and with expensive care furnished himself a study overlooking the miniature lake ('Well, a pond really,' Di would say to old friends when he bragged of it). The study was lined with shelves and alcoves designed, in hope, for red government boxes with the gold portcullis emblem on them. It was, Philip's wife thought sadly now, a house deliberately chosen as suitable for a Conservative Cabinet minister, a knight of the shires, later a peer.

Now, she parked the car a little askew in the empty drive, reached for her battered leather bag, and prepared to face a Philip who was neither peer nor knight nor minister. Nor, since the 2001 election, even an MP. A brisk young woman with short glossy hennaed hair and strict views on foxhunting had beaten him, taking the seat for New Labour with no trouble at all. She had compounded her crime by ignoring the time-honoured custom of acknowledging, in her election night speech, her opponent's sporting and gentlemanly campaign.

Not, Diana thought privately, that it had actually been a particularly gentlemanly campaign at all. Philip — needled by his foe's frequent self-righteous references to the Fanfair Finance scandal — had told local reporters to investigate her status as a single mother and her history of drawing benefits while working part-time for the Labour Party. Moreover, when interviewed by a magazine as an example of men who are even more handsome when they go grey, he had made unnecessarily sharp remarks about women with dyed hair.

She pushed the front door open and called in a studiedly hopeful tone: 'Hello! Philip — you home?' Thick silence met her, with no movement except the dancing of dust motes in the rays of sunlight from the landing window. Her real hope was fulfilled: he wasn't home yet. Sighing with relief, Diana wandered through to the kitchen and riffled through a pile of unopened post. It had been an early start at the radio station. Just as she was having breakfast the manager Steve had rung and said: 'Di, Maryanne's gone sick. We've got the roadshow out today, any chance you could cover? It means carrying on till four at least, do you mind?'

'What about reception?'

'Joanne can come in. But I'd be happier if Roger had you along. He's still got his tummy bug, apart from anything else.'

'Sure, I'd love to. Be with you in twenty minutes.'

When she had put down the phone that morning, her husband's cool pale eyes were on her back. She could feel them.

'I'm sorry,' she had said, turning. 'I have to go in early. Maryanne's gone sick, and I have to go into town with the Henry Windsor team. It's an outside broadcast. They need a timekeeper and general gopher.'

Philip winced, and wiped a crumb of buttery toast from the corner of his mouth with silent deliberation. At last he said: 'You know my feelings. Particularly in such a very public forum, and with some disc jockey . . . '

'I've been working at Two Counties Radio for two years!' said Diana. 'On the reception desk! This is a chance to do more work with programmes. And it's not as if — '

She bit her lip.

'Go on then, say it,' Philip had replied, picking up the newspaper and wincing in irritation, as he generally did, when the first headline met his eye. 'Say it. It's not as if I were still the MP'. His voice was cold, but the hurt in his eyes touched his wife, and Diana made an impulsive movement towards him.

'I didn't mean — '

'Yes, you did. Well, enjoy your day.' He raised the paper, said, 'Christ! Blair's Britain!' and began to read. Long experience had made his wife decide not to bother cajoling him out of this mood. It had to run its course.

'Thanks' she muttered. 'I'll go, then.'

Since this inauspicious start, the day had grown steadily better. Diana had learned to help out from time to time with a stopwatch when one of the trained programme assistants was away, and she thrilled to the immediacy of live programmes, especially when they involved Henry Windsor, the station's most unpredictable presenter. Henry was never content to settle for a steady phone-in with records and the occasional guest, but — with or without his producer's agreement — used scraps of tape out of his private pirated archives, threw recorded versions

23

of their earlier interviews at surprised and hostile council functionaries, allowed infuriated or starstruck members of the public to take on his guests directly, and generally blurred the division between entertainment and news to an extent which had the management of the little station trembling in their shoes.

But his ratings were good, the best in the region. Neighbouring stations were irritated by evidence that their own borders were lined with listeners tuning carefully and twisting aerials around when it was Henry-time. The BBC opposition virtually gave up during his hours on-air, and put their dullest shows out. Other 2C presenters — Sally Beazeley, Mark Hampton, Anwar Aziz — did well enough, but nobody raised the passions that Henry could. The advertising breaks in his programmes were fully booked months ahead.

To do a Henry programme was a feather in Diana's cap; she was, after all, only the receptionist. A Henry outside-broadcast was even better. On last year's Coming 2CU tour he had taken the radio microphone and impulsively waded thigh-deep into the river while interviewing an environmental health officer standing safely on the bank, about its increasing filthiness. Emerging, he invited the officer — a woman — to feel how oily his trousers were, and squeaked in mock enjoyment when she took him up on it. Listening behind the reception desk, envying the team in the field, Diana had liked that moment very much. Its irreverence was, she told her friend Lizzie, pure refreshment for the soul after eighteen years as a Conservative MP's wife. So on this day she rejoiced in her chance, marshalled her papers carefully, checked her stopwatch against the studio clock before they left, and determined to be as efficient as could be. If there was a proper job with programmes coming up soon, Diana planned to have it.

But, she told herself out in the sunshine of the Market Square, even if she never did advance in this late-flowering little career of hers it would be worth it. Even if she just stayed behind the front desk, checking in visitors and answering the telephone. After years of political wifehood, dutiful motherhood and pinprick humiliations, Two Counties Radio had, she felt with no sense of hyperbole, saved her.

Philip had been against it. Now, in the kitchen with the light fading, Diana sat for a few moments in the gloom, fiddling with junk-mail envelopes and remembering. She replayed the first angry scene of five years before, when she came home from the interview with a light step and golden news.

'Phil — I've got a job!'

He had stared at her, looking up from a pile of paperwork, shuffling something out of her sight with a quick instinctive movement. Even before the Fanfair Finance débâcle he had always been secretive about his business life.

'You don't need a job,' he'd said flatly.

'We agreed. When Manda went to university, I'd go back to work.'

'I don't know what you mean by *back*,' Philip had said, scornfully. 'You only ever worked for

25

that year at NatWest after we were married.'

'Don't I know it?' was the bitter rejoinder. Philip was taken aback; he had never known his wife to be bitter. She sat down foursquare opposite him and went on.

'I need to work, now. It's nearly the twenty-first century. Women do work.'

'There's an election coming. I need you to help me fight it.'

'I've helped you fight elections for twenty years. I'm tired of bloody elections. It's my turn.'

'For what, precisely? You've got all the housekeeping money you could possibly need. If you want more you only have to ask. We're not paupers.' His hands rested, long and white and protective, on the pile of documents before him.

'I want my own money,' Diana had protested. 'I want to earn it. But mostly I want to get out and be part of the working world. I do.'

'So you just want a hobby? And you'll take a job from someone who might need it? I thought you worried about that sort of thing.'

It was a low blow. Diana winced. Yes, Philip Hunton-Hall's wife didn't need to work, not for financial reasons. Yes, most women did need to earn these days. Was there a woman in the town, another candidate for the reception job, sitting at this very moment crushed with disappointment and worry about the family budget?

'It's been advertised for six weeks,' she said defensively. 'They say I was the first suitable candidate.'

Her voice wavered and Philip went on the

26

attack again, which melted her guilt and stiffened her resolve.

'What is this job, anyway? You've no qualifications.'

'Receptionist at Two Counties Radio.'

His thin face whitened, and his hands scrabbled in the papers on the desk.

'Why didn't you tell me that first? You know it's out of the question. Think of my position.'

'What do you mean?'

'I'm the local MP,' he said, with rudely exaggerated slowness. 'You're my wife.'

'So?' Diana was not normally truculent, but in fighting for this job she felt as if she were fighting for a child. She would not, could not, let this flicker of independence die. Philip had sliced through her anger with an irritable coolness.

'You know how aggressive these media types are about my party. They're all lefties. Face facts: the only reason they're offering you the job is to get a direct line to me. Just grow up. You've been had.'

Now it was Diana who went white.

'That is the most insulting thing anyone's ever said to me.'

'How so, precisely? It's the truth.'

'Don't talk to me as if I was a bloody Select Committee. Try and listen to yourself. They've hired me because I'm an intelligent, well-spoken woman who really wants the job. End of story. They didn't even ask what my husband did. Or whether I was married.'

'They knew,' said Philip. 'Don't be so naïve! You've had your picture taken opening enough fêtes in the local paper. They'll keep you till the election's over, and they've done me all the damage they can through you, then they'll dump you on your backside.'

Diana's response, she often thought over the coming years, banged the first long, cold iron nail into the coffin of their marriage.

'We'll see about that, shall we? I'll take the risk happily. Just like you've got to take the risk, even with a safe seat. But if you think the media are out to get you, perhaps you ought to look at why. It wasn't them who got you tied up with Fanfair Finance, was it? You did that all by yourself. Don't blame other people if your career took a dive. You shouldn't have been so greedy. We didn't even need the money.'

She had walked out, then. It was a bad and cowardly thing to do. Diana, who was habitually hard on herself where personal morality was concerned, understood as much even while she did it. If she was going to rake over the ashes of that particular conflagration in their lives, she should have stayed to see the matter out. As it was they hardly spoke for two days, but at the end of that time it was Philip who extended the olive branch, not her.

'Look,' he said over the third silent breakfast, 'if you want to work for these clowns at Two Counties, go ahead. At your own risk.'

It would not, Diana thought, have looked much like a tender olive branch to anybody outside their marriage. But to her, who knew Philip's nature all too well, it was as good as a sobbing operatic aria of repentance. She got up, walked round the shining mahogany table, and hugged him. For a moment, his narrow silver-haired head rested deliberately on her shoulder, in a gesture of dependent ownership; then he resumed his breakfast, with clucks of annoyance at the front page of the newspaper. The following Monday, Diana started her new job in a pale-blue skirt and sweater which it had taken her three agonized hours to choose.

'Do I look too like a Tory wife? Truly, tell me?' she asked her friend Lizzie Morgan, when she met her at the coffee-shop during the first lunch-hour. 'Honestly, do I?'

'You look perfectly nice and normal,' said Lizzie. 'Tidy and professional.'

'They're all so *young* there,' grumbled Diana. 'And hip. Bare bellybuttons on the girls, and one of the young men has dreadlocks almost to his waist.'

'Oh, come on,' said Lizzie. 'There are some pretty ropey middle-aged nerds in there, too. I've seen them. Look at that manager. He turned up at the school fête in an Argyle sweater-vest thing with a hole in it.'

'Well, that's another thing,' said Diana fretfully, tugging at the waistband of her own jersey. 'If they're not hip, they're sort of don't-care. Bohemian. Arty-looking. As if it didn't matter having awful corduroy trousers or hair like a bird's nest.'

'Fact is, it doesn't matter,' said Lizzie, who herself was rather less soignée than her friend. 'So long as you're comfortable. For God's sake, life's too short.'

'That's what I *mean*,' said Diana. 'I'm a tidy, formal, conventional political wife. I'm the sort of permed clone who ends up in the tabloids, being photographed on the way to church with an erring husband, promising to stand by him. I can't shake it off.'

'You will,' said Lizzie.

And sure enough, after a couple of years Diana's neat perm had given way to a younger cut of straight, layered hair with streaks of brighter blonde, and her wardrobe had acquired all manner of previously unthought-of clothes. There were a couple of thrift-shop antique leather jackets, numerous practical trousers and chunky boots, and some vivid T-shirts whose necklines and logos Philip could hardly glimpse without shuddering.

'I fought the 'ninety-seven election, though,' she said to herself now. 'I wore the tidy suits, I smiled the smile, I actually worked harder than I had in any of the others. Which is saying something. And we won.'

She grimaced at the memory. Philip had held the seat narrowly in the 1997 Labour landslide, despite the continuing reverberations of the financial scandal which had cost him his ministerial job. The succeeding years, however, had brought no satisfaction. The Parliament he once so loved had changed utterly with the new government. The levers of power were beyond his reach now, and the very idiom of the place was so different that every time he came home to his newly energized wife he was angrier and more bewildered.

The press would not leave him alone, either. There were no more major pursuits or doorstepping, but Philip Hunton-Hall's name kept cropping up in every trivia quiz or political comedy show, accompanied by puns on 'Fanfair' and bracketed with those of colleagues in far deeper trouble: Aitken and Hamilton and Archer. Philip was only a junior member of this crew of contumely, never having been taken to court over his association with the disgraced finance house, and having sidestepped the accusation of abusing his position on their behalf. But all the same his name kept coming up, making it unsafe for his family to open any newspaper or magazine without bracing themselves. It seemed to his wife that every joke, every newspaper reference to his association with 'Tory sleaze', leached a little more of the life and spirit from her husband.

It would have been better, she thought, if he had been thrown out of Parliament cleanly, in 1997, as far more senior figures had been. Instead he limped on, useless and ill-tempered in the House and hardly bothering with his constituents, until his defeat at the hands of the brisk Labour Mizz in 2001.

The last years of his political career had taken their toll on his wife as well, and her friends saw it clearly. Despite the pleasure Diana was taking in her new job she seemed edgier, more anxious, and on mysteriously worse terms with her student daughter as well as with Philip. 'Why he fought that election at all I will never know,' said Lizzie Morgan, outspoken as usual. 'Politics!

Why doesn't he just pack it in and do something else?'

'He's afraid,' said Diana. 'Afraid he won't exist if he's out of Parliament. He feels old.'

'He's only fifty-seven,' said her friend scornfully. 'That's right, isn't it? Thirteen years older than us? That's no age.' Her own husband Andy was sixty, the kind of headmaster who still ran marathons and did sponsored sky-diving for charity, and whose governors would never let him retire while there was breath in his body. 'For God's sake, Philip's got years. Time for another career if he wants it. These days . . . '

Modern longevity was a great theme of Lizzie's. It had, ironically, continued to be a theme of hers even after she was diagnosed with breast cancer and entered the cruel cycle of treatment, remission, operations, scans, more treatment and precarious remission.

'Life's so *long* these days,' she would say. 'Historically, we've got twenty or thirty years more than our ancestors, and look what they did with their lifetimes.' Lizzie's grandmother, dead at forty-three, had been a militant suffragette and a pioneer of girls' higher education. Her mother had been an eye surgeon. Her sister had held high office in the Ministry of Defence. Lizzie herself taught French and Russian in the sixth form of Andy's school, translated textbooks between the two languages, ran a charity for Russian orphans, and nonetheless considered herself the dull one of the family.

When, in the dim empty manor house on a spring afternoon, her train of thought and memory reached this point, Diana got up from the kitchen table, snapped on the lights and picked up the phone. She stood for a moment listening to the ringing, thinking of it echoing in the anxious spaces of the Morgans' house. When it was answered she said without preamble: 'Hi. How was the scan?'

'Mmph. Not fantastic,' said Lizzie's voice. 'Can I ring later? Tell you everything then. Andy's just coming up the path, and Freddie's in the house.'

'OK,' said Diana, and put the telephone down, as gently and carefully as if it were a thing of fragile human flesh. What were her own domestic troubles next to the timeless terror hanging over her friend?

3

The four friends sat round a café table, in an alley far enough from Rynek to bring the prices down. A high wall kept the sun from them, and they shivered a little from the excitement and the cool spring breeze. If they sat outside, though, they could get away with spending more time over one small cup of coffee or the childish treat of a squat bottle of banana-flavoured Kubus. The young men were laughing excitedly, and had for once ordered beer.

'I don't believe it!' said Staj. 'Is this money real? When do you get it?'

'I have to go to the radio station and they give me a cheque. See — this is the promise.' Tadeusz spread out a document on the table, signed by the manager and accountant of the radio station. The four craned over it respectfully.

'Looks real,' said Eva. When they'd found her behind the fountain, Staj had insisted she join them for the celebration. 'And you have witnesses!'

Tadek looked at her, his eyes eloquent. Halina was silent, turning her bottle of Kubus in her hands, staring fiercely at the label with its cartoon figure of the bear in dungarees holding a banana. Eva, suddenly protective, put her hand on her friend's arm. Halina gave her a brief, startled but not entirely hostile glance and went back to turning the bottle, balancing it

34

diagonally on its lower rim so that it made a hollow, uneasy sound against the wooden table.

Eva was about to speak again when another figure appeared, blotting out the thin sunshine.

'Matziek!' said Staj. 'Guess what?'

'I know,' said the boy. 'Tadeusz won the competition. I saw Jan and his new girl, they were watching but they lost you in the crowd. So now what, cousin? Where will you go?'

'Poland,' said the young man, with a grin. 'I have a job, remember. At police headquarters. I start next week.'

'You're joking? You've got to travel!' said Matziek, dismayed. 'I saved only five hundred and eighty zloty and I went to France, Italy, and Sardinia. And even Malta on that boat. Your brother went to Bulgaria and Turkey, and Radek and Krystyna — '

Tadeusz raised his hand, and the newcomer stopped. 'Everyone goes travelling now,' he said gently. 'What's the point? It's not real life.'

'But you have to see the world!'

'And come back poor? If I put this money in a bank — in dollars perhaps — I can use it for my real life. To find an apartment away from my parents, get married maybe.'

'Ah, God, no!' groaned Matziek. 'You're trapped, boy. What's the point of a free country if you don't even climb the bowl and look over the edge?'

'That's wrong! Travelling's just a waste of money. Tadek's not so stupid he'd waste all his money wandering around like a tramp!' said Halina, looking at the winner with even more admiration than usual. Eva seized the chance to distance herself still more from her awkward suitor.

'I think Matziek's right,' she said robustly. 'Poland is not the whole world. It's like when you grow up, your parents are not the whole world anymore. The modern way is to travel. I'm going travelling as soon as I have saved a bit more. Maybe this summer. I've got six hundred and fifty zloty in my bank.'

'Two thousand six hundred and fifty,' corrected Tadeusz. 'By tomorrow. You're on twenty per cent, remember? So I have to pay you two thousand.'

Hubbub broke out at the table when they saw that he meant it. Halina flushed angrily and began to remonstrate, then stopped when she saw Eva's transported expression; perhaps it occurred to her at that moment that if her rival had money, she really might go abroad. Far away, out of Tadek's sight and thoughts.

The other young men exclaimed and shook their heads in amazement.

'Are you in love with this little madwoman or what?' asked Staj. 'Two thousand!'

'It was a deal. It's fair. She put the German's guidebook in my bag,' said the winner, steadily. 'Otherwise I wouldn't have won, would I? I said ten per cent, she said twenty . . . '

'If you are sure?' said Eva a little stiffly. 'It was a joke. I didn't think you'd be serious about it.'

'I am always serious,' said the young man. He looked at her, his eyes eloquent, and Eva looked quickly away.

'Well, I *do* want to travel.' She sounded younger than usual, squeaky even.

Tadek went on looking at her, brows knitted. 'OK,' he said. 'Come on, let's go and get it. No,' as the others made to rise, 'Not all together. Just me and Eva.' Halina glanced at him, flushed, and bit her lip.

'I don't want to lose sight of my new rich friend,' grumbled Staj. 'I want to see all that money!'

'Later, then,' said Tadeusz mockingly. 'Wait by Fredro!'

They all laughed then, even Halina. If you are brought up in Wroclaw, one of the first things you learn is that a tryst by the statue of the playwright Aleksander Fredro is code for a meeting that will never take place.

* * *

Half an hour later, in the bleak concrete outskirts of the city, Tadeusz took Eva's hand. There was nobody they knew in sight so she let him, but offered no answering pressure to his big, warm, dry palm.

'Do you want to know the first thing I thought, when I won?' he said softly.

Eva was silent. He continued, more haltingly: 'I thought, now I can get married. I don't want to be thirty or forty, a sad old man, like my father. We could marry now. We could afford to rent an apartment. Near the stadium, there's a block I know — '

'Tadek!' said Eva. 'I told you not to talk like that.'

'Yeah, that was fine back then, because we couldn't even think about it when I asked you before. We were like children, with no money, living with our parents. Now, I think we could manage. And if you want to travel, we could take a holiday, in Greece perhaps.'

'I don't *want* a holiday,' said Eva. 'And I don't want to be married. I want to see the world. I want to feel it, smell it, argue with it. I want long times in new places, learning about them. I want different people. Different cities. Wonderful countryside, strange farms. The sea, the land. Adventures and stories!'

She knew she was sounding childish in her urgency, and tried to pull away her hand. 'Dear friend! I have said I can't be married. Not now. I am only twenty-two. And' — she gathered all her strength to say it — 'I can't be married to you anyway. Never. We don't want the same things.'

He walked on then, silently, dropping her hand. She scuttled to catch up with him and, although it tore the heart from her, said urgently. 'But to show I'm sorry, please don't give me the two thousand. You keep it for your own life. You should marry Halina, she really likes you and she never wants to travel.'

She did not hear distinctly what he said next, but knew it was 'I love you'. Miserably, she trailed behind him for the last few hundred yards to the radio station office, then stood outside, uncertain what to do, while he went in. Eventually he came out, followed by a fat man jingling car keys, and said in a flat voice: 'They're driving us to the bank. It's not safe to walk around with all this cash.'

At a jerk of his head, Eva climbed in the back of the car with Tadek and sat huddled by the window, trying not to be thrown against him as the fat man swerved and hooted through the streets back to the city centre. In the Zachodni Bank Tadeusz punctiliously deposited eight thousand zloty in his own account, for his future, and stood by while Eva, hating herself, paid two thousand into hers.

'That's done, then,' said the young man finally, and stood looking down at her. For the first time, there was a glint of severe judgement in his eyes, which daunted and distressed her beyond anything she could have imagined possible. 'I'll go home.'

'See you,' said Eva, her heart hammering unpleasantly.

'See you by Fredro,' said Tadeusz, and turning on his heel, he stalked away along the cracked and rutted pavement.

★ ★ ★

Hours later, just before dusk, Eva got home and climbed the seventy-two steps to the apartment, for she hated the shaky and malodorous old lift. Two rooms and the kitchen lay open to view, the chill light glimmering in the open doorways. Her brother's door was shut. Max worked night shifts at the Glowny station, and liked to sleep through the late afternoons. Her father should have been home by now; wondering a little, Eva went into the narrow kitchen and began peeling potatoes and making salad with hard mountain cheese grated over it.

Eventually the front door rattled open and her father appeared. He went straight to his room with a curt greeting. When more than one door was closed the tiny landing between the four rooms was dark and claustrophobic. When her mother had been alive, the internal doors were usually open, and the family called and laughed from their various rooms — Eva's was the smallest, a mere sliver big enough for a bed and desk. In those days they all ate together in the biggest one, where the parents slept. Now, it was usually just Eva and her father at table, and rather than fold up his bed and rig the dining-table they sat on the tiny kitchen bench and ate swiftly, silently, side by side before each retiring to their own territory.

Max never ate with them, and rarely cooked or prepared food. There was a snack bar at the station, and he seemed happy enough to eat there. He came to life among his friends in the bars and cafés of the city. Home was merely where he slept. At twenty-six, thought Eva, he was far too old to be still in his parents' home, but on his wages where on earth else could he live? Perhaps Tadek was right. Perhaps the only sensible use for a windfall was to leave home. Perhaps your own place, in your own country, however drab, was worth any sacrifice of life and experience and colour and joy.

She put down the paring knife and went to the

kitchen window: it had the best view of any except her father's. Kneeling on the bench she could see the mountains, dim and dreamy in the distance. Closer, the smoky skyline of the city was an elegant confusion of steeples, domes, and cranes. Nearest of all lay the cliff-like apartment blocks, tiresomely ugly, dirty white and orange amid the weary green spaces and the scatter of cars.

All her life Eva had seen this view. Tiny on her mother's lap she had sat in this kitchen, pulling at the bright dyed hair; from her mother's funeral she had come home to this place to make a herring salad for her father and brother, at eighteen years old symbolically taking up the responsibility of home-making. But never, she thought, even in babyhood, had she looked at this kitchen prospect without wanting to burst from the window and fly over the rooftops to the far mountains and beyond.

Onion tears stung her eyes as she passed her hand across them. She would go. She had to go. Another month behind the hotel desk, another month to explain to her father and Max, another few painfully saved zloty in the bank. Then, before the desperate baking heat of the Silesian summer, she would go.

Covering the salad with a mesh dome, she went to her room for a few moments to collect herself, and to take a refreshing glimpse at a certain bundle of letters in a broad, childish hand. She had friends, after all, out in that other world. There would be a welcome. She would take them honey. 'Always take honey to a friend,' her mother used to say, quoting the farm people of her childhood. Eva went back into the kitchen, peered in the cavernous cupboard, and pausing only to kill two earwigs with her thumb, pulled out a dusty jar of mountain honey and took it to put in the drawer with the letters.

4

On the night of the outside broadcast, Philip Hunton-Hall eventually came home unusually late, at almost ten o'clock. Diana was annoyed because she had made supper, but not worried. Once, she thought sadly, it would have been the other way round. In the early days of their marriage, and of motherhood, she would have been worried but not annoyed.

Twenty-three years of marriage, however, had taught her many things about her husband and erstwhile representative in Parliament. She knew, as well as she knew her own shoe size, that Philip drove carefully, kept himself safe, never got into fights or deviated from his routine haunts. He always thought before he acted, and was the last man of their mutual acquaintance who might be expected to be unfaithful. Sex, in any case, meant little to him, and women even less. If he was late for dinner there would be a good, and dull, reason for it.

The front door opened and closed at last. She glanced up from her book as he entered the long dim beautiful sitting-room of Garton Manor, and briefly found herself admiring the upright grace of his form against the glow of the hall light. Philip dressed wonderfully well, his extreme adherence to convention offset by the sheer quality and cut of his suits and the soft silken beauty of his shirts and ties. He did not look his age, but rather an ageless, iconic figure of conservative British style. You could have put him in a Jermyn Street window as a model. His narrow patrician features were topped by a still vigorous growth of silver hair, well brushed but never oily; his eyes were large, pale blue and well-set, his chin firm, his nose just aquiline enough to make a susceptible woman catch her breath. As he stepped forward into the circle of light around his wife, he managed a fleeting smile.

'Sorry. Got held up at Deutsche Intell. Chairman asked the non-execs to stay on for a briefing on the East European projects. Ties up with my own stuff.'

'Have you eaten? There's lasagne in the fridge, ready to go,' said Diana.

'They brought in soup and sandwiches. Euagh!' He yawned. 'I'll have a shower and finish off some paperwork.'

'You out tomorrow?'

'No,' he said. 'Not till evening. Got dinner with Edmund.'

'Oh,' said Diana. Edmund was the local association chairman. He wanted to replace Philip with a younger, more centrist candidate before the next election, but wanted Philip to resign of his own accord. An awkward ritual dance had been going on between the two of them these past months, and it was taking its toll. Diana could not decide whether Philip genuinely didn't want to leave, even after his humiliating defeat in 2001, or whether he was perversely manoeuvring himself into a position where Edmund and the others would have to sack him overtly, thus giving him yet another grudge against the world. On the whole, she thought, the latter. So she just said: 'Fine. You tell him!'

'Tell him what?' The brief truce of his arrival home, and the peace of the long room, lay shattered. His voice was up an octave. Diana raised her hands defensively.

'Whatever you want to tell him. Tell him you'll go, or tell him you won't go till he makes you. All I meant was that it'll be better if everything's out in the open!'

'How long,' asked Philip with biting sarcasm, 'have you been a political wife? Do you understand *nothing* about this life, about my party, and the nature of discretion and party loyalty?'

'It's all changing,' said Diana gently. 'Everything. Not just politics. Life's changing for all of us. All the time. You have to roll with it. At the radio station — '

She had been about to tell him that Alec, the manager's long-serving deputy, was under notice to take early retirement or redundancy; that the experienced programme assistant Maryanne, whose job she had taken over for the day, was on renewable four-month contracts. Her own job, though on the staff, was susceptible to having the plug pulled any time at three months' notice. She might have gone on to tell him more: that down at the school Andy had been forced to lay off two teaching assistants, one a single mother; that there was a petition going round in town

45

because the ironmonger's had closed down through inability to take the competition from the DIY superstores. She had wanted, with these tales, to draw Philip in to the freemasonry of modern insecurity. She had hoped to laugh with him — as she did with her colleagues — at the fact that nobody was secure for life anymore. Members of Parliament were no longer alone in their constant, haunting fear of rejection.

But Philip cut in angrily before she could go on.

'Oh, for God's sake. You and that tinpot radio station. I never hear about anything else. I'm going for a shower.'

Diana sighed and returned to her book; but her concentration was broken, and after a moment she switched on the television news and watched the flickering of quarrel and disaster without taking much of it in. She had played her wifely cards wrong again. She should have asked him about Deutsch Intell and what his own East European project was. Some jejune plot, presumably, to rip off the poor Iron Curtain countries before they saw the rapacious West coming. But it would have made him feel important and valued if she had asked about it. She could not settle, but got up and went to the foot of the stairs.

'Drink?' she called hopefully, hearing his heavy step on the bathroom landing.

'Not now,' said Philip's voice.

'Well, I will,' muttered his wife, defeated. Back in the sitting-room she poured herself an unusually generous measure of vodka, and topped it with sharp cranberry juice and crushed ice from her beloved new American fridge. 'Mega!' she muttered, sipping; then smiled, realizing she had used a Henry Windsor word from the DJ's patter. She had teased Henry about it that afternoon, saying that her daughter stopped using that dated word two years ago. Henry merely giggled and spent the rest of the hour using the most obsolete slang he could think of, strafing the placid country-town audience with 'faberoonie' and 'babe-olicious' and working his way back to 'corking', 'epic' and 'jolly D'.

Henry at least made her laugh. Working with him, she thought that it would have been nice to have had a son, and have him grow into a mocking, good-humoured, high-spirited young man.

For some associated reason, halfway down the drink Diana decided to ring her daughter Amanda.

'Hi. It's Mum.' She put all the brightness she could into the greeting. 'How's things?'

'Fine,' said a cool, thin voice on the phone. 'You and Dad?'

'Fine. How's Art?'

'In Amsterdam, on a course.'

'So,' said the mother, groping for words, 'everything's OK? Just wanted to catch up.'

'Yup. Look, I've got people in — '

'OK. Well, talk to you soon.'

Amanda, in her neat one-bedroomed flat in the maze of London docklands developments, almost always claimed she 'had people in' when

47

her mother rang. Diana grimaced and shrugged: she herself had been married at twenty-one, after all, and immediately moved well out of her parents' orbit of acquaintance and understanding when she began to live in Philip's smart world. She had certainly not confided in her mother on the phone every other night. Any confiding had been in Lizzie Morgan, who at the time was still in teacher-training college, still single, and always able to laugh her out of social terrors and emotional confusion.

Obviously, Manda had friends in her own world to talk to. Why on earth should she confide in her mother, or Philip? They had not, Diana told herself, given her the best of themselves. The girl's childhood and most of her teens had been spent as an MP's daughter, her interests secondary to those of constituency and career, her slightest school difficulty met by angry injunctions from Philip not to 'show him up' or 'give more ammunition to the bloody press'. She had been rising ten when they moved full-time to this pretty rural place, forced to leave her fashionable London school and hip, knowing friends for a stodgy local girls' academy which she hated. On top of it all she had been 'shown up' herself, embarrassed beyond toleration, at the time of her father's plummet out of the lower ranks of government and into the scandal-sheet headlines.

Small wonder, thought the mother ruefully, that Manda had gone to the most distant university she could arrange, studied the dry but profitable business of economics and accountancy, and acquired a well-paid job in the City which made it unnecessary ever to ask her parents for anything. Philip had given her fifty thousand pounds deposit for the flat, but otherwise Amanda made no demands whatsoever on her parents, and in this past year had avoided contact as far as possible.

Lizzie, whose adult son Joe and student daughter Marie were forever lounging around the untidy Morgan house at weekends, squabbling with fifteen-year-old Freddie and cooking fish fingers, told Diana not to upset herself over this coolness. 'It's common enough. They've got to find their own feet. Ask Andy. Some of our sixth-form girls at the College hardly talk to their parents, even at eighteen.'

'Yours do. Joe's always at your house, and he's Manda's age.'

'Boys are different. Less worried about finding their feet. Prob'ly' — Lizzie frowned with pretended thoughtfulness — 'that's because their feet smell so terrible. You could find them in a pitch-dark cave.' She grinned at Diana's involuntary giggle and continued, 'Face it, Joe and Marie come home weekends because their flats are so horrible, rotting concrete and drug dealers everywhere. Manda's a proper yuppie, you told me, with an entryphone and private gym and pool in the atrium. You should be proud that she does well enough on her own not to keep coming home and cluttering the house up.'

Diana tried; but it seemed to her that her real daughter had vanished a long time ago, somewhere between elections. Affectionate, biddable little Manda had been spirited off and replaced by an icy changeling. Perhaps if there had been more siblings, a proper family like Lizzie's, it would have been different. Philip, however, had been dead against having more children. An MP, he said, needed a wife who wasn't distracted. Sometimes, since the last election, Diana would look at news pictures of the young Prime Minister and his four offspring and almost choke with anger and envy. They had it all. She had only the memory of years of dutiful contraception, years of wasted opportunities, all for nothing but failure and sourness.

But at least she had the job at Two Counties, and Lizzie to laugh with. ('Well, as long as Lizzie lives,' said a hateful little voice in her head. She pushed the thought away.) What did Philip have? Money, directorships, dust and ashes.

The bathroom door slammed upstairs, and his tread on the wide old staircase roused Diana from her reverie by the telephone. Draining the last of her own drink, she called in a light and friendly tone, 'Drink now, darling? Whisky Mac?'

5

The deputy manager of Radio Two Counties took his early retirement without much sadness, and announced his intention of joining his brother in a market-gardening enterprise. When Diana Hunton-Hall's assessment interview came up, however, she found herself surprised by good news.

'You've been on reception for ages,' said Steve the station manager. He turned over the pages in front of him. 'Had you thought about moving on?'

Diana, heart in mouth, kept her voice neutral. 'Leaving, you mean?'

'No. Applying for something else. Here.'

'I didn't think about it much,' said Diana, not wholly truthfully. 'I'm aware I haven't got much of a CV as far as work's concerned.'

'Maryannne's finally got a job in telly,' said Steve. 'Cable lifestyle stuff. Seems to be what she wants, God knows why. She's leaving at the end of the month. What I should say to you is that we're not looking for a direct replacement. What we're doing is getting someone on contract to do her job, less some stuff that Roger will take on directly, but adding on the half-job that the trainee was doing in the newsroom.'

'Mmm,' said Diana, cautiously. The manager looked at her, consideringly. 'It's a lot of work. There's the Henry Show, which also involves

51

research as well as logging and letters; plus Maggie's Music, which is mainly music reporting; plus three afternoons or evenings in the newsroom. You're happy with the IT there, aren't you? On the whole? I mean, not the online editing, but the scripts and website stuff?'

'I did the full course,' said Diana. 'Including online editing.'

'Did you now?' He frowned at the papers before him. 'Bloody hell, that's a turn-up.'

Diana's chest was tight with hope and excitement. This was a real job he was talking about, a job requiring brains and nerve and invention. 'I did it all,' she continued, 'just before you took over here, on an enhancement scheme that someone else didn't want to take up. It was in the evenings. I think it was funded by something, Investors in People, that sort of thing. I just thought it was a good thing to be familiar with programme stuff, even on reception. In case of emergencies.' She paused. 'Do you really think I ought to apply for this job?'

'I'm more or less offering it to you,' said Steve. 'But I have to tell you that it is a contract, not a staff position. That's the way things are these days. Technically you'd have to resign. You'd earn a bit more, but for a lot more hours and without even the security of a three-month notice period. I mean, it's three-monthly renewable but not rolling. Which means we could get to two and a half months and suddenly say it's goodbye in a fortnight. It's not the way I like to work with people, but it's the new age.'

'I'm really grateful,' said Diana slowly, 'that

you're laying it all out like this. But really, it's such a fantastic chance I'd be mad not to take it. Especially at my age.'

'What age?' Steve smiled now, his worried hangdog face creasing into life. He looked down. 'Forty-four? No age.'

'For this kind of job, it is.'

'Lucky old us, then. Getting all those years of experience on the cheap.'

She left the room floating on air; Steve had set out the fuller conditions of the contract he was offering, and ordered her to think about it for at least twenty-four hours and 'discuss it with the family'. If he saw her wince, he pretended not to. The thought of telling Philip that she would be doing longer hours, and more unsocial ones, threatened for a while to cast Diana into low spirits. As it happened, though, he was out that night at dinner with Edmund and a few others from the local Association including his agent. This gave Diana the chance to call round at Lizzie Morgan's house to deliver her news and garner moral support.

'Fantastic!' said Lizzie, who was drinking herbal tea, propped on sofa cushions in a dim, cluttered living-room. 'You'll take the job, obviously? God, it's got dark. I was listening to Mahler, I was miles away.' She snapped on the light by her side.

'Too damn right I'll take it.' Diana looked hard at her friend in this new illumination, and was startled to see how waxen pale she was, how thin, and how sunken were the vivid brown eyes beneath the jaunty red knitted brim of her hat.

She had got used to seeing the hairless transparent look of a cancer patient under treatment, but Lizzie today looked a great deal worse than she had lately. Her friend did not, however, like discussing the progress of her illness, so Diana valiantly continued with her own news.

'I'll tell him tomorrow that it's yes. And I suppose I'll tell Philip tonight. They want me to start the newsroom shifts on Monday week.'

'You haven't told Philip?'

'Well, no. I only heard today and I haven't been home.'

'Ring him!'

'He's going out to dinner with Edmund and the party bigwigs.'

'Oh, dear,' said Lizzie. She fidgeted with her hat. An absent look came over her face, and for a moment Diana thought she might be about to divulge more about the progress of her cancer. But it was Philip, it seemed, who occupied the invalid's mind. 'Do you think they're going to make him walk the plank?'

'The sooner the better,' said Diana vehemently. There was a pause, then in a softer tone she added: 'But as you very well know, you're the only person on earth I can express that sentiment to.'

'Manda?'

'Manda, insofar as she takes any interest at all, quite liked her father being an MP. It did her no harm at work. Even the memory of the Fanfair scandal was a kind of feather in her cap, in that world. They like to think of themselves as hawks

54

not chickens. She was quite put out when he lost the seat.'

'He'd be far better off making a clean break, though, wouldn't he? It's not as if he needs the salary. And it's not as if he's actually all that likely to win the seat back next time. The Labour woman had a good majority, didn't she? Cut your losses, I say.'

'I wish he could see it like that, Lizzie, I really do. But it's like someone once wrote — being an MP simultaneously feeds your vanity and starves your self-respect. It's a self-esteem thing. He needs to know that people still think he's a winner, and that it was only a fluke he lost. If the local party throw him out and find another candidate, he'll crack up.'

Lizzie was silent. It seemed to her that Philip Hunton-Hall had always had rather more self-respect than he was entitled to, and rather less respect for his wife than she deserved. She had known Diana since university, and had had a ringside seat observing the couple in their courting days. Lizzie, then starting her teacher-training, lived in a council bedsitter off the King's Road in London, barely a stone's throw (though a million miles in ambience) from Philip's elegant Chelsea flat. Diana, on her way to each date with the beautiful, brilliant man of her dreams, would drop in on Lizzie's damp cavern of study papers and education textbooks. She was always early and eager, her neat little shoes pattering excitedly up the filthy outside staircase and along the walkway strewn with broken glass. She generally wanted reassurance.

'Lizzie, do I look OK? I mean, smart? He's taking me to meet some of his political friends, and they're all so grown-up!'

'You look fine. You can give all those old boilers a good twelve years' start, so why worry? Go in jeans and a T-shirt and you'll still make them look like old mutton-bags.'

'I don't want to show him up. Oh, Lizzie, I think he might actually propose. I can't imagine what he sees in me! Oh, God, I could die, it's so exciting!'

Lizzie would survey the vivid little blonde creature sprawled on her bed with pity and affection. She privately thought Philip was a cold fish, far too old and chilly for the trusting Diana. Her friend was, in Lizzie's view, still absurdly young for her age: a dreamy country girl from Derbyshire who had hardly even dated at university, preferring cosy girl-talk round a gas fire. It was a thousand pities that her first explosion of romantic love should be wasted on this Philip creature. He talked down to her. He clearly despised her degree, himself possessing a Cambridge first. He bored on about politics. He plainly loved himself more than anything, and the Conservative Party more than his girlfriend. Moreover, it seemed more than likely that he would be elected to Parliament in 1979, and as far as the independent-minded feminist Lizzie was concerned the life of an MP's wife must be atrocious. She hinted at these things to Diana, but never got far because she could not bear to hazard their friendship. Once, when Diana came by the bedsitter at 9.30 after a quick supper with

Philip, Lizzie peered suspiciously into her guest's bag, and prodded a thick sheaf of paper.

'What's this? Writing a blockbuster?'

'I'm typing some stuff up for Philip. It's a report' — she glowed with pride — 'for the Shadow Chancellor's Office!'

'He's got a secretary!' squawked Lizzie. 'And he's rich as a pig, he could afford a typist! You're not a skivvy!'

'I said I'd do it. I've got Mum's portable at home. It jumps a bit, but it'll be OK if I'm careful.'

'You type half the day at your job! Bloody hell, Di, he takes you for granted!'

Diana's reply echoed down the years, so that Lizzie seemed to hear it now as clearly in her comfortable, cluttered, invalidish front room as when she had heard it long ago, in that manky little room in Chelsea.

'That's fine. He can take me for granted. I love him. I *am* granted.'

The reply had silenced Lizzie, withering the words of satirical scorn on her lips. Diana looked so beautiful, so shining in her devotion to Philip Hunton-Hall, that her friend could not bring herself to jeer. What would be, would be.

Since that time she had witnessed the wedding — a grand, brittle affair at a London church nearer to Philip's home than Diana's ('because he has to invite a lot of his political friends, and they haven't got time to travel'). She had rejoiced at the arrival of baby Amanda, a mere week after her own Joseph; and remained as close to Diana as their lives and jobs allowed for twenty-three years. Andy's acceptance of a headship in Philip's constituency town brought them geographically close again, and left Lizzie better able to judge what had become of the union. Seen from the perspective of her own rough-and-tumble family happiness, Diana's life in the beautiful, orderly, silent manor house dismayed and chilled her.

And now Diana was here, sitting by her sofa, worrying what effect her tiny step into independence would have on a man who had never given a damn about the effect his all-consuming political career had on his wife. After a pause Lizzie said: 'Well, you take the job and to hell with him, I say. He was the MP for twenty years, and even if they de-select him, he's got a life. All these directorships and deals and whatsit.'

'It meant so much to him, being an MP,' mourned Diana. 'They all hate leaving Parliament. He still thinks he can go back to it, maybe at the next election. If I say anything which implies he won't ever be an MP again he goes spare.'

Lizzie flinched a little. Her head was throbbing and there were stabs of the new pain, the deep pain which had occupied most of her thoughts, and Andy's, for the past couple of weeks.

'Oh, Di-ana! Just forget about Philip's feelings, can't you? Just for a bit? He's healthy, he's rich, he's got you, he's got boardroom tables to sit round. He can't have bloody everything. It's a lousy business being an opposition backbencher anyway, I wouldn't make my dog do it. It's your turn to make the decisions. Take the new job.'

But Diana was looking attentively at her now, instead of listening, and merely said: 'Pain? Do you want your injection thing?'

'No,' said Lizzie bleakly. 'I try to hang on as long as I can. It's a sort of game. Makes me too sleepy, anyway.'

'Oh, Lizzie, I wish you — ' But a thin, raised hand stopped her.

'Shut up. No hospital talk. I've got the new drug coming on stream next week. You just bugger off and take your job. Best thing you can do for me is to bring home all the gossip.'

'I am going to take it. It's just I worry — '

'Don't. Stupid thing to worry about. *Che sera sera*. Go and work in your newsroom and stir up dreadful scandals about the new MP, then they'll have a by-election and Philip can return in glory and sing your praises forever.'

'I wish,' said Diana.

Leaving her friend so pale and wrecked on her sofa, she felt a stab of guilt at the lightness of her own heart. But then, an hour with Lizzie always eased the load of her feelings about Philip. It would have surprised Lizzie Morgan very much indeed to know how welcome this service was. Nobody but Diana herself knew, or ever would know, just how much of the old infatuation had condensed and hardened, over two decades, into a burden of dreary loyalty that was well-nigh unbearable.

6

Philip let himself into the darkened house, took off his pale Burberry raincoat, and shook the fat heavy drops of rain from it. He hung it on its long-accustomed hook, then abruptly put both hands against the half-timbered wall of the hallway and rested his forehead for a moment against the coat's damp warmth. His wet hair lay plastered in dark-grey strands across his nape, and sent drips down the back of his shirt collar. Arriving home half an hour earlier, seeing the bedroom light twinkling through the trees, he had been seized with the impossibility of going back into the Manor. Not for the first time on such an evening, he parked his car on the bumpy grass by the far end of the drive and walked for a while under the trees, stumbling often in rabbit-holes and over molehills. There was no moon, and the little belt of woodland smelt sharply of fox and carrion. He could lie down, he thought dully, and never get up, but let the wild things find and eat him.

At last he returned to the car, and drove slowly towards the house's broad uncaring bulk. Ghosts of past garden-parties flickered around him on the broad lawns. The figure of his erstwhile Prime Minister, bouffantly blonde, tripping like a partridge in her high heels, had moved among his guests at one memorable event in the mid-1980s when she still commanded the height of her glory. With his hand on her sleeve, Philip had steered her through the admiring crowd — his crowd, his voters and workers, standing round in smart ties and hats like a bouquet he had gathered to lay at the Leader's feet. In his immaculate drawing-room Margaret Thatcher herself had taken a cup of tea before the long black car took her back to Downing Street.

He remembered every detail: she had admired the curtains, and asked Diana for the name of the pattern of pheasants and curlicues. Diana had not known its name, or appeared to care very much. 'Oh, one of those Colefax and thingummy patterns. Actually, we bought them off the people who sold us the house, didn't we, Phil? They were chintz freaks. You should have seen their sofa.' He had reddened and changed the subject. Later, his wife had dropped a disparaging remark about the Prime Minister — some wisecrack from her leftie friend Lizzie, no doubt — and he, Philip, had been too angry to speak to her for the rest of the evening.

He was never sure whether or not she had noticed this: a characteristic of their life together, even during Amanda's tiring babyhood and the tension and disruption of general elections, was that his wife's equable good humour did not change. He might snap and snarl and offer her small but deadly insults, but Diana would always smile. Sometimes, her smile made him lonely.

Self-pity welled within him, for he was not entirely sober. The Party no longer wanted him. They had come right out with it. They wanted a younger, more fashionable type. A woman probably, or a homosexual, or somebody with a Northern accent and a childhood in clogs. They had made it clear that he had better jump before he was pushed; Edmund had even had the nerve to draft a letter to Central Office for him to sign.

None of it was Philip's fault. How could it be? Politics — real, grown-up politics, a man's game — had been his life. He had been held back, no question! by this naïve wife of his. Too kind, too ready to sway to any wind, no real interest in public life, all surface sweetness and no grit. He should have married a woman like Sandra, his secretary in the Commons: dark, sharp, ambitious for a seat of her own. She would not have let him take the few false steps which had cost him his promotion in the black days of 1993. She would have advised and helped him. Perhaps he should have cut free from Diana, openly, and married her. Sandra liked him well enough; certain glances and smiles made him sure that he could have made her his mistress just as many of his colleagues did their secretaries in the good old days. He could have done just that: she would have been his helpmeet in politics.

Why had he not? Caution? Timidity? Lack of desire? Loyalty to Diana? Had she deserved it?

Philip raised his head from the damp coats on the rack, and looked blearily around. Bedtime. As he went into the hall, his foot caught on a shabby leather bucket bag, Diana's ubiquitous holdall for work. He kicked it, viciously. Like so many other things connected with her work and her life, the bag was solid proof to him that she had no respect for his position. It was not the sort of bag that the wife of an eminent man should be carrying. It was not, come to that, a bag which his elegant and detached daughter Amanda would be likely to carry.

Philip kicked it again, harder. The drawing-room door was ajar, and without turning on any more lights he made for the heavy oak cupboard in the gloom.

Upstairs, half-asleep, Diana heard the door open and close, a long silence, and then a muted clink of glass and bottle. She pulled the covers over her, and huddled deeper into the pillow.

★ ★ ★

The night bus from Bordeaux was full, and the woman next to Eva overflowed her seat and snored with terrible intensity. For the first hour, Eva yawned and tried to read her book, an English crime novel she had found abandoned on the beach days ago. Reading these books, she always thought, would improve her colloquial English, but some of the slang was so unfamiliar she could not grasp it at all. She had managed to work her way through a couple of Dorothy L. Sayers novels, but this Raymond Chandler . . . he did not talk like the English people she listened to on the BBC World Service. Eventually the motorway lights flashing by made her feel sick, and she closed her eyes and tried to sleep. To lull herself she counted countries on her fingers, like rosary beads. She kept no diary, it would have been just one more weight to carry on her back, but there was great comfort in unreeling a mental film, the unwritten journal of her travels. So many borders crossed already!

The Czech Republic first, but that hardly counted. She had been lucky to get that lift with Matziek's friends, but the drive towards Austria had been a blur, literally, blurred with rain streaming down the windows of the old Lada whose windscreen wipers hardly worked. Even if the views had been good, though, Eva suspected that she would not have paid them much attention in those first two days. Too vivid in the foreground was the memory of her father and Max, standing together stony-faced, wishing her a good journey. Max could fend for himself in the station canteen, but she shuddered with worry about what her father would eat when there was nobody to cook for him. She would always, she thought, associate those little grey Czech towns with guilt.

'Don't let them hold you back,' Matziek had said firmly. 'Parents must not do this, not in the modern world.' But, thought Eva, she did not have 'parents', a cosy pair looking after one another as they had before she was born. She had one parent, alone and embittered, with only his big slow son for company. She had consciously abandoned him, knowing precisely what it would cost his comfort.

They had stopped outside Prague, and slept in the car. Eva wanted very much to go into the city; but the boys began arguing about money, and about how early to leave, and anyway they had all agreed it was best to sleep in the vehicle and keep moving. So in the end it was simpler to buy bread and cheese at a small village shop and carry on towards Austria at dawn the next day.

Josef picked up two hitch-hikers near the border, a Romanian boy who claimed his name was simply 'G', and his silent black girlfriend. Joe bargained with them over payment for a share of the petrol, and they accepted his terms with such suspicious alacrity that Eva was almost sure they were smuggling drugs. G and the girl sat squashed with her and the luggage in the back seat: they wore heavy, puffed-up anoraks through which she could feel small bulky parcels; once on a bend, when the girl lurched towards her and her mouth gaped open. Eva had to stifle a wave of nausea. The girl's teeth were all rotten, brown and yellow stubs of corruption, and her breath deadly. The pair left without warning once they were inside Austria, vanishing into the trees near Gmund.

'You shouldn't risk hitch-hikers,' Eva said crossly. 'It's crowded enough already, in this car, and these were bad people. I think he had a gun.' The two Polish boys laughed and shrugged, but they were shaken and she saw that despite their van and their surface swagger, they understood little more than she did about the world. At Salzburg they dropped her at the bus station, and, as Matziek had promised, she found it easy to get a cheap ride into Italy.

So that was three countries already, in the first three confusing days. She had not truly wanted to travel alone, but in Wroclaw among the students the word was that no backpacker from the old Iron Curtain lands need ever be alone for long. Even in places where Westerners looked down on you, with your shabby clothes and meagre supply of money, there were always others like you to share your secret laughter and secret envy, and to tell you where the hostels and the illegal jobs were to be found. 'It's a kind of invisible club, you don't see it till you're there,' said Matziek. 'Even Russian kids, they're part of it. We've all had the same shit life, compared to how they live in the West. But obviously, it's better if you find Poles.'

In Milan, in a hostel, she met Vessela and Reni, two pretty, carefully groomed girls from Bulgaria who giggled a great deal. They conversed easily enough in a mixture of German, English, and scraps of their own languages. They were her first friends outside Poland, and Eva prattled to them as if they were kindred spirits; she never noticed the amused, catty glances between them when she told them about Tadek and her dilemma about love and freedom. They intrigued Eva, not least because they had cheap-smart suitcases and vanity bags instead of backpacks, and wore shoes which were, by hostel standards, exotic and wildly impractical. They spoke chiefly of men, but not in the tender, puzzled tones of their new Polish friend.

'Watch the Italian men,' said red-headed Vessela. 'They are not sincere. Not serious.' Reni went off into peals of dirty laughter and shook her tumbling henna-brown curls. 'That's why we go to Germany next. No more sleeping in these hostel bunks. There are insects, you know?'

'Insects don't stab as deep as Italians,' said

Vessela, and snickered.

Eva did not understand, but spent a sociable evening in a bar with the girls, culminating in half-an-hour of terror when three Italian boys in leather jackets homed in on them, and proved beyond doubt that they were far from sincere in their intentions. In the end the three girls took to their heels, dodging at last out of the frightening streets and alleys into a broad square by a great cathedral, where there were enough lights and passers-by to deter their attackers.

'He had a knife!' panted Eva, terrified, her back against the old stone walls. 'He had a knife! He would have cut us!'

'That's nothing,' said Reni, airily. She had taken off her shoes to run, and was dangling the strappy fragile things in her hand. She bent and slipped them back on, and resumed her more normal stance, pelvis tilted provocatively, chest thrust out. She had told Eva she was a psychology graduate from Sofia. 'Italian men do anything they want. Look!' She rolled up her sleeve and showed a row of cigarette burns. 'My fiancé!'

'You were engaged? To an Italian?'

'Booked, not engaged,' said Vessela, cattily. Eva suddenly saw under the street light that despite her glamour she had the suspicion of a moustache.

'What do you mean, booked?' Eva still did not understand.

The two Bulgarian girls, lounging now with studied insouciance, glanced at one another and giggled.

67

'Oh, tell her! It's no shame!' said Vessela. She shook the cloud of curly hair that cascaded red over her shoulders.

'We are wives by Internet,' said Reni. She made the shape of a computer screen with her long, expressive hands and began to quote, in sing-song English: ''Bulgarian women are cheerful and sociable, warm-hearted and charming, and make devoted mothers and faithful wives.'' She grinned at the thunderstruck expression on little Eva's face, and continued in the same tone. ''But the best things in life are never free. If you want a truly grateful and docile woman to make your home a heaven'' — at her side, Vessela did a satirical caper, and flapped her arms like wings — ''why not browse our lovely listings of sincere girls, and register with our responsible agency, www.encountersofiagirls.com.''

'You were *advertised*?' Eva tried to hide her scandalized expression in the darkness of the cathedral's shadow. She had heard of these agencies. Students spoke about them with giggles, but educated Polish girls had only scorn for the Ukrainans, Bulgarians, Slovaks and Romanians who were reputed to fill the websites. 'They have pictures, imagine! For men to look over!' Halina had said, closing her eyes in horror. 'Like a shop window.'

But Reni and Vessela were unashamed, giggling about the two rich Milanese — 'Fat buckets of pasta!' said Reni — who had paid their fare to Milan, given them trinkets they could re-sell, and been swiftly discarded.

'We want Germans,' said Vessela firmly. 'Rich, industrial Germans with nice houses. Who go out to work in banks all day and leave us in peace.'

'Or Englishmen,' said her friend thoughtfully. 'Lords.'

'Lords don't marry agency girls!' said Eva, unable to help herself. Despite the difficulty of following the tatty paperback novels she had found in the hostel, Lord Peter Wimsey had found his way into her private pantheon of model men.

'We-e-e-ll,' drawled Vessela, 'they can keep me as a mistress, then. If they are rich.'

Eva felt awkward with them after that; tainted somehow, as if she herself were part of some cynical and sordid trade. Before, her comparative poverty in this rich land had seemed to be merely a small burden of her own. She stood outside shops and theatres and the grand Opera House watching the sleek Italian crowds without envy or rancour, only wishing she could talk to them and know about their homes and lives. After Vessela and Reni, a darker understanding oppressed her. A poorer person was always, she thought, a menace: a leech, a beggar, a taker of favours. In the hostel there was a savage-faced girl with slanting eyes and a crooked arm, which looked as if it had been broken long ago and badly set. She was aloof, sly, and walked the streets each evening, returning with rolls of Euro notes which she hid in her underwear, spitting like a cat at anybody who looked at her with curiosity. Eva was afraid of her and said something disparaging to Reni, but for once the Bulgarian girl was not catty or censorious. 'She is Chechen,' she said simply. 'Everyone in her family is dead now, I think. She has no papers. She is seventeen. The police came for her once, and she had to do blow-jobs to get free. The Italians who brought her here to work are looking for her too because she ran away from the house in Rome. I don't know what she will do.' After that, Eva tried smiling at the nameless, angry girl, but never received a smile in return.

After some excursions, including a dreamlike coach trip to Venice which used up a frightening amount of her money, Eva took a bus from Milan and travelled right through France into Spain — countries four and five! — and fell in with a couple of cheerful, reassuringly respectful Russian boys. They went a long way towards dispelling her dislike of their compatriots, and also her sense of inferiority. 'We work harder than Western boys and we are cleverer,' they said. 'They only want to surf and skate and be lazy. So there are always jobs in the summer.' They were working an ice-cream barrow on the beach near Blanes, efficiently and cheerfully, and let her help them with the refilling and cleaning in return for a spare wooden bunk in the staff quarters of the hotel which owned the business. Here, after a few days, Eva was roughly summoned by the proprietor and given a proper cash job unloading the big industrial dishwashers in the heat and clatter of the kitchen. Earning her first Euros, albeit illegally, for real work was a balm to her pride.

On Wednesday, their day off, she and the boys would take a bus into Barcelona and wander the streets, admiring the people and the shops. In the third week they all got two days off and went to Madrid on a train, which took up most of their week's wages. Vladimir, the richest of them, insisted that they ate *tapas* in a restaurant, and grandly paid Eva's share; then outside the bullring, they all had a vehement argument about cruelty, and later sprawled on the dry grass for a free outdoor concert. The music transported her; after the month of hard work and uncertainty it seemed to offer a high plateau of dignity and peace, on which her mind could rest for two blessed hours. Just thinking about it now, weeks later, she could feel the grass prickling through her T-shirt and taste the garlicky bread they all shared between them. On the night bus back to the coast, she slept so deeply that waking up with her head on big Vladi's shoulder, she muttered the baby word she used for her father: 'Tatusiu?' The Russian laughed drowsily, and pushed the cushion of his jacket more firmly under her head. She slept again, an absurd sense of safety cradling her. He was strong, he was carelessly kind, he would not harm her.

But after a few more weeks Eva grew uneasy with her life. Her horizons began to broaden again, and when she mentally stood back to contemplate her own existence she felt demeaned and disgusted. She was doing menial work, swimming in the sea in her shabby T-shirt in the evenings, and attracting scornful glances

71

from the European holidaymakers of the Costa Brava. She was a little grey Polish mouse, insignificant, downtrodden. In the cities — Milan, Barcelona, Madrid — she had seen girls her own age dressed with casual elegance, going into theatres and opera houses and restaurants, laughing and secure in their place in the world while she shrank into the shadows. Only in free museums, galleries and libraries was she able to remember that she was educated, cultured, the daughter of a proud nation and holder of a respected university degree.

Once more, her comparative poverty began to weigh upon her spirits and dull the exhilaration of seeing new worlds. The Russian boys — there was another one now, snapping at her heels for the dishwasher job — were happy enough as long as they had beer money, and Vladi, her favourite among them, had hatched a plan to get a boat to Ibiza and 'meet English and German girls at the big discos'. Eva understood perfectly that she, a serious Pole, was not what they were looking for. They treated her with casual affection, like a younger brother. With her dark hair now cropped shorter than ever she looked the part.

So, after a while, she had got on a bus again, chumming up with Annie, an Australian girl she met on the beach. Annie was blonde and vivid and uncomplicated, and claimed to know Europe well from the previous year's travels. She bombarded Eva with questions about the former Iron Curtain, most of which she could not answer ('I was only little') and organized an alarmingly cheap bus ride over another border, back into France.

Annie, who seemed to have an inexhaustible notebook full of contacts and tips from other backpackers, had blagged them both work on a campsite by a broad and beautiful river in the south. Here, in return for cleaning and removing rubbish from vacated tents, they could sleep in a battered spare tent which leaked slightly in the occasional rain showers, and use the ablutions block freely. The hot modern showers, thought Eva, were almost the best part of that interlude. Annie was a sunny-natured girl, and together they spent their time off walking by the beautiful tumbling river, trying out canoes which the Czech hire-boy gave them free, fraternizing with the horses at the riding centre, and hitch-hiking into the nearest town to sit outside cafés admiring the peeling, tumbledown elegance of the houses. Eva's French remained sketchy, but with the prevalence of British holidaymakers her colloquial English grew better each day, although her BBC World Service and Dorothy L. Sayers vocabulary was by now tainted beyond recognition by Annie's breezy antipodean profanity.

The job ended abruptly, in the way of all irregular employment. Eva and Annie were told to collect their things together and vacate the shabby tent the same day. There was, muttered the proprietor, some kind of official inspection pending. He gave them a lift into town, weaving terrifyingly through the lanes at high speed, and left them with their backpacks in a sunny market square. They sat together at a table and counted over their money.

'Where you going next?' asked Annie. 'I wanna see Greece.'

Eva looked across the square: there was a church, with a weather-vane swinging lazily in the breeze. North, south, east, west? How strange, she thought, how strange for it not to matter which way she went. Through school and university there had always been a direction. One day, she supposed, she would have to get a job and lead a real life, and have appointments and be busy. Now, there was no reason to go anywhere rather than anywhere else. She had gone, flown from the high kitchen window and travelled beyond the distant mountain view until there were no rules any more. She tried to think of her father, and Max, but their images had blurred; the picture of Tadek swam into her mind and was far more solid, but she banished it with a shake of her head.

'It doesn't matter,' she said aloud.

' 'Course it does,' said Annie. 'I wanna see as much as I can. Next year it's back to college, then work all my bloody life, or bring up kids. I haven't seen Greece and Turkey yet. Temples. Really old tombs. Snorkelling. Jeez, yeah. That's where I'm going.'

Eva was silent. Annie looked at her with impatient affection. She liked the company of this little Polish kid, so lively and cheerful and willing to do the crappest jobs. Some of her compatriots had been sorely lacking in any sense of adventure, and merely settled down in London as nannies for six months at a time, so

74

they could go clubbing. At least Evie wanted to travel. But, Jeez! thought Annie, she was young for her age. More like sixteen than twenty-two. Beneath her breezy exterior the Australian girl had a strong maternal streak, and at that moment did not want to abandon the care of this dreamy little creature.

'You come too,' she said. 'You've got the bus fare. There's all sorts of hotel work in the Greek islands. I got some addresses. My friend Lisa worked last year on Skiathos. That's an island.'

'I think,' said Eva, who was tidying her small change into piles, 'I truly think I would like to go to England.' She glanced up at the wind vane. It was pointing north. 'Yes. England.'

'Nah,' said Annie, taking this as merely a starting point for discussion. 'You don't want to go to Britain. No way. It's not like the rest of Europe.'

'Have you been there?'

'Yup. I worked as a nanny in London for a coupla months. Never again.'

'Why?'

'How long have you got?' Annie exhaled with a loud 'Whoo!' sound and began counting on her fingers, her sunbleached ponytail bobbing emphatically as she made each point with a nod of the head. 'One — it's bloody cold most of the time, and it rains like hell. Two — it's expensive. Jeez, you would not *believe* what they think they can charge for rubbish food. And the hostels . . . I was OK, I lived in a little room at the top of a big posh house looking after these kids in a place called Kentish Town. Which brings me to point *three* — Britishers are mean as hell. Work you all hours and pay as little as they can get away with. You know how Monsieur Hirsch let us have the food from the campsite café every night?'

'Yes?'

'That's because he wasn't British. A Brit would have thrown it away and whinged about hygiene regulations, and made us buy our own. Strewth, Evie, you don't wanna go there.'

'I don't think they're all like that,' said Eva flatly. 'Maybe you worked for a mean family. I think British people are kind and friendly.'

'Ask anyone,' said Annie. 'It's an interesting place, sure, with the Queen and the history and everything. But it's expensive, it's wet, it's unfriendly, it's harder to get work there than in Europe, and besides the Brits prob'ly won't let you in.'

'For a visit, I think it's OK,' said Eva defiantly. 'I am not an immigrant.'

'They'll think you want to work illegally or use their hospitals for an abortion,' said Annie flatly. 'Forget it. Come to Greece. See temples and all that shit. We'll have a blast.'

'I think they'll let me in' said Eva thoughtfully. 'I have a letter from my friend's brother in Scotland, saying I am a visitor invited by him.'

'Scotland!' Annie almost shrieked. At a neighbouring table, a dumpy black-draped Frenchwoman glared at them. 'That's wetter and more expensive than England, even.'

'I'm not really going there,' said Eva. 'But it was quickest to get the letter from Adam. Really,

76

I am going to see my penfriend Manda. I was writing to her since I was sixteen. In my school, three of us wrote to English girls. It was part of her school project studying politics, and for me to practise English.'

'Well,' said Annie, still doubtful but a little reassured, 'that's a bit better, if you've got people to stay with. They've invited you, then?'

'Yes,' lied Eva. And, because she disliked lying, added more truthfully, 'I wrote to Manda before I left, she'll be expecting to see me before September anyway.'

'How long since she wrote to you?'

Eva didn't answer. In the silence between them, Annie guessed it was a matter of years rather than months. Finally she said: 'It's your funeral. I'm going to Greece. But I can give you the griff to get to England.' She riffled in her battered notebook. 'Cheapest way is the bus from Bordeaux to Paris, then another bus to Calais, and then the ferry. I'll write it down for you. If you stay in Paris, for God's sake use a hostel and don't think you can afford to buy anything in a restaurant. Better to wave at the Eiffel Tower and blast on quick. Once you're in England, money's still the problem. It's bloody expensive getting anywhere and you do not want to hitch on your own.' She looked narrowly at Eva, who was still enwrapt in the silence, trying not to think about Manda's failure to write. 'Will this English girl come and get you by car from Dover?'

'Oh, probably,' said Eva. Her hand stole into her bag and closed around her purse. She had saved in Spain, and a little on the campsite. There would be enough money. Perhaps. Or another job soon.

Next evening, on the night bus from Bordeaux, the memory of this moment made Eva wriggle uneasily in her seat. She must earn a bit more money. Soon. But never mind. There were always chances. And it was good that Britain would be country number six. Six was her lucky number.

It was a pity Manda had not written back before she left, but it was probably the fault of the post.

7

If it had not been for Philip's depression over his rift with the Party, thought Diana, this would have been a summer of soaring happiness. Not only was her new job pleasantly tiring, taxing and fascinating, but against all expectation Lizzie Morgan's latest round of treatment had brought improvement. When the sickness abated after the radiotherapy, her new drug regime seemed to leave her with more energy and cheerfulness than had been evident in months. One evening, she and Andy even came to dinner at the Manor for the first time since before Christmas.

Philip, surprisingly, rather liked Andy Morgan. Although their political views could not have been much farther apart they shared a passion for music, and could exchange animated views on musical education and the merits of notable conductors. In this area even disagreements seemed to form a kind of bond. They had long reached a silent ceasefire on political issues and matters like private education, and could spar quite happily about treatments and tempos and orchestras. If anything, Andy was more conserva-tive than Philip in musical matters, which balanced out their temperaments nicely. So if Diana was careful with the seating plan, it was possible for a whole dinner to pass without Philip remembering how much he disliked and distrusted Lizzie. She always looked as if she was laughing at him. Philip hated that more than anything.

For this reason, Diana preferred not to make their dinners together into cosy foursomes, which would inevitably entail putting Philip fairly close to Lizzie. On the other hand, she doubted whether the Morgans would want a big crowd. Six should be fine. She wondered for a while whether to make the evening into a kitchen supper. But Philip preferred formality, and this was Lizzie's first social outing since the apparent remission of her cancer: she deserved a bit of silverware and ceremony and an excuse to dress up.

The question was, who should the other couple be? Diana longed to bring together the two halves of her own life by asking Roger, the producer of the Henry Show with whom she worked most closely; he had a nice wife, who taught at the school and was friendly with Andy Morgan. But no, that might be provocative. Philip seemed to accept her job now, albeit grudgingly, but Roger talked constantly about broadcasting because it was his whole life. To have this stranger talking shop to Diana over their own dinner-table would ruin Philip's mood in no time. (As the thought went through her head she could almost hear Lizzie saying, 'Who cares? You spoil that man. He's not made of glass! Let him sulk, he'll come round.').

Eventually she settled on friends they had not seen for a while, Marianne and Tony Hamilton. Philip liked Tony, who was a strong Conservative supporter and taught Latin and Religious

Education at the local private school. He was a bit of a bore as far as Diana was concerned, but Marianne was fun: plump, pretty and flirtatious, an enthusiastic drinker and a great but not too irritating giggler. She also thought Philip very handsome, and was prone to hang on his words and flutter her long false lashes at him to pleasing effect. He referred to her as 'that ridiculous woman' but all the same, thought his wife, he was not wholly immune to admiration. What politician could be?

But when Diana rang with the invitation, Marianne said two things which blew her hostess right off course.

One was, 'Yes, I'd adore it, thank you so much, you've no idea how few invitations one gets. In the circumstances.' And the other, following a murmur of puzzlement from Diana, was, 'Oh, dear, perhaps you didn't know what circumstances I mean. Tony left me.'

'God, no — I mean, how?' sputtered Diana.

'Sixth-former. Well, one of last year's, she'd left. Busty little tart with a turned-down mouth. Shelley Martin. He just came right out with it, said he'd never been in love till that moment. It happened four weeks ago. On a Tuesday morning. They've gone to Tenby, of all places. The only good thing is, I've lost a stone.' Her voice rattled with misery.

After suitable commiseration, Diana put the phone down and clasped her brow. Marianne was coming to dinner, alone. Uneven numbers would not matter to her, but Philip hated them. He belonged in his mind to an earlier, posher and more formal generation which could not digest its food properly if there was a dangerous unpaired spectre at the feast. Diana sighed and ran her hands through her honey-gold hair. She was tired. Work was wonderful but the newsroom shifts in particular were surprisingly wearing, and even with their thrice-weekly cleaning woman it was difficult to keep the house the way that Philip liked it, as well as leaving him meals in the freezer and directions on what to do with them.

She often wished they were poorer. If her salary were vital to the household, it would be easier to tell Philip to get his own supper and put up with a bit of muddle and un-plumped cushions. But since his investments alone brought in a far higher income than her forty hours a week at Two Counties Radio, this seemed impossible.

So all right, it was silly and ridiculous, but she needed a spare man — not a woman — at short notice to fill the gap in her dinner table, and she was desperate to find one. The absurdity of the dilemma grated on her far more than it would have done six months earlier. Her work in the radio newsroom and her dealings with callers to the Henry Show had completed the process which began five years earlier when she went back to work. The fact was that Diana Hunton-Hall no longer belonged in her own world. The informality, the perpetual teenage casualness of modern life, had seduced her. Her working world was friendly and easy and larky and had no dress codes, while her married life was still the opposite: cautious and tactful, sober and civilized.

'I have,' said Diana aloud to the kitchen wall, 'been trapped inside a napkin-ring for twenty sodding years.'

She rang the vicar, who said he would have loved to come but was at a diocesan conference that night. She looked through the address book by the phone, and found two other men without partners, but realized just in time that both were part of the constituency association cabal which had so recently and woundingly ousted Philip as candidate. 'Hellfire!' she said, again aloud. 'So much for our social life!' More of it had been tied up with Conservatism than she had realized. She would not miss the political friends, but thought with dismay that Philip undoubtedly would.

Perhaps there was a new teacher at the school, some young single man who would already know Andy, and enjoy a square meal. As a last resort, with two days to go, she rang Andy and suggested this stratagem.

'Uneven numbers don't matter,' he said.

'They do to Philip.'

'Well, I've got two single men on the staff. One's gay, and comes with a partner who's a hairdresser with an eyebrow stud.'

Diana moaned, and Andy's laughter came down the line. 'The other is a very presentable lad with a public-school education and a degree in Classics, who plays the cello and — '

She broke in. 'Fantastic! What's his name? Gimme!'

'Let me finish,' said Andy. 'I was just going to tell you the snag.'

'What snag? There can be no snag. Public-school, classics, cello!'

'Ah. But he is so left-wing he thinks Tony Blair is practically Hitler, and that Thatcher was the Antichrist incarnate. I'd give him three minutes in a room with Philip before blood started seeping out under the door.'

'Damn! He sounded so perfect'

'Stop worrying. Five is a good number.'

But Diana did worry. This dinner, insignificant though it seemed, marked three important transitions in their lives. Firstly, Lizzie's apparent reprieve. Secondly, a slight but comforting easing of the frostiness between herself and Philip. Thirdly, it was her chance to prove to herself and to him that even with long hours and a demanding job she could still choreograph a pleasant social life to suit them both. There must — damn, damn, damn it! — be a spare man somewhere. She must use her talent to find one. She had, in her daydreams, thought of applying for a BBC researcher's job one day, down in London. They would throw tasks at her like finding a disabled gay couple who wanted to adopt a baby, or pinning down a former Royal footman to spill the beans on etiquette. This was child's play in comparison. Almost any man would do. All she wanted was to feed him in return for some uncontroversial conversation.

With this on her mind, she went into work next morning to be informed that Roger was ill so she would have to see Henry through the

84

mid-morning show alone.

'Fine,' she said, and began gathering interview notes and records, enjoying the relief of feeling her own ridiculous social and domestic problems recede and shrink in the face of work ones. 'Where *is* Henry, though?'

'Dropping his kid back with her mother. He'll be here by nine-thirty.'

In the event it was ten-fifteen when Henry ran in, damp and dishevelled, out of the rain.

'Flat — bloody — tyre,' he said. 'Would you credit it? I was just leaving Ali's and, crack! It went down on the rim. Nasty. I didn't have a spare in the car.'

'What?' said Diana. 'No spare wheel? Why not?'

'\'Cos I is feckless,' said Henry, dropping into patois and out again, and pulling off the striped hat he affected in his mock-Rastafarian moods. 'Why d'you think? Because I burst the other tyre on Friday night. And having Marley for the weekend, I didn't want to bugger up our access-time sitting around in garage waiting rooms. Blowouts never happen twice in quick succession. Never. Some evil deity is throwing tintacks under my chariot wheels. Someone up there hates me.'

'Someone is going to hate you down here,' said Diana in a tone of soothing menace, 'if you don't get on the air on time.'

Henry slid a sidelong glance at her, crackling with mischief, and continued his plaint.

'Plus, Marley woke me up at twenty-past-four this morning to make him a model of an electric cat. Christ knows where that came from.' He sat down on the bench in the control cubicle, yawning.

'You've got *ten minutes*,' warned Diana.

'I'm fine. I can busk it,' said Henry, looking vaguely around for his running-order. 'It's only the quiz in the first half. I'll put some nice long records on. Where's 'Bohemian Rhapsody' when you need it?'

Diana slapped a clipboard down on his lap, quite hard.

'Roger moved the quiz to Wednesday, remember? Today is the consumer interview. And listen up, Henry: we have to do it right up the top of the programme because the punter's due in court as a witness. It's legally complicated. You *have* to read the brief.'

'Oh, shit.' He took the papers from her, and frowned over them. He dropped his flippant manner and moaned, 'Diana, I can't take anything in. I'm finished. Help!'

She laughed at him, took the brief back and sat down on the bench beside him, pointing to salient points she had underlined and put into bold type.

'OK. It's not that bad. The basic story is that she went on holiday and the hotel was double-booked. Why it's complicated is that the tour operator claims it was under a local Spanish legal restriction . . . '

By ten-twenty-five Henry had grasped the issue. In heavy felt pen on his own pad, Diana wrote down for him again the name of the client, the tour operator, the disputed law in question and a few other keywords. He went into the studio at ten-thirty, uttered his usual exuberant greeting to the region, and put on a music track. The interviewee, a middle-aged woman of commanding aspect, was ushered into the studio to sit opposite his control desk, and squared herself to make her case. Diana watched her double-take at the sight of Henry's dark face, ringlet dreadlocks and exuberant parrot-patterned shirt, but then saw the presenter tilt his head at her engagingly as he made some observation. Instantly, she could see from the relaxation of the woman's shoulders that she too was smiling. Diana in turn relaxed. Henry would cope. He always did. The song played on, light and bouncy; Henry jigged a little, threw another melting smile at his interviewee, and slotted a jingle into the cartridge machine.

When the music faded, Diana sat in the control room with her clipboard of notes, marvelling at his smooth, assured, colloquial but intelligent interview. Oh, yes, he was worth his money. He always came through. The scatty, chaotic, flippant creature of the green room was a hundred per cent professional in the studio. Henry could play the jackass around in the office and be funny between records, but he always knew precisely how to pitch himself. With the alleged holiday-company victim he was articulate, attentive, and challenging without rudeness. She glanced down the running-order. She must remind him soon that they had a three-minute-23 tape of their tame chef, the Flying Foodie, to fit in before the eleven o'clock news.

He was doing polenta.

Her thoughts drifted, predictably, back to the dinner party. Not that Philip would eat polenta, but come to think of it, there had been a recipe a few weeks back which had sounded rather promising. Easy to do for six. No. Five. Damn!

She was looking straight at Henry as he wound up the interview and gave a helpline number for other disgruntled holidaymakers. The connection was inevitable. There he was: the answer to her prayer, a single man who was forever grumbling about his own cooking, and who knew how to pitch himself to any company.

Diana trembled a little at her own daring, but rebuked herself sharply for doing so. After all, she was not some twenty-two-year-old PA nerving herself to ask out a big star. She was a grown woman, wife of an ex-MP, who had entertained two Prime Ministers. She was perfectly entitled to ask a promising young presenter round to dinner. He would know how to be tactful with Philip. He would not get drunk or foul-mouthed. Above all, Lizzie would love him: she was always saying how much she envied her friend's modest brushes with showbiz. He would soon get the measure of Marianne Hamilton, who would be all aquiver with the pleasure and danger of light flirtation with a handsome young black man. Oh, if only Henry could be free!

It was the thought of Lizzie's pleasure which finally, after a couple more hours of intermittent doubts, nerved Diana to say as they cleared the studio at one o'clock: 'Henry, I was wondering if you might like to come to supper?'

She did not want, for some reason, to call it dinner.

He looked up vaguely from the CDs he was stacking.

'It's not suppertime, it's lunchtime. And do I need food! I think I've got this blood sugar thing. Going hypo. Pub. Urgent.'

'No — I didn't mean now — but yes, I was thinking of going to the pub if you are.'

It was their habit, with Roger, to spend half an hour in the Golden Lion eating soggy chicken pies after the programme.

'Good,' he said. 'See you down there?'

In the pub, turning a glass of cola on the table as she spoke, Diana courageously returned to the subject.

'When I mentioned supper just now, I meant at our house. On Wednesday. Philip and I have got a couple of friends coming who I think you might really like. He's head at the Leasmount School.'

Henry looked at her over his glass and, sounding suddenly far younger than usual, said: 'Hey, that's really kind. Are you sure?'

'Of course. And' — she hesitated, but ploughed on because his look of innocent youthfulness seemed to deserve honesty — 'it's not really kind. You'd be getting me out of a jam.'

She explained, and as she did so the usual mischief returned to the young man's features.

'Yo! You mean your husband really doesn't like dinner parties that don't balance? What do you do when you ask two gays round?'

'We've only done it once,' confessed Diana. 'We're ever so straight, you know. Philip was a Tory MP in the olden days when they didn't approve of that. But the time I did have the two gay partners round — they were musicians, so Philip didn't mind so much — we got two women to balance them.'

'Lesbians?'

'Not everything is about sex, you know.'

'Yes, it is.'

'No, it isn't. Anyway, it's a lot easier to get single women than single men, I don't know why. Men are like gold dust.'

'Hence, yours truly,' said Henry. 'Delighted to oblige.'

Diana was horrified. 'No, I didn't mean that. Well, even if I did at first, the *moment* I'd had the idea of asking you I realized that Lizzie would just adore to meet you. She's had really serious cancer, you see — '

Henry was laughing aloud now, drawing irritated glances from the staider corners of the pub.

'Yeah, as well as being usefully rare, I do go down particularly well with people who've got terminal illnesses. They can't run so fast.'

He stopped abruptly, seeing the look on Diana's face. 'Sorry. Shouldn't have said 'terminal', should I? You love this Lizzie, right?'

'I do,' said Diana. A small, observing corner of her mind murmured how un-English it was of Henry to use the word 'love' in the context of dinner-party friends of the same gender, but a far greater part felt pure relief at saying for the first time that yes, indeed, she loved Lizzie Morgan. 'Like a sister,' she added. 'I never had one, you see.'

'I did,' said Henry. Then, more quietly, 'Haven't seen her for years and years. We got adopted by two different families. I wrote once, but she didn't answer.'

'I'm sorry,' said Diana. There was a pause, but not an awkward one. She smiled, and Henry smiled back.

'Anyway . . . ?'

'Yes, I'd like to come. Thank you. Another drink?'

That evening, Philip was at home listening to Mahler when she arrived with her shopping bags from the supermarket on the town bypass. He looked up, and said, 'Have a good day?' It was a rare moment. He did not often ask.

'Yes,' she said. 'I've asked a nice boy to join us on Wednesday, so that'll be company for Marianne. Take her mind off things with Tony.'

'Tony Hamilton!' said Philip musingly. It was so unlike him to gossip — with her at least, maybe he did with his political friends — that Diana stayed where she was, in the doorway, rather than taking the shopping through to the fridge. 'Tony Hamilton! I still don't believe it.'

'Well, young girls . . . she was one of his pupils. He's not the first man to be carried away.'

'Stupid,' said Philip. 'Though, mind you, he might have had provocation. Marianne's a bit . . . you know.'

'A bit what?' This was such a novel

91

conversation for the two of them to be having that Diana felt quite light-headed: maybe there really was a new chapter opening in their marriage.

'Nympho,' said Philip. 'I didn't tell you this, but she made a hell of a pass at me, a couple of years back.'

'No!' Diana considered for a moment. 'Well, perhaps if she was really pissed . . . '

It was a wrong note. His face became shuttered once more, and he just said coldly, 'I hate that word. On a woman's lips especially.'

'That's a bit old-fashioned,' she protested. He went on, though, in a flat bored voice.

'Well, I'll have to get used to it, I suppose. You always come home from that radio station of yours swearing like a fishwife.'

Diana took the shopping through to the fridge. She was all the more annoyed because she realized the accusation was perfectly true. Everyone in the office — except perhaps Steve — used words like pissed, crap, fuckwit, bugger and shit on a daily basis and did not even notice. It sometimes seemed miraculous to her that they never got on the air.

8

The sea voyage was thrilling. Eva thought of it as a sea voyage, although it was only a couple of hours; just a thin sleeve of water after all, smaller than the great Masurian lakes of her childhood holidays (memories foamed in the ship's wake: Mother laughing, Father younger and full of energy, Max trying to tip the rowing-boat over by rocking it). The ferry had few passengers, and she roamed around it, up and down the stairs, excited at being on a real ship, bearing her away from her continent for the first time. The ship was so empty that she risked leaving her backpack on the luggage shelves, and ran about free and unencumbered like a child on an outing. She patted metal bulkheads with their curious round-topped rivets, and popped out on to the deck when she saw a door to the outside.

There was nobody else out there, and many gangways and stairs were barred; but Eva found that she could go to the very back of the ship and lean on the rail, where she stood watching the clean wash splaying and bubbling astern, and the land vanishing into the mist. At last she was forced indoors by driving rain, and — wincing a little at the reminder of money — spent some of her Euros on a plate of sausage and chips. As the ship approached Dover, the rain eased and she was able to go out again, warmed by the food, and stand shivering with excitement on the upper deck, watching the misty grey cliffs and the curving line of the harbour wall.

The emotion of the moment filled her eyes with tears, and the wind tore them away and drove them backwards across her cheeks. This was England, Britain — she never knew which to say, and feared very much that she would give offence to English (British?) people. Was it OK to say England if you actually were in England, and Scotland in Scotland? Was it truly one country, or four? No schoolteacher in Poland had ever managed to give her a satisfactory answer to this point, and when Halina — whose degree was in modern politics — told her that you should always say 'Britain', her advice was immediately devalued by the omnipresent news items about the England football team in the World Cup.

But whatever you called it, this was the place. The BBC World Service news came from here, which even her father approved of. He could not always understand it, and would make Eva translate, but told her that with her mother, he had listened to Polish and Russian language news from the BBC all through the bad years, and also through the time of Solidarity and the Velvet Revolution in Czechoslovakia and the great changes of the 1980s.

And Shakespeare came from here, and Kipling. Her mother used to recite Kipling, a poem called 'If'. '*If you can bear to hear the truth you've spoken, twisted by knaves to make a trap for fools*'. This had seemed to mean a lot to her; she had always been the most political person in the family. Eva looked at the looming cliffs through the drizzle, and thought how pleased her mother, at least, would have been that she was seeing England. It eased her guilt over Tatusiu and Max, and made a counterweight to a certain sense of chilly dismay at the forbidding aspect of autumnal Britain.

In Spain it had been hot, in the French campsite pleasantly warm. Today, the first of September, Britain presented a bleak aspect, and with a shiver of worry Eva realized that she had not brought any of her warm clothes from Poland. When she had talked of travel with Matziek and the others they spoke only of heat, and beaches, and a gentle Mediterranean lifestyle. Adam wrote from Scotland that it was cold, but Scotland was far away in the north.

Still, she could ease the pressure in her heavy rucksack. While the ferry docked, Eva pulled on an extra T-shirt and her two thin sweaters together. With the waterproof anorak over the top, there was far more room in the pack. Hoisting it, she walked down the gangway clutching her passport and the letter from Adam, and prepared to face the immigration authorities.

Ten minutes later, baffled and delighted by the insouciance with which she had been waved through, she was walking towards Dover town, unhindered and unnoticed. It must be true what Matziek said: 'They have strict days and days they don't seem to care. If you're lucky and the ship's half-empty, you'll walk through.' She had, on his instructions, assured the bored immigration lady that she was only in the country for a fortnight, with no intention of working. It was a lie, but never mind that. She was here. The rain had eased, and outside the bus station Eva could stand and read the timetables and consult her faded book of maps. She had to go through London. That would be an adventure in itself. But she would not stay to see the capital city, not yet. There was a friend to find and honey to deliver.

★ ★ ★

Henry was, as Diana had guessed, a perfectly pitched guest. He had even taken the trouble to wear a suit. Philip did a swift double-take when he saw that the newcomer was black, with dreadlocks, and darted a reproachful glance at Diana for not having warned him; but his courtesy held, and he was disarmed by Henry's finely calculated deference and the artful way that he had brought with him not a bottle (which Diana had feared) but a newly released review CD remastering of Sargent conducting the Eroica. 'I know you're interested in interpretations, and this really is a collector's piece, sir.'

The 'sir', thought Diana, was particularly masterly. She had in fact clean forgotten to mention her visitor's race, and felt a little remorseful when she saw Philip's naked amazement. This was provincial England, his world, not Notting Hill. It would have been tactful at least to have mentioned it. She absolved her husband of racist feeling, though: it was pure surprise on his face, as if her guest had sported an unforeseen Mohican haircut or a wooden leg. Henry rapidly consolidated his strong position by weaving into his conversation a warm accolade for one of the former Conservative culture ministers as 'the only man in that job who's ever understood what the arts are about'.

Lizzie, already there when Henry arrived, was delighted with him: he was everything she liked, young and vital and (tactful treatment of Philip apart) pleasantly irreverent. He was, as Diana had hoped he would be, a more than welcome visitant from a vigorous outer world, unlikely to ask boring and intrusive questions about chemotherapy and prognoses and the whole dreary business of her cancer. She bombarded him with questions about his job, and demanded to know what was the difference between rap and dub poetry. Diana teased her a little about this feeble middle-aged attempt to get up to speed; Andy and Philip looked at the Sargent CD cover notes. Altogether, by the time Marianne Hamilton rang the doorbell, the party was going with a swing.

Marianne was already drunk. Well, tipsy. Diana realized that she should have been prepared for this. It had been stupid of her not to ask Marianne over for six o'clock, and serve her deliberately weak drinks while she got her grievances off her chest in comparative privacy. She must have needed a great deal of courage to come out to dinner alone, and had clearly opted for the Dutch variety. Now, decked out in a tight black shiny skirt and shrieking turquoise blouse with a very low neck, poor Marianne was in such a condition that she plainly should not have driven her own car to the Manor.

'I forgot to ask,' said her hostess quickly, as a slight lurch towards the coat-rack betrayed Mrs Hamilton's state, 'would you like to stay over, in the blue spare room? It's all made up ready.'

'YeshIwould,' said Marianne. 'Breakfast with you and lovely lovely Philip. Mush more intimate.' Then, with the inconsequential interest of the tipsy, 'Who the hellisthat?'

She was gazing raptly at Henry's back view, where he stood deep in conversation with Lizzie Morgan. 'Lovely shoulders! Shnake hips, too.' She was not in full control of the volume of her voice, and from a slight tremor in Henry's shoulders Diana realized that he had heard.

'It's Henry from work' she said more quietly. 'He's a presenter on Two C Radio.'

'Henry who? I could put it in my little black book.'

'His surname is actually Windsor,' began Diana, who had been failing to mention this picaresque fact in Philip's presence for the past twenty minutes. 'But he was a foundling, so he was given that name because that's where the children's home was, before he was adopted. I mean, they found him and his sister under a tree in Windsor Great Park, when they were too small to say anything but their first names.'

'Romantic!' said Marianne, weaving a little but lowering her voice.

'Then,' said Diana, 'he went back to that name

when he grew up, because his adoptive parents are called Henryson and he says he felt like an Icelander, calling himself Henry Henryson.'

She was steering Marianne into the drawing-room now, and planned to leave her there while she brought the food through. Philip would be annoyed at such precipitate starting of dinner, but from long experience Diana knew that the only thing to do with drunken guests was to feed them, fast.

Henry turned, politely, as she brought Marianne close to him, and the hostess could see that he had sized her up at a glance. Placing a firm hand on her arm he said, 'Just what we need. Mrs Morgan and I were arguing about colours, and I can see you're on my side. Bright is best. Gorgeous blouse.'

'Yes,' said Lizzie, equally willing to come to the aid of the party. 'Henry was saying he likes Caribbean colours, like that red shirt he's got on now, and I was saying I'm a monochrome girl. Grey, beige, black — Armani all the way.'

Philip and Andy had moved up to the far end of the room, and were talking earnestly. Diana saw that her two friends would, between them, contain Marianne for a while, so she handed her a supposed gin-and-tonic with no gin in it, and retired to the kitchen.

'Five minutes,' she said to Lizzie as she left. 'Can you chase everyone to table in five minutes?'

Lizzie nodded, and returned to the technico-loured conversation that was developing between Henry and Marianne. The big woman was leaning forward, showing abundant pink flesh, and jabbing her forefinger at Henry's red shirt. He was looking down at her, flirting obediently, offering full eye contact and broad white smiles.

'What a lark he is,' Lizzie murmured to her friend a few minutes later, in the doorway of the dining-room. 'No wonder you like work!'

'I can't believe how marvellous he's being. Even Philip's charmed,' said Diana. 'It was a desperate last-ditch throw, you know. I needed a man for tonight, any man.'

Henry, whose hearing was exceptionally acute, a tool of his trade, turned his head and winked at her, to Diana's considerable mortification. Marianne, suddenly sharper, saw the wink and offered a most indiscreet thumbs-up.

'Jusht the ticket, darling,' she said between courses, bringing her soup plate out to the kitchen against Diana's express pleading for her to stay still. 'Your Henry's gorgeous. You desherve a little fling. Wish I'd done more of it while bloodybloody Tony was bunking up with his little tarts.'

'No!' said Diana, horrified, her blushes veiled by clouds of steam rising off the casserole. 'He's not — I'm not — good grief, Madge, he's way too young for me! He's someone I work with! He's got a girlfriend, I think, and a four-year-old kid by another ex-girlfriend!'

'Thassyour story,' said the tipsy woman complacently, picking a cherry off the elaborate pudding on the worktop. 'Shtick to it, thassagirl.'

'Philip — ' began Diana, but stopped and laughed. 'Never mind. Just go back and sit down.

I'll bring the food through. Everything else is out on the sideboard.'

The nods and winks, however, continued, becoming increasingly boisterous as Marianne worked her way through the nearest bottle of wine. Mercifully Philip did not seem to notice and Henry played a deadpan game of pretending not to, even when Marianne squeezed his knee and slurred, 'Luckylady, Diana.' Lizzie watched with wary amusement, and the two older men carried on a completely independent conversation.

At twenty-past-nine, just as the casserole plates were being cleared, an unexpected noise echoed through the house, making all five seated diners raise their heads questioningly.

'Is that the *doorbell?*' asked Lizzie, surprised. 'At this time of night? Who're we expecting?'

'Nobody,' said Diana, poised with a pile of plates. 'Philip? Are you?'

He was on his feet, a flush on his cheeks. In his days as an MP, during the recess it was the habit of his local chairman to call round in mid-evening with news or progress reports on constituency matters. A call right now could only be Edmund, bearing apologies and the association's penitent desire to keep him on as candidate.

'I'll go.'

'Thanks.' His wife's eyes followed him, uneasy and anxious. A strange feeling shook her. Glancing round the table, she suddenly seemed to see all the guests with new eyes: Lizzie pale, thin and sick, Andy worn down with concern,

101

Marianne a fat pasty overdressed caricature of a woman. Even the youthful Henry became suddenly just an overly sharp-faced, watchful young man in a slightly spivvy suit with too much of a waist to it. The leftover stew congealing on the plates in her hands looked equally disgusting: fragments of vegetable and fat glued together in its vinous viscosity. It was as if the whole room was a picture jolted out of its frame, hanging precarious and askew, suddenly tawdry.

On the front step, meanwhile, Philip was looking down at a small, urchin figure with a rucksack. It took him a moment to realize that it was not a boy child but a young woman. There was no car in sight so she must have walked from the bus stop in the village: if so, it must have taken her an hour at least, for the last bus passed through shortly after seven. Her damp, mud-splattered and windblown appearance confirmed this theory.

The figure said, in piping girlish tones: 'I am sorry to disturb, but is this the right house for Amanda Hunton-Hall?'

9

Philip looked down at the urchin figure on the doorstep, took a breath and said bemusedly: 'Well, Amanda is my daughter. But she lives in London now.'

Eva stared in horror at the handsome, silver-haired old man before her. She blurted out: 'Oh — but I have just come from London! I was there one whole day!'

Her stare was direct, limpid and innocent. Philip could not, despite a sense of helpless irritation, prevent himself from saying: 'Well, do come in out of the rain for a moment or two, and we'll see if we can help you get in touch with her.'

He stood back, holding the door open. The girl reached down for her vast rucksack — an appendage which he had not noticed before — and lugged it over the sill. Weak with misgivings, forgetting his manners, Philip stood by helplessly while she hefted the shabby bundle in and leaned it carefully against the coat-rack in the lobby.

The girl straightened up, and ran a hand over her damp hair. Philip was doing and saying nothing, so she took the initiative.

'Perhaps you have got an address for me to find Manda in London?'

'Well — yes.' From the dining-room came hubbub and laughter; the sound of Henry's voice

103

telling some story about the radio station and a deep laugh from Andy Morgan. Philip's instinct was to fetch his wife and let her sort out this big-eyed changeling, but curiosity overcame him.

'How do you know my daughter?' he asked.

'She has written to me in Poland. She is my penfriend. See?' From a small leather shoulder bag the young woman pulled out a bundle of letters, six or seven of them, in the careless scrawl he remembered from Amanda's home-work days. They must, he calculated, be five or six years old: certainly Amanda's writing had been far more adult than that by the time she went to university. Maybe they had been corresponding by e-mail more recently? He looked at the scruffy, workmanlike appearance of this girl, at the shabby jeans and the hooded sweatshirt beneath her anorak, and began to doubt it. She did not look likely to be a recent friend of his cool, soignée daughter.

'Is she expecting you?'

The little figure seemed to shrink. 'Perhaps not,' she agreed. In the dim light of the hallway the clock chimed the half-hour into the ensuing silence, and a door opened on to a lighted room and the silhouette of a woman.

'Philip?' called Diana. 'Who is it?'

He glanced back at her, then said to the dripping girl 'Wait a moment.' He hesitated, looking at her condition, and then glancing into his pristine living-room. 'Perhaps the bench?'

Eva took the hint and sat obediently on the wooden settle against the wall. She watched with interest as the tall, dignified man walked away and drew his wife into some side room off the hall. A door closed, and she heard nothing except a blur of conversation from the dining-room. The smell of food made her feel faint. She had eaten a burger-house miniature pizza in London at lunchtime, but nothing else all day.

In the study, Philip was saying to Diana: 'It's some Polish girl. Seems to have been a penfriend of Manda's, when she was at school, and now she's turned up here.'

Diana stared for a moment, then said, 'God, I remember. When Miss Harrington was into all that global citizenship stuff. There was a scheme where they wrote to Eastern Bloc kids and got letters back. I remember, because the PTA raised money for international postal credits because we thought it wasn't fair on the Poles and Russians to have to buy stamps.'

'Was she a close friend, do you suppose?'

'Well, I don't know. You know how secretive Manda always was. I do rather doubt it.' She exhaled, frowning. 'We'd better ring her straight away.'

'Our guests?'

'Oh, shoot. Yes, you'd better get back in there and pour some more drink. Not for Marianne if you can help it, she's already pawing poor Henry to pieces.'

When he had gone, she dialled Manda's number in the London Docklands and waited.

'Yah?'

'It's Mum,' said Diana.

'Oh, hello.' The young woman's voice was flat,

distant, faintly surprised.

'The thing is, it's a bit strange. A girl's just turned up here, literally on the doorstep. From Poland, apparently. Philip spoke to her. She says she was your penfriend at school.'

Silence hummed between them.

'Eva,' said Amanda at last. 'From Warsaw or somewhere. God, yes. I wrote to her perhaps half a dozen times. We had to. It was coursework.'

'Well, she seems to know you.' Diana tried not to be irritated by her daughter.

'Nah,' said the high distant voice. 'The deal was that we wrote about life in our country, politics and shopping and stuff. And the penfriends wrote back. I got the stuff for my General Studies essay, then it tapered off. I don't actually know anything about her.'

'What do you mean, it tapered off?'

'Well, she went on writing to me — God, endlessly — but I didn't answer. It was just one of Harrington's citizenship projects. Once I'd finished the essay . . . '

Diana bit her lip. She had caught a glimpse, down the hall, of their waiflike visitor and an impression of big, trustful eyes in a thin small face. Not being proud of one's adult child was a hard thing, she thought: it implied such great deficiencies in oneself. She forced herself to brightness, but knew what the response would be.

'Well — shall we send her up to see you? That'd be nice.'

A long, gusty sigh came down the line.

'I've hardly got time for my actual *friends*,'

said the young woman crushingly. 'Mum, do not, do absolutely not, stick this one on me. You handle it. Tell her to take a hike.'

Even through the heavy oak door of the study, Diana could hear Marianne's high uncontrolled voice from the dining-room, and the words, ' . . . in our bed, I suppose, the little trollop!' She had to get back there, rescue the party, stop Philip being embarrassed, make it a nice evening for poor Lizzie and Andy. She could not argue all night with her cold daughter. And the little stranger was still sitting in the hall, damp and patient. All at once, she made up her mind.

'Well, I hope you think better of it. We'll keep her here tonight, she's wet through and hasn't got a car or anything. I'll talk to you tomorrow.'

'Art and I are going to Barcelona tomorrow.'

'How long — ' But the phone had clicked and purred, after a barely audible 'Seeya'.

Back in the hallway Diana said to the damp girl on the settle: 'Come on, then! You look as if you need a bite of supper. Amanda's — um — away in Spain right now, but we'll talk to her when she gets back. You can stay here tonight.'

'Oh, no!' There was genuine distress in the girl's voice. Her English began to crumble. 'I am not to trouble — I am fine — I can go away — '

'Rubbish!' said Diana heartily. 'Come on. Meet our friends. I'll heat you up the rest of the casserole while we have our pudding.' She pulled Eva to her feet and led her by the hand towards the dining-room. 'Now my husband Philip you've already met — and this is Lizzie, and Andy, and Marianne — and Henry!'

A murmur of greeting, most cordial from Henry and Lizzie, made Eva blush and stumble over her words.

'I am Eva Borkowska. I come from Wroclaw.' Her pronunciation, Vrot-slav, meant that none of those present recognized the name. 'I am sorry to trouble you in your party.'

'No, it's lovely to meet you,' said Lizzie. 'Have you been hiking? Walking, I mean?'

'Yes, from the bus.'

'Poor thing!'

'It was not so bad. It was a very nice bus, very friendly. And I am strong.' Eva smiled now, for the first time, and her small face was transformed. Henry looked at her approvingly, and Andy jumped up and pulled another chair to the table, between him and Diana. It was an upholstered chair, smart in Regency stripes, and the Polish girl hesitated.

'I am afraid my jeans are wet,' she said. 'I will spoil it.'

Henry whipped his napkin from his lap and laid it respectfully on the chair. Andy did the same. Emboldened by the double layer of heavy linen, Eva sat down, and Diana laid a plateful of reheated *boeuf bourguignon* before her, with the remains of the scalloped potatoes and some broccoli. Andy, to ease her embarrassment at eating alone, picked up the thread of his conversation with Philip, who responded enthusiastically. Henry talked to Lizzie, with occasional quizzical glances at his flustered hostess. Diana got the pudding out, and served Marianne first.

For she was by now eyeing the newcomer with the ponderous attention of the very drunk, and plainly shaping up for some epically tactless remark. Lizzie caught her friend's eye, and the corner of her mouth twitched. Diana raised her eyebrows to heaven and smiled; at that moment, the mere connection between herself and Lizzie gave her a rush of unexpected pleasure. So many years, so many stories, and both of them still there and laughing at the same things. Then the pleasure was rapidly tempered by nervousness at what Marianne might say next. Sure enough, once Diana had sat down with her own pudding, the big blonde leaned across to Eva and said, separating out the syllables with care: 'You're ter-ribly wet if I may shay so.'

'Yes,' said Eva politely. 'I had to walk. I did not understand how far this house is from the village bus.'

'Have you come as an au pair?'

Eva blushed. 'No — I am looking for my friend Manda,' she said.

'Manda?' said Marianne. 'She's never here! Stays in London, with her yuppie friends. No time for her parents at all. Terrible girl. Mind you, they are terrible. Girls. One little tart just ran off with my hushband!'

Eva understood, now, that this woman had had too much to drink. She smiled, that beautiful sunny smile which had captivated them moments before, and said gently: 'I am so sorry. The same thing happened to my best teacher in the school. She was a good lady and very beautiful too, but her husband went away with a

Russian girl. I hope you are not sad.'

Marianne blinked at this directness, and gave a loud, sorrowful burp. Henry hid a grin, holding his napkin to his mouth.

'Did you see *I Masnadieri* at the Royal Opera House?' said Andy desperately to Philip. 'I liked it. Melodrama needs to be done with full-hearted conviction like that. The critics were a bit harsh, I thought.'

'Wonderful pudding, Diana!' said Lizzie heartily. 'Did you use fresh ground almonds? The taste's just fabulous!'

It was no use. Nothing would divert the flood of emotion. 'Yesh,' said Marianne loudly. 'I am sad. That's just it. I'm bloodybloody sad.' Tears began to drip from her eyes, running fatly down her powdered cheeks and smashing into the remains of her almond pudding. 'I'm so sad I could shoot myself. Every singlebloody morning, so sad — '

Eva got up from the table, walked round, and put her arms round Marianne's chubby pink shoulders. She rested her cheek on the peroxide hair and said calmly: 'I am sorry. I should not have made you more sad. But it is good to cry. All your friends are here, and they love you, I can see.'

Five pairs of eyes dropped to the tablecloth, and Eva stayed with her arms round the sobbing Marianne until at last Lizzie broke the silence.

'Tell you what,' she said, 'that's the nicest thing I've ever seen happen at a dinner party.'

Diana roused herself and said, 'Yes. Thank you, Eva. You put us all to shame. Come on,

Madge. Let's go upstairs and get you a hot water bottle. Eva, if you come too I can lend you some dry clothes. Philip, will you make the coffee?'

Released from this appalling scene, he thankfully fled to the kitchen. In his absence, after a moment or two of silent contemplation, the other three began to laugh, and laugh, and laugh. Henry actually sobbed, in the end, and rather inelegantly blew his nose on his napkin. When Philip and Diana got back from their various errands of mercy and began to pick up the threads of the evening, he had kicked the napkin under the table like a guilty child and was trying to discuss football in a choked but level tone with Andy. Eva, who had burst into weary tears herself once they were upstairs, stayed in her room at her own earnest request, and was taken up a plateful of almond cream by Diana ten minutes later.

But it was too late. A soft tap on the door produced no response, and when Diana put her head round, she saw that the warm room had done its work already. A heap of clothes lay on the floor and Eva, wrapped carelessly in a towel, was fast asleep on top of the counterpane.

10

Later, lying sleepless in her half of the vast
marital bed, Diana listened to Philip's quiet
breathing several feet away and imagined that
she could hear also the rustle and sigh of the
other sleepers under their roof. It was, she
realized, a long time since they had had
house-guests. When Philip was MP there were
many. Weekend after weekend, she had made up
beds and filled bedside carafes for colleagues,
party officials, and best of all for young
researchers whose resilient enthusiasm and
chatter at the breakfast-table made even Manda
smile and laugh. Although some of these political
creatures were not to Diana's natural taste
— indeed their obsession with Westminster often
struck her as decidedly odd — she had enjoyed
mothering them, and having her ideas challenged
with bouncy youthful confidence over a mouth-
ful of bacon-and-egg.

And then there were the other nights, before
Andy and Lizzie came to live in the town, when
they and assorted friends and children would
come down from London for the weekend,
mob-handed and high-spirited, to argue politics
with Philip and sprawl companionably around
the kitchen with Diana.

She snuggled down, yawning. Yes, it was good
to have a houseful again. Poor Marianne,
though; she would be mortified when she

remembered the scene she had caused at dinner. Certainly she wouldn't want to face Philip, who at the best of times wore a forbidding aspect in the morning. Breakfast in bed would be best for her, decided Diana.

Suddenly she was wide awake: in remembering the old days of political houseparties she had clean forgotten that she herself was now a working woman, expected at Two Counties Radio by nine-fifteen at the latest for a live broadcast. Marianne's breakfast! She would have to take it in at eight to have any chance of stirring her friend up before she left. Oh dear, though: eight was surely too early for a hungover Marianne. Diana squirmed and frowned in the darkness. No help for it: she had to leave early for the Henry Show. Worry tugged at her, shredding her cocoon of sleepy comfort.

What about the Polish girl? She had to be thought about too. She would wake in a strange house, in a strange country, with no idea where to find this 'friend' on whom she had set so much store.

'Hell,' said Diana, aloud but under her breath. Philip stirred irritably on the far side of the bed. Hell! The kid would simply have to be woken up when she herself got up, at seven. There would be time to talk a little before Philip appeared on the dot of eight for his breakfast. Little Eva might want to be driven to the station in town, to head back to the bright lights of London. If Diana left fifteen minutes early, there would be time to detour by the station and drop her off without being late for work.

But then — oh, hell, again! — that meant bringing Marianne's breakfast in bed forward even earlier, and risking one of two equal evils. Either she would get up early and lumber around in a borrowed dressing-gown, harassing Philip while he tried to read the paper; or else fall asleep again and later disrupt his quiet morning in his study with bleary enquiries about where the tea-bags were. Maybe the best thing was to leave a note — no, three notes.

Prodded and teased by domestic detail, tugged by small insistent phantom hands of duty and kindness, Diana lay awake for a while longer. Her last waking thought was a wish that it was still possible to do as she had in the earlier days of marriage and roll over to cuddle Philip's broad warm back for comfort. Ten years ago, this immensely wide new bed had seemed a comfortable idea. Today, it was like a desert, with armies encamped on its edges and bare unbreachable territory between.

★   ★   ★

In the event, Eva woke long before the rest of the household. She had drunk very little of her wine the night before, and the early sun woke her easily. The room was cool, too cool; she stretched, yawned, and looked down in surprise to see that she was covered only by a bath-towel and a corner of quilted counterpane which she must have hauled over herself in her sleep.

Manda's house. Of course. Manda's parents' house. She wriggled upright, feeling a twinge of

114

mortification. How stupid not to have realized that in Britain a girl of their age — twenty-two — was not necessarily going to live in her home town with her parents. The old man must have thought her very naïve, like some savage brought to the civilized world and refusing to understand that not everybody worships their ancestors. Adam had said, in his letters to his brother and cousins, that in Scotland he shared a house with some students, all of them far from home. The system was different here, that was all.

And now Manda was 'away'. For the first time since the exhilaration of the ferry, real anxiety pinched Eva. So far this had been an adventure, a merry quest. Travelling on the bus to London had been fine, and the hostel she was directed to by bored, accustomed staff at Victoria Coach Station lay barely two blocks away from it. It was all very easy and even fun: there were lockers in the hostel for your backpack, and some nice Austrian boys from Salzburg who took her with them for a pizza. They told her about England and warned her about the pimps who preyed on girls arriving without money from the Eastern bloc.

'There was a Romanian girl, they made her like a slave and never paid her.'

'I heard she was killed in the end.'

'No, I heard she was freed and got asylum and works in a proper job. It was in the paper!'

'No, she was killed.'

'Must have been another girl you're thinking of. They force them to have drugs until they are addicts and can't get away.'

'They make them smuggle drugs when they are no good for sex anymore.'

'They get AIDS.'

Getting out to the village, once she had looked carefully at the map, was not too difficult either. One bus took two hours to reach the nice little town with the market square, and another one (enchantingly, a double-decker) wound through country lanes to the village. Riding along on the top, looking over the trees in the dusk, Eva had felt like an invincible explorer. The walk in the rain from the station was long, but still exhilarating; for the first time in her travels she was quite glad to be alone. Manda was *her* friend, *her* contact, not just an address in a fellow-backpacker's notebook.

She had imagined arriving, relishing the surprise, laughing with Manda as she used to with Halina. In fact, the English girl's face, never seen except in one small blurred passport photograph when they first exchanged letters, had in recent weeks become merged in her mind with Halina's. Once, she even caught herself thinking that perhaps Manda was with Tadek now at last; then realized that she meant Halina. Sometimes she thought about how it would be when she went back to Wroclaw and those two were married, with their own apartment. Good, she told herself firmly. It would be good. They could both be her friends again.

For the moment her plans went little beyond the idea of staying for a few days with Manda, on a sofa or a floor or even a spare bed, exchanging talk and experiences and perhaps asking the

116

English family for advice on getting some work locally. Not serious work, that wouldn't be allowed, but perhaps a month or so as an au pair with one of their friends. Or as a cook. Eva was, she knew without false modesty, a very good cook. And economical, too. She had even brought with her the tiny notebook of her grandmother's recipes. To show Manda . . .

Sitting on the edge of the big double bed now, in a room she perceived to be luxurious if rather bland, Eva writhed at her own stupidity. These were rich people, busy important people — she had caught part of Philip's conversation and realized he was a politician. Her whole perspective shifted, and she saw with embarrassing clarity that it was as if some scruffy student from Bulgaria or Estonia had turned up in a government family's country house in Poland, expecting to be welcomed.

Nor was she entirely sure that she had acted properly in making that impetuous gesture towards the poor fat lady in the low-cut blouse. Matziek, she now remembered rather too late, said that British people did not appreciate this sort of display. They called it a Stiff Lip. Was that right? They must think her stupid.

For a moment she sat on the bed, cross and humiliated. She did not like to feel this way about herself. Wallowing in self-doubt was, in Eva's view, a weakness of character. If you had done something stupid, you had two choices: make something good out of it, or forget it. You had to know this, if you were a person who often did stupid things. It was genetic, with her. Her brother Max was shy and ponderous, Father was quiet and a little bitter, but Eva was — so the Borkowska aunts always said — her mother over again: rushing into things, surviving on enthusiasm, tangling herself up 'like a deer in a fence'.

But a deer, she thought fiercely, did not sit in the fence bleating and waiting for death, like a sheep. It kicked, struggled, and got free so it could bound on towards the next thing. So would she. She stood up, stretched, pulled the towel around her and went over to the broad window. When she pulled the dark-gold brocade curtains aside, a sight met her which changed her mood again.

It was just so beautiful, so beautiful. Tears sprang to her eyes now. Beyond the clean white window-frame there lay a miniature lake, rippled by a light breeze until it sparkled under the early sun. Broad trees surrounded it, their green fading to red and gold as the first leaves turned; behind them, a line of darker pines, rocketing heavenward into the pale blue morning. Over to the right, a broad field of golden stubble rose and fell in gentle, barely discernible undulation to another line of green hedgerow; on the left a long, red-brick barn sagged benevolently under a rakish iron weathercock which swung south, south-west, and south again.

Eva stared, entranced. Leaving the double-decker bus the previous evening she had gone into a village pub, with some trepidation, and asked the way to the Manor; a man behind the bar with a large red nose and a grubby T-shirt had sketched her a little map on a beer-mat,

118

observing that it was a long way to go on foot. This map she had followed carefully for an hour before realizing that she must have missed a turning, retracing her steps and finally recognizing a grassy triangle with a sign on it on which her guide had laid much stress. It was growing very dark during this walk, and although a few cars passed her and splashed mud on her jeans, she obeyed the common wisdom of female backpackers and shrank back into the hedge rather than solicit a lift. So she had seen nothing of the potential beauty of this fold of the countryside. The winding driveway of the property had been a particular trial, seeming to take her too deep into unknown and un-public territory. It had taken courage to knock on the door and not to turn tail and run at the forbidding sight of Philip. The last thing she had expected was that the house and its grounds would be beautiful.

So this unexpected idyll of lake and trees and golden field came on her like a thunderbolt. Whatever happened now, she said to herself with a lift of the heart, she had come to a beautiful place. It was more lovely, she thought, than the rushing river in France — where, to be fair, the campsite spoilt the scenery — and certainly closer to her innermost desires than the brash seaside scenes of the Costa Brava or the vivid urban muddle of the cities she had passed through.

Eva stood for a long while contemplating the picture before her, watching the changing light and the slow, high clouds; then she turned back to her pack, and pulled out a pad and pen. By the time Diana knocked lightly on the door at seven, she had written out part of a poem from memory and was frowning as she tried to remember its translation. Of all her foreign languages she loved English best, and now there was pleasure in using it in its own homeland — far more than when it simply formed part of the utilitarian patois of international companionship in the hostels. She wrote carefully, in a neat schoolgirl hand. When Diana entered the room her young guest looked up, still clad only in the bathtowel, smiled, and held out the notebook towards her.

'It is very beautiful here,' she said without preamble. 'I have been looking out of the windows and remembering a poem by Adam Mickiewicz. See. I have forgotten how to translate some lines. But a very clever Englishman called Mackenzie did a translation we studied at university.'

Diana, amused, took the notebook and glanced at the words. Lines were missing and scribbled over, with evidence of childish concentration:

There stood a manor house, wood-built on
  stone;
From far away the walls with whitewash
  shone . . .
(????about the trees — poplar?)
. . . It was not large, but neat in every way
And had a mighty barn, three stacks of hay
. . . ????) . . .

Everyone could tell
That plenty in that house and order dwell.
The gate wide open to the world declared
A hospitable house to all who fared.

'It's in English,' said Diana.

'I have remembered the translation we learned,' explained Eva seriously. 'You see, it is an ideal of the perfect house in the country. Adam Mickiewicz was put in prison, by the Russians, then he ran away to the West. But in Poland we always dream of the country. I live in the city, but when I was small we went to my grandparents in the mountains, but they are dead.'

Diana watched the girl, animatedly prattling, nervous but intense. 'Then we went to the lakes. In the north. But my mother died. I have not seen a beautiful countryside like this for three years.'

'I think Poland's got more countryside than we have,' said Diana inadequately. 'Anyway. Thank you for showing it to me.'

'I will remember the rest soon. Or look it up in an internet café,' said Eva. Diana pressed on.

'But we've got to have a council of war about what you do next. Manda's in Barcelona, on holiday, and the trouble is that I don't know how long for. I just rang, but she's got the answering machine on.'

'It's OK,' said Eva briefly, tucking the towel more snugly under her armpits. Her face had lost its animation now, and become a polite

121

blank. 'I think she is busy. I am just passing through.'

Diana smiled at the expression; it sat oddly, and rather sadly, on the lips of a girl who had come a long way to see her daughter. But the subject of Manda was beyond her, this early in the morning.

'Well, come down to breakfast,' she said. 'Straight down the stairs, and I'm in the kitchen. It's the door opposite where we all were last night. I have to leave in an hour for work. You found the bathroom? Good.'

Ten minutes later, showered and dressed in her jeans and a clean T-shirt, Eva joined her hostess in the kitchen. Seeing her glance around, Diana said, 'My husband generally has breakfast about eight, in the other room. He hates eating in the kitchen.'

'It is a nice kitchen,' said Eva. It was. Framed by dark beams but high and spacious, it was about the size of the entire apartment back in Wroclaw. Ranks of pale blue, delicately marbled wooden cupboard doors set off a floor of rough dark blue tiles, and even the untidy heap of pans and cooking trays in the sink was upstaged by a family of gleaming steel appliances whose various purposes Eva could barely guess at. She blinked, and identified among this magnificence the hob, on which a pan of bacon was efficiently crisping, a toaster with glowing red jaws, and a hissing coffeepot.

'I like it in here,' said Diana. 'I don't cook enough, really, but there's only the two of us. I'm going to sort out some hot breakfast for

Marianne, though. Philip just has toast. Would you like some bacon?'

Eva sat down and accepted toast and bacon; following Diana's example she made a sandwich and ate it in her fingers. After a few moments of silent chewing, she said: 'Mrs Hunton-Hall, I want to say I am sorry for arriving with no warning. It was a stupid idea. I wrote a letter to your daughter two months ago but I think perhaps it did not arrive.'

'To be honest,' said Diana, 'Amanda is quite forgetful about — ' She was going to say 'about people', but it sounded too harsh. Lamely she concluded: 'You see, she lives for her job. She's very busy.'

'Yes,' said Eva. Silence stretched between them. 'Perhaps I will ring her up in London when her holiday is finished.'

'What are you planning to do next?' asked Diana. 'Do you have other people to see? Do you want a lift into town?'

Eva wriggled uncomfortably. Diana glanced at her watch, then at the stove, hating herself for not making more effort with this poor child. She was too anxious about work and the Henry Show, and the other two breakfasts, and Philip's reaction to being left in the house with a shambling hungover Marianne and possibly a Polish stranger as well.

Eva saw the movement and suddenly said: 'May I help a little today? You are very busy. I could make a good breakfast for Mrs — uh — Marianne, a strongly cooked omelette perhaps. I do this when my brother Max has had

123

too much drink. Protein is good. And coffee. I know how to work this coffee machine because it is like the one in the hotel where I have been a maid. Then I can make everything tidy, and leave later in the morning.'

Diana looked at the pans in the sink and back at Eva, then said hesitantly: 'I couldn't ask — '

Eva straightened her back, triumphant.

'I would like to. I can repay your kindness,' she said grandly. 'And Mr Hunton-Hall's.'

'Well, it would be rather nice,' said Diana. 'I could get off early to work, which is wonderful because I can get ahead of myself with the paperwork before Henry comes in. Henry — the one who was here last night — I work with him, you see. He's a radio presenter.'

'Yes,' said Eva. And returning to practicalities: 'So I will make toast for eight o'clock for Mr Hunton-Hall, in the other room, and take breakfast to your friend later?'

'About nine, or half-past nine even,' said Diana. 'Her room's the one with the funny pointed wooden arch thing over the doorway, on the landing opposite yours. I'll tell Philip you're here. But' — she hesitated again, wondering whether she was courting trouble — 'please don't go away. Stay tonight. You can make yourself a sandwich at lunchtime from the stuff in the fridge. Go for a walk, perhaps. It's a lovely day. Then we can talk properly when I get back from work. Should be about four o'clock, it's one of my short days.'

Eva looked out of the window at the sagging, graceful red barn and the fields. Despite her audacious offer to cook the breakfasts, she had fully nerved herself to leave all this and head for the London bus, the hostel at Victoria and the uncertainties of finding illegal work in some café to earn the fare back to Poland.

'Is it really OK if I stay today?' she said.

'Yes, of course. We'd love it,' said Diana, and this time there was real warmth in her tone. 'To be honest, it solves a problem. My husband is not a great friend of Marianne, and he likes to be left alone in the mornings.'

'I think,' said Eva, and as she spoke her smile broke through the clouds of anxiety and diffidence like the sun, 'I think I will take her for a walk outside, after her breakfast.'

'Excellent' said Diana; and, complicit at last, the two women allowed their eyes to meet. Both grinned.

A few minutes later, having briefed Philip through the bathroom door about the morning's arrangements, Diana slipped into the car, kicked off her shoes, and manoeuvred round Marianne's carelessly parked Volvo to speed off down the driveway. It was only half-past seven. Diana Hunton-Hall was, for once, ahead of her day's routine. After the night's anxieties, the relief was immeasurable.

11

Henry was in the office early too, for once. Arriving at twenty-to-nine, Diana found him in conclave with Roger, arguing about a quiz.

'It's rude,' Roger was saying. 'Steve will hate it.'

'It's not rude, it's erotic,' said Henry.

'Kids might be home from school . . .'

'Kids know a lot of stuff. Even Marley. Think of it as sex education.'

'It's out of the question, no!'

Diana grinned. One of Henry's quirks was devising shocking little proposals to horrify Roger. It constantly amazed her that the producer did not notice his intention sooner: having grown up close to a family of boy cousins, she was attuned to the idiom of the youthful male wind-up. But Henry was a past master at adjusting the level of outrageousness downward until his suggestions hovered on the border of probability, and made it seem just possible that he was serious. She glanced at the piece of paper they were arguing over and laid a hand on Henry's shoulder with motherly firmness.

'Show him the *real* quiz, Henry,' she said. She felt his shoulder begin to shake, and reached across to pull another sheet out of the presenter's untidy red manila folder. 'Is this it?'

An unexceptionable, though sharply witty, quiz script lay before them. Roger glanced at it,

126

snorted, and stumped off towards the coffee machine, muttering, 'Pillock.' Diana shook her head at Henry.

'You are so mean. You know his stomach's still playing up.'

'Nice evening yesterday,' said Henry, ignoring the reproof. He slid her a sly sidelong glance. 'I like your friend Marianne.'

'Oh, please!' groaned Diana. 'She's going through a marriage break-up. She's a really nice, kind woman really.'

'What did I say?' complained the young man. 'I like her. Honestly. She's upfront. Says what she means. And your little Polish girl . . . wow! Like having Oprah or St Bernadette crashing your party. She made us look so British it wasn't funny anymore. Well, it was . . . ' He giggled.

'Yes,' said Diana, 'there's a problem about her. Look, give me the music list, I'll do it now. We might as well get ahead, since we're all early.'

'Why is it a problem?' He handed her the list. 'She's an au pair, isn't she? Nice kid.'

'No — she's not an au pair, she's a sort of school penfriend of my daughter's. Only Manda seems to have forgotten all about her and gone to Barcelona.'

'I hope Marley starts writing to gorgeous Polish girls when he's bigger,' said Henry. 'Then he's welcome to forget about them, and they can come and stay with me. Yum!'

Diana was filling in music forms with rapid, practised ease.

'Is she that gorgeous?' she asked idly. 'A bit tousled, I thought.'

127

'Ah, but the eyes!' said Henry. 'I've got a mate who loves those little tomboy types. P'raps I should ring him.'

'She's a very different type from my daughter, I can tell you. Pale ice maiden, Manda is. Makes me feel like a great sweating lump with trick hair whenever I see her.' She finished the list of records with a flourish, and slotted it into her folder. 'Talking of kids, how's Marley?' she asked. 'I didn't really ask you the other day.'

'Gorgeous. A winner. Better every day,' said Henry. 'Four years old and king of the damn world.'

'Is everything OK with your — um — ex?' asked Diana casually.

'My babymother, you mean?' said Henry. There was a faint chill in his tone now. Diana interpreted it correctly, and decided to meet the issue head-on.

'No,' she said. 'Your ex-girlfriend. Ali, isn't it?'

'Ali it is.' There was a soreness in his voice, an edge of bitterness.

'Henry, don't involve me in this feckless-black-man-babyfather nonsense. All I know is that you lived together, I presume in all seriousness, that you had Marley, and then it broke up. Happens to lots of people. Same as divorce.'

Henry looked at her for a moment over the stack of CDs and notes, and then nodded. 'OK, I'm sorry. But some of the comments kind of get me down.'

Diana smiled. She had wanted to smooth this ruffle in Henry's relationship with his colleagues for a while now. The 'babyfather' expression had lately been popularized by a television series about feckless young black men who scattered illegitimate children around with insouciance and lightly abandoned their 'babymothers', except for occasional *droit de seigneur* visits and impulsive moments of tyranny over their neglected offspring. Knowing Henry a little better than some, she had always accepted that it was not so between him and the absent Alissa. She knew his devotion to Marley, and suspected that it had caused a frost with the present, rarely spoken-of girlfriend, Sue. But Henry never usually complained at being treated or talked to differently because he was black. At public events he deftly turned aside both the surprise and the over-emphatic kindness of the Middle-England constituency of his local radio listeners. The rawness of his response just now must mean that the 'babyfather' gibe was one which truly hurt him. She remembered suddenly that he himself had been abandoned as an infant, presumably by both mother and father.

'Henry,' she said gently, 'you know I don't think that way, so don't get chippy with me. Everyone's different, nobody's a type. You're not a gangsta stud anymore than I'm a cartoon Tory wife.'

'Yeah,' said Henry, abashed. He began to spin a CD on the table, on its edge, watching it flash under the ceiling spotlights. Diana took it from him, as if he were a child, and put it back in its case.

'I just wanted to know if things were OK,' she said. 'I've had plenty of friends go through divorces and it's horrid when there are children.'

'Yeah,' said Henry again. They were alone. The stack of music notes was finished, the running-order and quizzes ready; there was time before the programme. Roger could be heard down the corridor talking to someone by the coffee machine, and there was a sound of intermittent metallic thumping which indicated that the apparatus was once again in need of a slap or two to make it function. 'Yeah. OK, thing is, I could do with some advice. Ali wants to move to London with her new guy. He wants to do minicabbing there. And I don't think I've got any legal right to stop her.'

'No?' said Diana, dismayed. 'Oh, that's awful. You'd still have the same access, right? But, oh, dear, the geography!'

'Yeah. Oh dear is about right. I couldn't have him odd nights, I couldn't drop in and see him at bedtime. Her guy — Donny — he's OK about all that. Amazingly OK, for a yob like him. When I come round he just slopes off to the pub or somewhere, as often as not. But if they're in some skanky flat in Deptford it'll be two hours' travelling each way every time. Plus, what's that going to be like for Marley? If they stayed here he could go to a really nice friendly little school — be part of a nice friendly little town — '

Diana looked at Henry, and saw that there were tears in his eyes. She put her hand on his arm and said steadily: 'Lunchtime. After the show. Shall we shake off Roger and go to the pub? I might have some ideas. It'll be OK. Honestly.'

'OK,' said Henry. 'Oh, shit. Got a show to do.' He began singing, off-key but with vigour, 'The Sun Has Got His Hat On'.

★ ★ ★

At eight o'clock, Eva gave Philip his toast and coffee with all the discreet impersonality of a hotel waitress, and melted back into the kitchen for an hour. Here she scrubbed the pans inside and out, enjoying the way that the copper shone and twinkled under the spotlights. She found them homes on high hooks or deep in the bewildering cupboards, and discovered that one of the steel fascias concealed a dishwasher full of clean crocks and cutlery from the night before. She stowed it all according to her intuition, and stood back to enjoy the neatness and newness of everything.

Then she took three eggs from the fridge (after a false start when she opened the door of the microwave by mistake) and found a bowl to whisk them in. Despite the palatial, almost hotel-like dimensions of the kitchen, it suited her very well to be in a private domestic setting again after the weeks of continental wandering. Beating up the eggs with a fork, she closed her eyes for a moment and imagined herself back home, with Max and Tatu behind their bedroom doors and her own city spread far beneath the high kitchen window. She had gone beyond the mountains now, beyond the sunset, and found a strange new world. It was disappointing at times; frightening, sordid, scruffy in places, this wide world. But sometimes there were pockets and havens of peace, prosperity, gentleness and music. When she had made the omelette and the fresh coffee, she piled toast on the waiting tray and added, as an afterthought, a large glass of tap water. Philip, by now in his study, raised his head briefly as she passed the door and said: 'All right?'

'Yes. I will take Mrs Marianne breakfast, then we will go out for a walk.'

'Good, good.' Absently, he turned back to the note he was writing, in graceful old-fashioned script on thick white paper. In his black polo-neck he looked, thought Eva admiringly, like a monk working in his cell.

Upstairs, she tapped on Marianne's door and received a groan in reply. Pushing the door open, she saw the big woman in bed, a tousled mound.

'Good morning,' she said cheeringly. 'I have brought you some good breakfast.'

Marianne raised herself on one elbow and looked around, bleary and bewildered. Her bleached hair, flattened by the pillow, showed itself as thinning and brittle with advancing age.

'Oh, God. I made a fool of myself,' she said. 'Oh, my head!'

Eva put down the tray on a side table, and gravely handed her the glass of water. Marianne drained it and handed back the glass, flopping back on to the pillow.

'I've got some Paracetamol in my bag,' she said, pointing with one flabby white arm at the pile of clothes on the floor.

'Try breakfast first,' said Eva. 'My brother

Max always wants to take pills for his head, but food and air work even faster, and don't cost money. My mother said that too many pills make you weak.'

Marianne sat up, reluctantly, and allowed the girl to stack pillows behind her back. This room, thought Eva, was even more luxurious than her own, with a great bay window and thick dark rose-coloured carpet. 'Ooof,' said the invalid. 'Actually, do you know, that does smell rather good.'

Eva put the tray on her knees and slid from the room. Passing the doorway of the long sitting-room on her way back to the kitchen, she saw the mess of ash and charcoal in the fireplace and scattered on the hearth. After some careful opening and shutting of oak doors in the hall, she found a cleaning cupboard and equipped herself to deal with it. Then she plumped the cushions, gathered up a few sticky glasses, and opened the window to let air through. In the dining-room she wiped down the mahogany table, eased off some specks of candlewax and polished it with a dry duster; she did not dare use the unfamiliar brands of furniture polish in case she did some damage. She straightened the rugs, flicked the curtains into a tidy fall, and put the chairs neatly round the clean table.

All this while Philip continued to work in his study, with the door open, glancing up occasionally as the stranger busied herself round his house. After a time, he flicked a button on his CD player and filled the house with a rising, joyful Bach prelude. Outside, the sun sparkled on the last puddles of rainwater and the weathercock swung lazily, gently to the south-east. A distant plane flew overhead. On board, though he did not know it, were his daughter Amanda and her boyfriend Art, bound for Barcelona.

★ ★ ★

'You'll never guess what my *parents* have done,' said Manda to Art, settling in her Club Class seat with a yawn. The pair had met at the airport, since Art had just flown in from New York. 'They've produced this Polish girl I used to write to when I was *sixteen* or something. She's actually here! They want me to nanny her!'

'Why'd they do that?' asked Art, who was even sleepier. 'Whass the deal?'

'I think Mum's making a point about me being a selfish yuppie. As per usual,' said Amanda. 'Would you believe it?'

'Gross,' said Art, and unfolded his newspaper.

12

Eva tapped on the study door, open though it was, and said shyly: 'I am going for a walk with Marianne. Is this OK? Mrs Hunton-Hall said that it would be a good thing if she had a walk before she starts to drive the car.'

'Yes,' said Philip. He looked at the slight, vivid figure framed by the pitted oak doorposts of his room. 'Thank you. That's very kind. My wife says you're, er, staying tonight?'

'If that is OK?' said Eva. 'She wanted to talk about your daughter, I think.'

'Mmm,' said Philip cautiously. 'Well, you're welcome. Thank you for clearing up like that. You didn't need to. We have a cleaner who comes three times a week. Usually, anyway.' Irritation flickered in his handsome face. Mrs Carter had been a little erratic of late; Diana kept saying she would 'sort something out', but never did so. Philip's annoyance was increased rather than otherwise by his suspicion that she did not want to offend Mrs Carter. That it might be his job to go through the harrowing process of offending her into better performance did not occur to him.

'It was a pleasure to care for the house,' said Eva. 'Your home is very beautiful. It made me think of a poem by Adam Mickiewicz. About the manor house.'

Philip looked at her more sharply. 'Yes, of

course. The opening of 'Pan Tadeusz',' he said. 'A friend of mine set that to music once, at Cambridge.'

'*Really?*' Eva was too astonished now for shyness. 'A Polish poem? You know it?'

'Only bits, from the oratorio. I sang in the chorus. Mickiewicz isn't just a Polish poet, he's a world figure. Fits into the Romantic tradition with our Shelley and Keats,' said Philip, with a touch of smugness which Eva was too unpractised in his ways to detect. 'I suppose — yes, I suppose his world standing wouldn't be stressed in education yet, in your country. He wasn't exactly beloved of the Russians in his own time.'

'Do you study poetry? Are you a poet?' Eva was immoderately excited at the idea: the old beams of the study, the white hair and high brow of this senatorial politician seated against a background of learned books, seemed to be a noble scene for the writing of poetry! Vaclav Havel had been a poet and playwright as well as a politician, after all, and poetry had fuelled the Czechs' Velvet Revolution which inspired her mother to political raptures when she was small. She gazed at him, entranced.

'No,' said Philip. 'I'm in business, and politics, and my degree was in economics. But if you care for music, you care for poetry, I think.'

'It is the same,' agreed Eva gravely. 'Like a great bell that rings in your heart. My mother said this.'

Behind her, at the far end of the hall, the heavy tread of Marianne echoed on the bare

136

polished floorboards between the long rugs. Eva glanced round, and before Philip could compose himself to make some response to her poetic outbreak, said more prosaically, 'I will find Mrs Marianne some boots, I think.'

Abruptly the doorway was empty again. Philip looked at it for a moment then turned back to his letters.

There were long rubber boots in the lesser hallway between the scullery and the back door, and seeing the puddles on the drive outside, Eva had found a pair to fit her. When Marianne appeared, she led her through to look for some; but it rapidly became clear that her plump legs were too wide to hope for any degree of comfort in Wellington boots.

'I usually wear galoshes,' said Marianne, tears welling behind her eyes again. 'They pull on over your shoes.'

'Like these?' said Eva. There were some limp plastic socks of inordinate size lying in the corner on top of a mop-bucket. They had puzzled her but now she said, 'Galoshes?'

'Goodness, yes, how clever to spot them. They're a different colour from mine.' Marianne put them on, pleased, and together they went out into the garden.

'Where shall we walk?' asked Eva. 'Do you know this place well?'

'Absolutely,' said Marianne. 'Up the drive, through the wood, and that gets you into a footpath round the five-acre field and down towards the river. I feel better already for the fresh air.'

And indeed, with her hair blowing free, no make-up and a faint pink blush in her unhealthy, veined cheeks, Marianne looked considerably better. On an impulse, Eva put an arm round her shoulders and gave her a brief hug. Then she blushed and shook her head.

'I am sorry for your trouble.'

'Don't be. How sweet. Your mother's a lucky woman. My niece hasn't hugged anyone since she was twelve, and as for that terrible Manda!' She shuddered. 'Poor Diana! Cold as charity, that girl!'

Eva saw that Marianne had entirely forgotten her reason for being here, if indeed it had ever penetrated her fuddled mind the night before. Anxious not to embarrass her, she ignored the strictures on Manda and said merely, 'Alas! My mother is dead.' Then, seeing Marianne's eyes begin to fill, with the easy sentimentality of the hungover, she added quickly, 'But I have a father and a brother and many friends.'

They walked on, up the drive and on to the pathway; coming out of the trees, Eva gave a little skip and said chattily, 'We have a poem about a place like this. What is it?' She began to mutter in Polish, then slowly translated.

'"The cornfields like a quilt, silver rye, gold wheat fields, amber and snow white flowers" — I do not know the names in English!'

'It always makes me think of 'The Lady of Shalott',' said Marianne surprisingly. '"On either side the river lie, long fields of barley and of rye, that clothe the wold and meet the sky' . . . I used to know it all, I got a prize for reciting it at school. It was,' she added cryptically, 'that sort of school.'

'A poetry school?'

'An old-fashioned girls' school. I think that's why I never really understood about men. What they want. I was married at eighteen, you know. Just after A-levels. I thought Anthony was Sir Lancelot.'

'Sir Lancelot?'

'In that poem. Gosh, I liked reciting it! I did it at Prize Day. The worst bit was '*the shallop flitteth silken-sailed*'. If you didn't trip over that, you were fine till the end.'

'Do you know it now?' asked Eva. 'I like the pattern . . . what do you call it? The rhythm?'

As they walked on together, Marianne pieced together her memories of that girlhood recitation, arriving finally and with an air of triumph at:

> ' . . . *he said, 'she has a lovely face,*
> *The Lady of Shalott!*' '

'This is very sad,' said Eva. 'But I love it. I must read it. Poor lady!'

'She looked back,' said Marianne, with a return of her former gloom. 'She looked back. She tried to see out into the real world, instead of watching everything second-hand through a mirror, embroidering it prettier than it was in that web thing. It was probably a lovely dim old mirror, sort of goldy, where everything looked better. Women are meant to see the world like that, through lovely dim family mirrors. Until one day they crack. I never thought of it that way before, but when I was remembering the poem just now it struck me. We're all Shalotts.'

They were almost back now, following a little stream uphill and getting close to the barn wall. The chimneys of the Manor looked to Eva for a moment like battlements, and she frowned in concentration and then abruptly pointed and said:

> '*Four gray walls and four gray towers*
> *Overlook a space of flowers . . .* '

'Goodness, — you're quick,' said Marianne. 'Do you remember quotations all the time?'

'No,' said Eva. 'But if I really like them. I think this place is like Shalott.'

'Paf! No way. Diana got sick of looking in Philip's magic mirror years ago,' said Marianne, pursuing her theme with all the intensity of a woman wronged. 'She turned right round and got out into a job, and nothing broke at all. Best thing to do. Stop living second-hand, take some of your eggs out of the marital basket. Wish I had.

'*I am half sick of shadows, said the Lady of Shalott!*' '

'I could never grow tired of this place,' said Eva, not understanding at all. 'It is beautiful.'

'I need a cup of tea,' said Marianne. 'I do feel better for the walk, though. Bless you.' They slipped quietly into the house, but Philip had gone out; his long car was missing from the drive and the study door shut. Together, at Marianne's insistence ('Diana won't mind!'), they heated up some soup from the fridge; then the older woman left, splashing through the puddles in her little car, and Eva was alone with the old Manor, the grey walls and the roses. She passed the afternoon by making all the beds and Hoovering the floors, stopping every time she came to a window to enjoy another new-framed view. After a while she found some dusters and crept round polishing all the mirrors, looking into their dim antique lustre for enchanted glimpses of the world beyond the windows.

★ ★ ★

Diana and Henry found a table in the corner, relaxing into the dim light and warm beery smell of the pub.

'I suppose it gets into the carpets,' said Diana, referring to the smell. 'I sort of like it. Reminds me of my barmaid days.'

'You were never a barmaid!' said Henry. 'You?'

'You think I'm too posh, don't you?' said Diana mildly. 'But I was from a very ordinary family, and when I was a student I had to graft away like anybody else in the vacation. I liked bar work best. More sociable than being a waitress. You lean your bosom on the counter and let them tell you how their wives don't understand them, and then they tell you to have one yourself. You can make a lot more that way than on waitress tips.'

'My old man wouldn't let me do that kind of work,' said Henry. 'Nothing menial. He was born in the Cape, see, before they got away to live here and adopted me. In the holidays I had to be an office-boy in my uncle's window company in Birmingham. God, it was boring. I fancied being a waiter in the wine bar like my mates, but my father said he wasn't having me handing plates to white bosses like a houseboy.'

There was a brief silence while Diana considered this admission.

'Gosh' she said. 'I suppose that he felt that waiting at table had a bit too much of an — well — an edge. For you. You being — '

'Black? Yeah. Rastus, see? Faithful old southron slave material. Whereas you were always bound to be a white madam when you grew up — '

' — so it was OK for me to wipe down bars and simper for tips!'

'Yeah. Because nobody would assume you were there for good.'

They both laughed. 'I don't know much about your family,' said Diana, sipping her lager. 'I know you were adopted, because you told me about being found in Windsor Great Park and called Windsor. Did your new dad really come from South Africa?'

'Yup. Political asylum. He ran an illegal newspaper with some white guys. One of them was run over by a police car, accidentally on purpose. Then Mum and Dad's son got shot. I suppose that's why they wanted to adopt a boy years later.'

'How awful for them!'

'Anyway, some guys helped my parents out.

Dad's brother came the year after, and started the company with a five-hundred-quid loan from a bleeding-heart liberal bank manager he ran into. Uncle Jonah Henryson was the go-getter of the family.'

'So they adopted you when they must have been getting on?'

'Yeah, but apparently it's easier for black families wanting black babies. They were nearly fifty. I'm afraid I was a terrible handful for them.'

'You still are,' said Diana lightly. 'Shows what clichés we all think in, I just always assumed your family came from the West Indies.'

'Nah, that's the rap identity fooling you. African. Though, God knows, I suppose my birth mother could have been West Indian. But my Dad always said no, I didn't have the look. Apparently I have a different-shaped head. East African not West.'

'Your parents died, you said?'

'Yeah. But they saw the free elections on the news. They always thought I'd go to Johannesburg and pick up where their son left off. But I've never had the bottle.'

'Well, why should you? You're British-born.'

'Oh, because.' Henry sipped at his lager and sighed. 'I sometimes feel as if I'm on the wrong continent. Everything changing out there, new world being built, it feels like dereliction of duty.' He made a face; she had never seen him so despondent, but the next sentence gave her the real reason. 'Anyway, if Ali and Donny go south and I can't see Marley, I might as well go five thousand miles away.'

143

'Yes, that's another reason I thought you were Jamaican or something,' said Diana, with too much lightness; she suddenly did not feel equal to meeting his smouldering depression. 'Marley!'

'He was my hero too,' said Henry simply. 'And Ali's dad was Jamaican.' He brushed aside her unease and put his worry to her directly. She had, after all, explicitly offered to talk about it. 'Look, what am I going to do? You know this stuff, you're married to an MP.'

'Ex-MP,' said Diana. She frowned, took a sip, and spoke with what she hoped was judicious slowness. 'I suppose the best thing you can do, really, is not to tangle yourselves up with lawyers in the first place, but talk to Ali about it all. Are she and Donny stable, do you think? Will he stay around?'

Henry glanced towards the bar, flicked his hand, and the barmaid smoothly arrived, bore off their glasses and prepared to replace them with full ones. Diana marvelled: Roger never commanded this sort of service.

'No,' said the young man in reply to her question. 'I don't think Donny will stay around. He'll never bring in much money, and Ali hates losers. But once she's in London, there'll be endless other boyfriends. I do fear for Marley, with a succession of semi-Dads in and out of the house. With the two of them living here it feels great, as if things are really under control. Like, part of the same neighbourhood. It's cool that I can see him most days. Donny just keeps out of the way, which is excellent.'

'Well,' said Diana, 'There is another option, if

they do move to London.'

'What?'

She hesitated, surprised at how reluctant she was to put it forward. 'Well, you could look for work there.'

'One of the local stations, you mean?'

'No,' said Diana. 'You're easily good enough for the BBC. One, or Two, or Five, or Classic FM. Radio Four, even. You're educated. And since we're being so frank, it wouldn't actually hurt you, being black. They're all desperate for ethnic credibility. And with you, well, the advantage is sort of — ' She paused, embarrassed.

'That I don't sound too black to rock the applecart?' said Henry, in his best Bertie Wooster tones. Reverting, he crooned, 'Respeck!'

'Well,' said Diana, 'if it happens, and they do move to London, think about it. We'd miss you terribly, but it might be for the best for Marley.'

'Would you?' Henry's eyes were on her, steady and for once not laughing. 'Would *you* miss me?'

'You are the best presenter we have got,' said Diana calmly.

★ ★ ★

When she had done all the cleaning and tidying she could see, Eva wandered into the dark hallway and looked along the oak shelf of books outside Philip's study. A name caught her eye — Tennyson — and she pulled the old volume down, and sank gracefully to a cross-legged position on the rug. Here, half an hour later,

Philip found her in the same pose, reading by the one dim ray of light that fell through the stained-glass window above the stairway. When he snapped the light on she jumped, losing her place in the book. She had been too engrossed to hear his key in the front door.

'I am so sorry!' she cried, jumping to her feet with difficulty, her legs and ankles prickling with pins-and-needles. 'I hope you do not mind — I saw this book! And it felt so strange and wonderful to read it in a manor, an English manor!'

He took it from her. 'Ah, Tennyson,' he said. 'Not quite Mickiewicz, but the same taste for epic.' He turned a page at random and read:

'*Forward, forward let us range.*
Let the great world spin for ever down the
  ringing grooves of change!'

He glanced at Eva. 'I think he must have written that when he was excited by the invention of the phonograph. Ringing grooves of change, you see?' He flicked on further. ''*Sweet and low, sweet and low, Wind of the western sea*' . . . my mother used to sing that to us when we were little.' He smiled; it transformed his face.

'I was reading about Ulysses,' said Eva, emboldened by his interest. 'Going travelling in his ship. I don't understand all the words, though.'

'Ah, yes — '*to strive, to seek, to find and not to yield*',' said Philip, still riffling the pages. 'He

146

sails away from the humiliations of advancing age. We should be so lucky. '*Matched with an aged wife, I mete and dole/ Unequal laws unto a savage race*'. That's more like it.'

The girl looked up at him, curious at the sudden ring of bitterness in his voice. Then, jolted by the carven coldness of his face, she remembered that it was his book, his hall, and she an uninvited guest. She reverted to formality.

'I was thinking,' she said, 'that perhaps I might help to make the meal this evening. Mrs Hunton-Hall is working hard at her office. I can see what I could make, in the fridge?'

'Well, that might be just the ticket,' said Philip, putting the book back into its place on the shelf. 'You do what you think best.' He gave her a vague, unfocused half-smile and went into the study. This time, he closed the door.

Eva went back into the kitchen — now quite her favourite room — and began searching out the ingredients she wanted. There was some ham on the bone, she saw approvingly; she found potatoes in a dark earthenware crock by the door, and began to peel them and then grate them into a bowl. Eggs, flour, salt and sugar were located and mixed in one by one; then she laid a cloth over the bowl of potato batter and began to cut up a cabbage, very finely. When Diana got home, rather later than usual after her extended lunch-break, she found Eva presiding over a tidy, shining kitchen with two bowls and a plate all covered with clean white cloths. The visitor was sitting at the broad kitchen table, with a glass of water at her side and Philip's school-prize volume of Tennyson open in front of her.

'Well!' Diana said dryly. 'You have been busy!' Her voice rang hostile in her own ears, and she saw dismay cloud the girl's eager, elfin face. 'That looks exciting.' She tried to make her tone friendlier, but was thrown off-balance by the shock of finding her own house looking better than when she'd left it, with supper preparations clearly well under way.

'Mr Hunton-Hall said it would be OK if I made the dinner,' said Eva a touch stiffly, standing up and closing the book. 'I am very grateful to you for inviting me to stay one more night. I have made *Placki Kartoflane* and Polish cabbage with coriander seeds. It would go well with the ham. This English ham is very good'.

Diana smiled, more naturally now, and said 'Thank you. You've been to a lot of trouble, and you're quite right. A Bradenham ham deserves better than the boiled potatoes and Tesco salad I would have served. Was Marianne all right?'

'Marianne has taught me about Tennyson!' said Eva. 'She spoke a long poem and now I have found it in the book!'

'Blimey' said Diana, inadequately.

'And Mr Hunton-Hall has taught me about Ulysses' added Eva. 'He is a very cultured man'.

'Hmm' said Philip's wife. 'How nice. Anyway, do carry on. I need a bath'. She left Eva in the kitchen where, after a brief hesitation, the girl plunged back into her book.

Later on, after her bath, Diana found Philip in the bedroom changing his shirt. According to established custom she said brightly:

'Good day, dear?' but in shocking breach of the said custom, Philip replied with some animation.

'Yes, fine. Got some letters off about the Warsaw partnership. And had a most interesting chat with little Eva about Mickiewicz and Tennyson. She's very bright, you know. Supper smells good, too'.

Diana, caught in astonishment half into her sweater, reflected that it must be several years since Philip said anything so positive about a new acquaintance. Or, indeed, about anything at all.

13

'It is beyond anything.' said Diana to Lizzie, five days later. 'The house is spotless, every supper is amazing, Philip chats away about poetry and corrects her grammar and praises her *pirogi* and generally dotes like Heidi's grandfather. I'd almost forgotten what he looks like when he smiles. And best of all, I can get off to work in the morning without feeling like a deserter.'

'Your little changeling's still there, then?' asked Lizzie. She had come into town with Andy to see, she said, whether she was still capable of wasting a morning in the shops without toppling over exhausted. Diana had left the radio statio after the Henry Show to meet her for a quick lunch before she went back. Lizzie was pale and slow-moving, a green velvet cap pulled over her bald head, and had bought only a bathmat before giving up the shopping effort. But she was sufficiently fascinated by the Eva phenomenon to quiz her friend with energy.

'What about Manda? What's going on? Is the Polish girl going to London to see her or what?'

'Ah,' said Diana, prodding her Caesar salad with unnecessary viciousness. 'Manda is back from Barcelona but 'busy'. I suggested she show Eva a bit of London, and she says maybe next week. But she'll 'get back to me'.'

'So the kid's staying with you meanwhile?'

'I'm bloody tempted,' said Diana, 'to make it

permanent. Are you allowed to adopt adult Poles, I wonder? I can't tell you how much better life is with Philip not always in a mood. He had the official letter from the Conservative Association today, and didn't seem to care. Chucked it into the bin. You know he's not the candidate any more?'

'Hoo-rah!' said Lizzie. 'So you can have your life back, then. No more Mrs Tory Wife. But, seriously, what do you mean about making Eva permanent?'

'Well, she could be a sort of au pair, couldn't she?' said Diana a little uncertainly. 'She doesn't seem to want to leave for a while, and she's desperate to learn more English now she's discovered all these old poets of Philip's. He's started her on Milton and that's completely banjaxed her, it's all those Latinate words. He's even ordered a big Polish dictionary on the Internet so they can translate stuff like 'unannealed'. And she is cooking such wonderful suppers, and now she bikes into the village for fresh veg from the farm shop and just gets me to fetch the meat or fish. And she tidies things up! I don't have to listen to Philip going, 'Tchuh!' every time he goes into the living-room and the fire hasn't been swept out by me. And she smiles *all the time*. And Marianne keeps dropping in to go for after-lunch walks with her, instead of drinking gin all afternoon, so she's looking better too. Why spit on your luck, I say? Till after Christmas, at least.'

'Well,' said Lizzie, in a tone of mock solemnity, 'it isn't every wife who'd willingly introduce a doe-eyed gamine twenty-two-year-old into her household when she's out all day and her husband isn't.' She grinned. 'You're not worried about Phil *pouncing* on her?'

Peals of laughter from the two women made the elderly shoppers in the department-store café turn their heads and stare.

'I think it's a strictly cultural relationship,' said Diana at last, wiping her eyes. 'Yesterday he put a Chopin CD on after dinner, and she recited something in Polish by some famous poet who knew Chopin, and then she translated it: 'You have in your fingers an orchestra of butterflies'. Philip was so charmed he wrote it down in his diary.'

'Bloody hell,' said Lizzie reverently. 'An orchestra of butterflies? Well, you'd better find her a nice boyfriend, then she'll stay. I know girls. There has to be a boyfriend or they wander off. What about hunky Henry?'

'Now,' said Diana, with enthusiasm, 'that *is* a thought! They could go clubbing together at Hannigan's near the station, and do all those weird things kids seem to do these days.'

'You mean, jigging around with blank stares?'

'And drinking straight out of the bottle. Yep, all that. If Henry introduces her to his cutting-edge mates, she'll have such a great life down here that we might hang on to her for a bit longer. P'raps we could put her through driving lessons, even!'

★ ★ ★

152

Eva, meanwhile, found herself happy to take every day as it came. She had no yearnings for the flashing lights and alcopops of Diana's and Lizzie's imagination. The gentle, slow pace of her life at the Manor was exactly what she needed; gradually, day by day, she came to realize that her recent life had been winding her into a knot of nervous tension. It had twisted itself up tight through the last year of university, the exams, caring for her father, the situation with Tadeusz, the degrading work in the tourist hotel. Perhaps even her longing to travel had not been the romantic and adventurous thing she'd thought, but just a well-disguised need for escape. Yet the tension, undeclared until this moment, had actually grown worse during the months of rootless uncertainty and menial jobs in Europe, living out of a shabby rucksack.

During that travelling time, she realized, there had hardly been an opportunity even to read a book; she, who had read three books a week at home, was reduced to cast-off tourist paperbacks and reading barely ten pages a day. The febrile atmosphere of hostels and campsites was not conducive to private concentration: someone always wanted to chat, or grumble, or discuss the next move against or in favour of the current employer. Now, after her easy housekeeping jobs were done, she could sit for hours with a book in the hall or the kitchen, or even under a tree in the orchard when the morning was mild. Philip had shown her how to start the stereo in his study, so when he was out of the house she could fill it with Chopin or Bach while she read. The weather stayed clear and often warm, she chatted happily with Marianne on their walks, and rejoiced in the late vegetables from this mild and kindly earth, and the good meat which — according to each day's request from her — Diana brought back for the following supper.

In the big peaceful kitchen she cooked *bigos*, the hunters' stew, *Golabki* cabbage rolls, *kluski* and *klopsy*; she chopped bacon, fried onions, rolled meatballs and patted meat-loaf. She formed cabbage parcels as her mother used to do at feast days, and introduced Philip (normally, had she but known it, highly resistant to any foreign food except French) to the pleasures of sour cream. Each day she offered to cook 'something English' and read assiduously in Diana's collection of cookbooks; but each day the Hunton-Halls indicated that the new diet was suiting them very well. Philip said that his digestion had never been better. Sometimes, alone with the music and the sweet food smells, Eva talked aloud to her dead mother, saying: 'See, the things you taught me are helping me now.' She was, it sometimes seemed to her, like a culinary Scheherezade: as long as she could keep on offering new and delicious dishes every night to these people, she would be allowed to stay.

Sometimes, Eva tried to rationalize why it was that she so much wanted to stay. With reluctance, she admitted to herself that a great part of the answer was fear. In Italy and Spain, in France, in London, she had needed to live on her nerves, guarding her pack and passport, wary of every other human soul. The tales of enslavement and prostitution had preyed on her mind more than she had ever admitted to herself; the mocking spectres of Reni and Vessela and the desperate, snarling Chechen prostitute never quite left her. If you were a poor girl in a rich world, shame was never a distant possibility but a close, hateful shadow.

But here all was peace and safety, with the kind old man and his brisk, impersonally friendly wife. A slight shadow in her mind told her that she was a little uneasy about Diana; they seemed to have no real connection, and their eyes rarely met. But maybe it was because Diana was busy. Anyhow, Eva could not help hoping that for a few more days at least, she could stay. The idea of Manda had become a complication rather than a hope. Diana constantly said that Manda and Art were 'looking forward to showing her London' but Eva was not stupid. Manda was busy, had forgotten all about her penfriend, and was not inclined to put herself out.

She could not, in honesty, resent it. Things were different here. Even from her few encounters and overheard conversations in the village — where she cycled for bits of shopping on Diana's old bike — it was clear that the affluence and busyness and family fragmentation of British life created something quite different from the domestic culture she had come from. Manda, she saw, had become like a distant relative of the house: already a new unit with her own home and her own preoccupations. She was not a close part of her parents' universe. This must be how it was, in the West.

Eva's father, in a rare outburst of open anger, had once said that Poland had 'missed fifty years of progress' under the Soviets, and here in rural England she felt this more crushingly than she ever had before: more than amid the elegances of Milan and Barcelona. It was just so safe here, so peaceful, so carelessly confident. Even young people seemed to feel no terror of being alone in the world. Philip had explained the Welfare State to her one evening, in a conversation about William Morris apropos his study wallpaper. His view of it was not rosy, but the bare facts she gleaned from his tirade seemed next-door to miraculous. 'In Poland,' she had said, 'if you are very poor you must beg in the street, or go to the nuns if they will take you.'

'Better system, frankly,' said Philip. 'It'd give some of our shirkers an incentive to do some bloody work for whatever the market pays, instead of drawing benefits.' If Eva took a different view, she kept her own counsel.

On the evening after her conversation with Lizzie, Diana came home around eight-thirty from her newsroom shift — she had had a long day, doubling up for a sick colleague. She found the Polish girl as usual in the kitchen, grating the peel off lemons for a pudding.

'Eva,' she said, 'could I put a proposal to you? You must say no if you don't like it.'

'Yes?' Eva stood, the pile of shining moist gold before her under the kitchen spotlight, the lemon and grater poised in her small white hands.

'Would you consider working — sort of semi-officially — as a kind of housekeeper for us, until January at least?' said Diana, in a rush. 'I know it isn't why you came over, and you probably want to go off on the next adventure — heavens, you're young — but it's been working out so wonderfully for me these last few days.'

Eva was silent; Diana misread her silence for insulted shock. Rattled, she rushed on: 'Well, of course, I shouldn't have asked. You're a graduate, after all. It was just a thought, you have no idea how hard it is for Philip suddenly to have a working wife. And we could entertain a bit more if you were here. And — well, you know. We love having you here.'

'I love to be here,' said Eva, almost inaudibly. She bent her head, and a tear fell on the lemon zest, unnoticed by the anxious Diana.

'The thing is, we could pay a sort of au pair rate, say sixty pounds a week and your board and lodging, and you could have plenty of time to study as well. If you went to the college in town I could give you a lift, or if it was later on you could cycle to the bus.' It all tumbled out; during a quiet newsroom shift she had been checking out on the Internet the normal conditions of work for au pair girls.

Suddenly, forcefully, Eva said, 'I should not be paid! That you give me food and shelter is enough!'

'No, we have to. You'd need college fees, and money for books, and to save up a bit. We can afford it. Honestly, we can. You'd be doing us a favour.'

'Polish au pairs are not legal,' said Eva heavily.

'It is the rule. We hope this will change soon, but now it is the law that we must not work, even as an au pair.'

'Pish,' said Diana. 'Who's to know? We'd say you were a house guest, friend of Manda's. Pay you in cash. No names, no pack drill.'

'Mr Hunton-Hall is in the government,' said Eva uncertainly. 'It might be bad for his reputation to break such a law.'

'He's not in the government anymore,' said Diana happily. 'Not even in Parliament. He was voted out last election. I thought you knew that?'

'How,' cried Eva, distressed, 'could anybody vote against Mr Hunton-Hall? He is such a *good* man! I am sure it is because of cheating in the election, like under the communists. The free people would always have reverence for Mr Hunton-Hall.'

Diana, who felt with some dismay that this conversation was getting away from her, offered no contradiction but stored up the remark to hoot over with Lizzie another day. Eva duly agreed to the proposal, and became an official fixture at Garton Manor. That night, over a bowl of thin, scarlet *borscht*, the three of them drank one another's health in Philip's best claret, which was hardly richer or clearer than the soup.

Diana had particular cause to be cheerful, because Henry — between records — had reported to her that Donny appeared to have left Ali, by way of a couple of bruises and a police intervention. So Marley could stay put and not migrate to London, and the Henry Show would continue for the moment as the prime ornament

158

of Two Counties Radio. Diana was happy. The amusement and interest of her own job would not be compromised by having to work with some dull new presenter. And Eva, perhaps, might take up with Henry's young set and find some company to run around and drink out of bottles with. And she would stay, and life would be easy for a while.

★ ★ ★

'Art,' said Amanda Hunton-Hall, over their glass dining table a few days later, 'you won't believe this, but I've had a letter from my mum, and they've basically gone loco. You remember that Polish girl who turned up?'

'Yah?'

'Well, she's only bloody still there! They've taken her on as an au pair.'

'But they don't have small children, do they? You haven't got any brothers and sisters.'

'No. Just me. She cooks, apparently. So when Mum's out at work she doesn't have to bring home cook-chill shepherd's pie all the time like she used to.'

'Well, that sounds OK.' Art's attention span was short; he was a pale, jumpy young man with big green eyes and eyelashes which were almost white. These had, briefly, been fixed on his lover while she talked, but now he started to open his *Financial Times* to signal an end to communication.

'No, wait. It's not OK. What's going on?' cried Amanda, flicking her smooth golden hair out of her eyes. 'She's trying to get round them, that's what it is.'

'Why?' He put the paper down, resignedly.

'For their money, of course!' The young woman was almost squeaking now. 'She's battened on them. Next thing we know, she'll be *named in the will*.'

Art flattened his paper again and stared at her. He did not live with Manda for mercenary reasons, but the knowledge that a sizeable family fortune hung in her background was not unwelcome to him. If they stayed together, in ten years' time perhaps it would be bloody useful. A lot more certain than the stock market, as investments went.

'That wouldn't happen!' he said with some dismay.

'Bloody might. Mum's such a sucker for lame ducks, and Dad . . . ' She could not think of any reason why her father would be taken in but concluded, 'Dad would do whatever Mum made him do.'

'Perhaps he fancies this girl,' said Art crudely. Manda thought for a moment, then giggled.

'No,' she said. 'He's had plenty of chances over the years, all those House of Commons secretaries gagging for it, the whiff of power. No. It's my opinion that he doesn't actually have much interest in sex. Prefers his music and his books and his wheeler-dealer Tory tediosity.'

Art was a little shocked, despite himself. If he ever had a daughter, he thought hazily, he would not expect her to be so frank in her assessment of his sex drive. Still, she had a point about the

Polish girl. Feet under the table always spelt trouble.

'OK,' he said. 'We could go down. You say they're always nagging you to do that. And she's supposed to be your penfriend anyway.'

'Yeah', said Manda slowly. 'You know, I think we should.'

14

Marianne's afternoon walk with Eva became a ritual. She would turn up at about half-past one, usually with her dilapidated old Labrador in tow, and bang on the kitchen door. She wore her own Wellingtons now, bought from a company in town which specialized in boots with wide, comfortable legs. With a broad-brimmed waxed cotton hat jammed on her ever-looser peroxide curls, she looked every inch the countrywoman.

'I can't imagine why I never used to go for walks,' she said happily as they strode along in watery afternoon sunshine. 'It totally cheers you up, doesn't it?'

'Exercise is good,' said Eva, absently. She was looking towards the river, where a cold, lonely heron hovered over the reeds. 'My mother said that outdoor people, like my grandparents with their farm, were happier than city people who use trams and buses and cars always.'

'Tell me about your home,' said Marianne, swishing at the low hedge with her stick. 'What's it like?'

'A big city,' said Eva, who was having a homesick day. 'Very beautiful. Tall buildings. High pointed roofs. A big square . . . no, not square, what do you call it? A *platz*, in German . . . called Rynek. With a clock. And people selling things, and cafés. And a statue of one of our poets, Fredro. The children from my school,

Fredro School, were sent once a year to wash and clean him. I hated this, because it was cold and you got wet from the sponges when the boys threw them at the girls.'

'I went to Prague once,' said Marianne. 'With Tony. That's my husband. *An*-thony!'

Eva knew by now that it was wisest to steer Marianne off the subject of her marriage. But she was a little tired; she had not slept as well as usual, haunted by thoughts of her father and Max, and by irrational intimations that something was wrong. She had written two letters since arriving at the Manor, but received none in return. She wished that either of them would get used to e-mail: there was a cyber café at Glowny station but Max would never be bothered to learn. How would she know if things were not well with them? Perhaps she should ring Halina or Tadek? But that was difficult, too, as she was shy of asking to make calls from the Manor, and the coin-box in the village was old-fashioned and needed an absurd number of coins for international calls. And she was only in the village by day, when they were all working anyway. Perhaps her letters had not even arrived, and they did not even know which country she was in? The last card from them had arrived at the French campsite. Perhaps they were dead?

The morning brought relief from such morbidity, but now some small inner demon made her feel that it was the spoiled, comfortable Marianne's turn to be unhappy. She knew that once the erring Tony had been mentioned it would take no more than a nudge to push her new friend onward down this unfortunate pathway. She administered that push with the words: 'It is very sad when married people divorce.'

'I'm not divorced,' snapped Marianne. 'And I bloody won't be until he's realized he's going to suffer financially over this. I've had to suffer every other way, but my God, I'll hit him in the wallet!'

'Do you have children?' asked Eva.

'No. Tried for years. Didn't want to do that yucky test-tube stuff, so we gave up. Oh, God!'

The big woman stopped in her tracks, and turned in dismay to stare at her young companion.

'Perhaps that's it! Perhaps his little tart is going to give him a child!'

She was almost shouting. Eva winced. The distant heron was flying away, fishless.

'No! I am sure that is not true.'

Marianne resumed her walking.

'If he thinks . . . ' she said. 'If he thinks he'll get away with this . . . '

Eva, remorseful at having released such anger, sniffed, wrapped her scarf around her face and strode on, forcing the pace until Marianne began to puff and could no longer talk.

★   ★   ★

Back at the house Philip sat dreaming in his study, a quiet passage of Chopin shepherding his thoughts down old forgotten pathways. Before him, unheeded, lay a dossier on the proposed

164

partnership with a property company based in Warsaw and Gdynia. It would, his associates at the bank had assured him, make a great deal of money in the coming rapid expansion of the old Iron Curtain economies as they joined the European Union. This project, like several others, was a good ground floor to be let in on. He was the major investor, and there was a meeting in London next week to finalize the details. The risk was minimal, and the Polish partners were ready to come in on terms which were quite laughably favourable to the richer consortium from the West. There was nothing even remotely dodgy about the sources of secondary finance. In the old days he would have been elated by involvement in such a coup; it would have fitted in most satisfactorily with his idea of himself as an MP, lord of his own manor, friend of Prime Ministers, a man with his hands on the levers of international money and power.

He was none of those things now, no kind of master except in his own sphere of house and land. Until the last fortnight the unhappiness of being bereft of it all had gnawed at him without remission. The bitterness of rejection, the loneliness of being sidelined in politics, had been an agony to Philip: a long illness. Every newspaper he opened, every television debate, reminded him that he no longer mattered. '*They flee from me, that sometime did me seek*'. He took personally, and hard, the self-satisfaction and arrogance of the new government, prating popinjays who had replaced his leaders. Yet he also grievously resented the way that his own party seemed unable to elect a credible new leader or mount an efficient challenge to the incomers. The only figures in his own party now who enjoyed any popular esteem at all were either older men than himself, at the sour dog-end of their careers, or else ridiculous upstart opportunists who could be amusing on comedy news quiz shows. Dust and ashes, thought Philip, dust and ashes: it wasn't only he who was finished, but everything he had cared about, every structure of power and policy and established good sense.

All of it was blowing away. Bloody Britain! Bloody Blair! Soon his country would drift, rudderless and humiliated, into the sticky and permanent embrace of a federal Europe, its culture belittled, its ancient freedoms sold for a pittance to old enemies and replaced by a hateful new age of whining and complaint.

Yet even as these familiar thoughts went through Philip's head, he was realizing in astonishment that their power to hurt was gone. These things, or approximations to them, might indeed happen, but they could not bring him to despair. They could not cloud the sun, dim the brilliance of the music, or belie the poetry of life. He was, in short, better. The long illness was over; the sun was shining through the crack in the curtains and it was time to sit up and think about the future.

And the past. The music was reaching a glittering climax now, pouring from the discreet expensive speakers to fill the little room and roll down the hallway like a golden tide. As it rose

Philip realized, with even greater incredulity, that the debility from which he now felt himself arising was not brought on by his political failure at all, but had afflicted him long, long before. Perhaps depression had even been the motive force behind his ambition: maybe he had not been, as he thought, struggling bravely towards a distant star, but merely fleeing from the hounds of despair. Now he was reaching back further, with ease and comfort, into a youth he had too impatiently discarded. He saw that it was not only political decline and impotence but politics itself — his whole life, his whole career — which had been the illness.

He had embraced ambition, stifled originality and sentiment, acted pragmatically and ambitiously at every turn during his young manhood. He had taken on a suitable career in law and property; bought a suitable house; married a suitable and biddable wife. His daughter had once in a teenage fury called him 'Identi-Tory' and claimed that he could be ordered by the dozen from Central Office. Her ignorant gibe was, thought Philip in amazement now, nothing less than the plain truth. He had made himself into an imitation of something he admired, yet he had never learned to admire himself.

And now he was better. Bored by the business documents before him, alive with the joy of the music, he found his mind filled with long-forgotten poetry, a healing stream of high, impractical thought.

*The world is too much with us; late and
    soon,
Getting and spending, we lay waste our
    powers;
Little we see in Nature that is ours;
We have given our hearts away, a sordid
    boon!*

That was it, thought Philip. Wordsworth had
it. Getting and spending, ignoring the sea and
the winds and — what was it? Some sea-god?
— Triton, that was it, coming to '*blow his
wreathed horn*'. Horns of elfland — that was
Tennyson — '*blow, bugle, blow, set the wild
echoes flying*' . . .

The Polish girl had discovered that one in his
old prize volume of Tennyson, and loved it. Ah,
the simplicity of youth! For all the music that
he played, the operas that he visited with an
always reluctant Diana, how many years was it
since he, Philip, had truly been capable of
hearing the horns of elfland? A long time. Until
now. Now they sounded again from deep within
him, calling him to a long-forgotten land of lost
content. He smiled. He had no idea what to
do with this new resurgent life he felt within
him, and certainly no words in which to
express it to his distant, distraite wife. But for
the moment it was enough merely to bathe in
its splendour.

The phone rang on his desk, breaking into the
music and his reverie and making him jump.
Before he answered he faded down the Chopin,
slowly and respectfully. Picking up the phone, he

said the number in a neutral voice: 'Two six eight five.'

'Dad? It's Manda. Hi.'

It was a long time since his daughter had initiated any contact. Usually Diana rang her; occasionally Philip. He frowned at the receiver, as if it were an unidentified insect on a windowsill. Manda was, he realized, no part of his new feeling. Her conception, infancy, childhood and whole life so far had been things that happened during the dark years. He hardly knew her. Closing his eyes, he tried to visualize what she looked like: cool blonde, small triangular face, pale skin, no smile.

'Dad? Are you there?'

'This is is a surprise,' he said cautiously. 'How are you?'

'Fine. Art and I thought we'd come down at the weekend.'

Silence lay thick between them. After a moment Philip said, 'Well — that's fine. I'm sure your room is OK. Eva's using the south guestroom.'

'She's still there, then?'

'Well, yes. Till Christmas at least. I assumed that was why you were coming. To see her?'

'Right.'

There was nothing else to be said between them. When it had been agreed that Manda and Art would drive down on Saturday morning, Philip laid the phone down, carefully, as if it might spring dangerously to life again. He realized that he did not want to see his daughter. She was part of all the wasted years. To reconcile, to explain, to change the way they behaved together was not within his power, even if it were not such an excruciatingly embarrassing prospect. He might have suddenly become happier, for some unknown reason, but that did not mean he had turned into an *American*.

He turned up the music. No: what Philip wanted was not to rebuild his present life and relationships but to uncover something from the age before, something long missing: the invisible glory which had hovered around him as a boy in the school chapel and briefly shone between the spires of stone colleges in his youth. It had deserted him for long, arid decades of getting and spending. Cold brittle Manda would not bring it with her. Diana had no idea about it. If the fragile glory was to be reborn, he must guard it from all their heavy, trampling, insensitive feet.

An appropriately leaden tread and loud laugh from the kitchen hallway told him that Marianne had come back from her walk with Eva. Gently, so as to make no sound, he got up and pushed the study door shut.

Later, when Diana got home, Philip found her rummaging in her shabby bag in the kitchen. Eva was in the scullery, noisily grinding up peppercorns with a pestle-and-mortar somebody had given them for Christmas years before, but which had not been used at any time Philip could remember.

''Lo, Philip,' said his wife. 'I thought you were out. Have a good day?'

She did not look at him, and continued pulling crumpled papers out of the bag. He realized that

170

he was not the only one who had changed in the past weeks. Diana seemed less anxious about his state of mind, less placatory. It was, he thought, a relief. If there was one thing worse than feeling constantly angry and depressed, it was having a woman fussing around trying to stop you being either.

'Manda rang,' he said. 'Wants to come down on Saturday. Stay till Sunday.'

'Really?' This had got her attention all right. 'Crikey! Is she wanting to whisk Eva away? Only I've just got all the details of English courses at the F.E. college.' She glanced at the scullery, beyond the long broad kitchen. Eva seemed oblivious of their conversation.

'No,' said Philip. 'I got the impression she was coming down just for the weekend. There wasn't anything said about taking Eva back to London.'

Diana snorted. 'Huh! That doesn't surprise me. Well, OK, I'll do the bed. I suppose we can put them in together now?'

It had always been a bone of contention between them that Philip refused to have his unmarried daughter and her boyfriend officially sharing a bed in the parental home. He had some idea that if leaked to the tabloid press, the intelligence that she did so would be taken as proof that his party were hypocritical when they praised 'family values'. Now, as Diana correctly surmised, it did not matter.

'Put them wherever it's least trouble,' he said. 'I don't think we should disturb Eva, though.'

'Oh, no, of course not,' said Diana. 'They can have Manda's old room. It's a big enough bed.

171

They're both such skinny little shrimps.' Then she called out brightly to Eva, who had finished pounding at the peppery seeds.

'Eva, great news! Manda's back from Spain. She'll be here to see you on Saturday.'

Eva paused in the doorway of the scullery, holding the fragrant mortar between her hands.

'That is good,' she said carefully, and carried on with her preparations. She was, to tell the truth, shocked and unaccountably upset.

* * *

Henry went to visit Ali and his child in their flat. As he made his way along the outside walkway towards her door, his sharp eyes noticed every sign of disturbance and litter. Once he stooped to pick up a used hypodermic, with a dark stain on its needle, and carried it to one of the overflowing waste bins which the council so rarely emptied. It pained him to have Marley living like this, but Ali was a devoted mother and until recently Donny had seemed to be a reasonably inoffensive quasi-stepfather. Every time he came here Henry wondered whether he ought to try for custody of Marley, but every time he realized how absurd and unlikely that was, and how snobbish it was of him to assume that a clean privately owned flat in a nice part of town with some paid nanny and a part-time father was better for a child than a council flat with a mother who loved him. By the time he reached the door he had, as usual, gathered his wits and banished these uncomfortable thoughts.

'Hiyee!' he said as the dark, morose figure of Alissa opened the battered, yellow-painted door. 'Hey, Marley!'

The child, who was dressed in Spiderman pyjamas with streaks of green luminous hair-gel on his curly head, looked at him with steady unwinking eyes for a moment. Then his face split into a huge grin. 'I just farted,' he said with satisfaction. 'I can do it by trying, now.'

'Cool,' said Henry, whose heart had turned over with love at the sight of his little son. But Ali frowned and aimed a light cuff at the boy. 'That's rude,' she said.

'Donny always farts and doesn't say sorry,' proffered the child. 'Hey, Dad, are we going to McDonald's?'

'No,' said Henry. 'Well, unless your mother wants me to take you out for a bit. Tell you what, go and get changed just in case.' The child raced into his small room and slammed the door, shouting, 'Mega! McDonald's!'

'Do what you like,' said Ali brusquely. 'Anyway, whatch'ou want? You got Marley for the weekend, why're you here now?'

'I wanted to know that things were OK,' said Henry flatly. 'That you're OK for money, you two, and that you're not too — um — fed up about Donny leaving.'

'It was *me* who threw *him* out,' said Ali, between gritted teeth. 'Like, *nobody* hits me.'

'Right!' said Henry. 'Are you OK? And I mean, he didn't ever . . . ?' He glanced towards the door of Marley's tiny room.

'Are you mental? Of course not! I wouldn't

have let him,' flared the girl. 'Like, just because you work for the radio you think you're fucking Mr Perfect.'

'I don't,' said Henry. 'But look, I could help more. I've got a second bedroom plus the sofa in my flat. You and Marley could just come and chill out for a few days at mine. In case he comes back and gives you any grief.'

'Just piss off, right?' said Ali. As she turned to look at the door behind her, Henry saw a swelling bruise on one side of her jaw, and a cut just healing over.

'My God!' he said. 'That is terrible. Is that what he did?'

'Well, I don't do kick-boxing classes or wrestle bears' said Ali sarcastically. ''Course he did it, genius.'

Henry, not for the first time, raised a silent prayer of thanks for the short temper and lashing tongue which, long ago, had led to the break-up of his own love affair with this woman. At least she had the courage and cheek to stand up for herself. And for Marley. She would never be one of those sad dreadful women with no pride or courage who stood by while a boyfriend beat her child. Ali was a firecat, and spectacularly selfish in love, but she loved their son and would defend him.

Marley, at this moment, swaggered out of the bedroom with all the confidence of an approaching fifth birthday, this time wearing a dark blue tracksuit and a baseball hat in a vicious shade of green.

'OK. Burger time,' he said. 'C'mon, Dad!'

Henry swept him up, rather against his will, and gave him a hard determined hug.

'Lemme down!'

'Give us a proper hug, first.'

The child obliged, squashing Henry's nose against his chest in a businesslike rapid hug, and was put on to his feet. He danced on the spot.

'C'mon, c'mon, c'mon!'

'OK,' said Henry. 'But not McDonald's. We'll go to the American Diner and have a proper burger, and you've got to have salad as well.'

'And chips?'

'Some chips. Ali, I'll have him back by eight, that all right?'

'Yeah,' she said, and yawned. 'Tire him out for me. I'm going to the launderette, this machine's so crap it can only do one sheet at a time without dancing all over the kitchen.'

'I'll buy you a new one,' said Henry. 'Please?'

'Patronizing git you always were,' said Ali, but without much rancour. 'When I want more maintenance I'll ask for it through my lawyer and bloody well get it, yeah? You're not doing me no favours.'

'Shutup, shutup, shutup!' said Marley. 'I want a burger.'

15

Eva wanted to make a dish of carp for Manda's arrival, but carp were nowhere to be found in the shops. So a harassed Diana drove into town on the Saturday morning, and brought back six fine trout from the most expensive fishmonger, and a large bag of frozen prawns on which her young housekeeper looked with marked disfavour. Indeed, tempers at the Manor were less sunny than they had been for days. The short interval between the phone call and the arrival of the London couple saw a slight but perceptible rise in tension. Philip spoke less, Diana prattled more, and Eva spent the night before sitting alone in the kitchen, obsessively rolling tiny wormlike dumplings, instead of reading poetry by the fire.

In the morning, heavy-eyed, she fiddled with lunch and spent a lot of time wiping and polishing a jar of clear honey she had produced from the depths of her backpack. Looking at Eva standing preoccupied in the kitchen, holding the golden jar up against the light, Diana felt a stab of irritation towards her daughter. Home had run so smoothly in recent weeks! An unprecedentedly benevolent *modus vivendi* had been reached between the Manor's inhabitants, unknown for years and certainly unlike the time when Manda lived at home. The alchemy of Eva's presence, Eva's simple-hearted joy in small things, and Eva's food had smoothed the way for all three of them. Philip was not much more communicative towards Diana than usual, and as usual she knew little about what went on in his head; but he was distracted rather than depressed, as if he was thinking something through, and this made an immense difference. Relieved of her constant faint anxiety about his state of mind, she had enjoyed work even more full-heartedly than usual. She had invented a new quiz for the Henry Show, got better at editing clips of sound on the new computer system, and been entrusted with the writing of several local news bulletin items. Her wings were spreading, growing stronger by the day. She still dreamed of applying for a job as a researcher or producer, maybe with the BBC in London: she could even commute, if such a housekeeper were in residence. According to Roger ageism was the new racism, frowned upon by the vast benevolent Corporation, so she would at least get an interview. She had a chance, at last, to do something of her own.

To top off her delight, the final dismissal of Philip by the constituency party had set the seal on her freedom without worsening his temper. Something she had looked forward to with trepidation, as a dangerously mixed blessing, had turned out after all to be an unmixed one. Philip didn't seem to care in the slightest.

But now their daughter, a cool contemptuous creature from an alien big-city world, was coming home to cause trouble. Diana was convinced that her purpose was nothing less.

177

Unlike Philip, who seemed tranquil at the prospect and even hazarded the view that she was 'keen to meet Eva', Diana had a shrewd notion of what had provoked the unwonted visit. When it seemed that the Polish penfriend was only passing through, Manda had shown not a shred of interest. Now that Eva was a fixture, and an obvious asset to the household, she represented a threat. Manda was coming to spy out the terrain and satisfy herself that her interests were safe. The fact that the charmless and apparently money-obsessed Art was coming with her only confirmed the mother's gloomy suspicion.

She did, of course, feel guilty even as these thoughts formed in her mind. A woman should long to see her grown daughter. Lizzie always did: she glowed and boasted about her adult children. It should not be Eva who was fussing over food and honey and carrying flowers up to the bedroom, it should be Diana.

She shook her head to dislodge these thoughts, went into the kitchen and asked unenthusiastically, 'Do you need any help?'

'No, thank you,' said Eva. She sniffed. Diana wondered whether she had been crying, but felt so dissociated from her guest's emotional state that she had no idea. Was the child homesick, or uneasy? Had it been a stupid idea anyway to take her on as housekeeper, a mad fantasy bred of the brief honeymoon of hot fragrant suppers, tidiness, and a smiling Philip? Diana realized that she knew nothing of this girl, little about her own daughter, and less and less about her husband. Was it always like this when mothers returned to work? Was there just not enough attention and perception in one woman to go round? Did all homes gradually disintegrate into separate individual lives if there was no powerful, interfering female focus to hold them together?

Unbidden, the image of Henry swam into her mind. Oh, to be young and cheerful, with the whole world before you and nobody to please but yourself! She smiled, in spite of herself, at the memory of the strange dinner party with the Morgans and Marianne, and Henry catching her eye with irrepressible merriment across the table. She must, she thought, organize a young people's evening for Eva with him and maybe some of the other kids from Two Counties Radio. It might make Eva more contented, and more likely to stay on over the winter even if Manda made trouble.

Suddenly, with a snap of irritation, Diana pulled herself together. Of course Eva would stay! What right had a twenty-two-year-old, amply provided for and carefully educated, to dictate how her parents ran their lives? If Eva suited the Hunton-Halls as unofficial au pair for a few months, and was willing to be so, then Eva must stay. When she decided to travel on, they might advertise for another one, legally this time. Yes. They would have a series of nice girls, cooking nice Scandinavian or Croatian or Dutch suppers and keeping the house tidy, and Manda could mind her own damn business. She didn't live here any more.

It was the sound of the front door opening

which reminded Diana that her daughter still had her own key.

* * *

Henry was not, at that moment, feeling young and cheerful or as if all the world lay before him. He was standing aghast on the walkway outside Ali's flat, looking at a broken yellow front door hanging on one hinge, revealing its pathetic chipboard flimsiness where the paint had been kicked off. He saw an overturned mess of furniture, broken glass and toys, with Marley's plastic tractor lying on its side at the centre of it. He saw a dark stain on the cheap grey nylon carpet.

Behind him, a fat fair women he recognized as a neighbour stopped and said to his back view, with insulting emphasis: 'Police have called the man to board it up. They'll be back in a minute. A WPC's talking to them downstairs. You'd better piss off.'

Henry turned and said, 'I'm not . . . ' but the woman recognized him in turn and said in a more conciliatory tone: 'Oh. You're the old boyfriend, right? The little kiddie's dad? I thought you was one of them fucking yobs from the Towers.'

'Where are they?' Henry's throat was tight, but he was instinctively reassured by the woman's tone. She was known to Ali, he had seen her laughing at Marley on his tractor. She would surely not be speaking to him so matter-of-factly if anybody was dead. But even as the word

180

formed itself in his mind he grew dizzy and leaned on the splintered doorframe.

'Where's Marley?'

'WPC rang someone. Social Services got him by now, I'd think. That red-headed bint who was so rude about my Joshua was round here a couple of hours ago.'

'What happened?'

The woman, it transpired, had been attentive behind her curtains throughout the whole drama. On Friday night there had been, she said, a row. Donny — for Henry recognized his description without difficulty — had come round late on Friday night and started 'shouting the place down'. Ali had shouted back. The kiddie had started crying.

Henry closed his eyes, and concentrated on staying calm enough to listen to the rest. The woman saw his distress and said, 'I think she put the kiddie in the bedroom, though, when the guy left. Because he was def'nitely asleep in bed when the police came. They had to go through and look for him.'

'When was that?' Henry's mind was fogged.

'That was later. When he came back, I mean.'

With difficulty, Henry got the story straight. Donny had left, around midnight, still 'shouting the odds'. At two o'clock he had come back, with another man who, according to the blonde witness, 'Must've got the door down with one kick. 'Cos I only heard one bang and some splintering.' The unknown man had run away, his footsteps heard by several neighbours. 'We all reckoned it was him running off. The boyfriend.'

The next anybody knew was a scream, then shortly afterwards another burst of running feet. At this stage several neighbours had put their heads out, and the woman's boy Joshua had seen the door leaning wrecked on its hinge. Rather bravely, in her view — ''cos he's like that, never thinks' — he had gone inside and found Ali half-conscious, bleeding heavily. 'But she def'nitely wasn't dead.' Joshua had called the ambulance and the police: 'Lucky her phone was working, 'cos the bastards cut mine off.'

A knife had been found, not one of Ali's own kitchen implements but a huntsman's knife. The wound was in her stomach. She was in hospital. The WPC and a male sergeant had been asking everybody in sight questions, all morning. The kid had, incredibly, slept through the bang and the scream and been woken up by the policewoman, apparently unharmed, and carried off half-asleep down the stairway.

'Did he see the — did he see his mother lying there?' asked Henry, but the woman did not know.

He rubbed his hand through his hair, blinked heavily, and hurried back along the iron walkway and down the stairs. At the bottom, a young policewoman was talking to a man from a white van whose roof was stacked with planks. Peremptory in his anxiety, Henry interrupted.

'I'm the little boy's father. Marley. He's my son. Where is he?'

The woman in uniform turned and looked at him for a moment.

'Do you mean the child at number twenty-three?' she said. 'Your name, please?'

'Henry Windsor.' He registered, through his agitation, the usual lifting of eyebrows at his surname. Not for the first time, he wished his father had not abandoned the polysyllabic, clicking tribal name he'd brought from the Cape, thus landing him with a choice between the absurdity of Henry Henryson and the improbable name on his birth certificate. But it was on his passport now, and he was stuck with it.

'We'll need to interview you,' said the policewoman. 'Down at the station. My colleague Sergeant Wilson is back there. If you just wait a moment I'll take you in the car.' She turned back to the man with the boards and gave him a few more brief instructions, ending with: 'Scene-of-crime officers need access at fourteen hundred hours.'

'You mean, two o'clock?' said the man. Through his terror and misery Henry noticed the nuance of contempt. He didn't much like the WPC either.

'Yes,' she said. 'Right, Mr Windsor. In the car, please.'

'I have to see my son,' said Henry. His voice ran up an octave, breaking stupidly. 'Where have you taken him?' A vision of Marley's Spiderman pyjamas haunted him. Had the social workers taken any clothes? Or had they been in too much of a hurry to get him out of the bedroom, past the bleeding body of his mother? 'I have to see Marley.'

'He's in safe hands. If you'd just get in the

183

back of the car, please?'

He saw that there was already a policeman in the back seat, sitting in silence.

⋆ ⋆ ⋆

'Well!' said Diana. 'This is nice.' Her husband and daughter looked unconvinced. Eva sat next to Manda, darting shy glances at her, unhappy at not being allowed to serve the food to the Hunton-Halls before sitting down with them, as she normally did. Diana had, quite abruptly, told her to sit down and be served.

'You're a guest,' she said. 'Relax for a change.'

How could she relax with these intimidating people from London? Never, even in the richest, most shining streets of Milan or Madrid, had she felt shabbier or more naïve. She was from another world. All she had learnt at university, all the adventures she had bravely undertaken, meant nothing when set against the deadpan, disdainful, clipped and minimalist chic of Art and Amanda. The photograph she had kept with the school letters showed a plumpish blonde girl with a frizzy bush of hair, crooked school shirt collar and a surprised expression: a girl who might have been in any of her own classes, shared a Kubus with her at a café on Rynek or discussed dreams of travel. The young woman at her side now was thin, with slick blonde hair immaculately smooth, falling in a slight but perfect curve to the exact right point on her collar. She wore a green jacket and loose trousers which the most unpractised eye could identify as expensive beyond reason, a silk shirt as immaculately smooth as her hair, and had the finest of soft cashmere shawls draped over the back of her chair.

It would have been all right, though, if Manda had seemed glad to see her. Oh, she had been courteous enough, shaking hands and saying 'Hi', and introducing the pale, bored-looking young man with her as 'Art'. But every question Eva had rehearsed in her mind and falteringly ventured had been met with at most five syllables.

'Do you still like rabbits?'

'Rabbits? Why?'

'In your letters you told me you had a rabbit in a cage . . . what do you call it? . . . a hutch. He was called Possum.'

'God, I forgot. Weird.'

'Have you been travelling? I have been in Spain and Italy and France and Czech Republic this summer.'

'Yah. A bit.'

'Where do you like to go? I thought maybe to go to Greece with my friend from Australia, but I have come to England instead. It is very beautiful here.' Outside the window, the leaden autumn sky began to drizzle over the winter wheat. 'Do you like to go to the sunshine? Diana is telling me that English people love to holiday in the sun. Poles also.'

'Mmm. Quite like Thailand.'

'You have been to Thailand? Wonderful! Did you see the temples?'

'Art likes that stuff.'

185

So, waiting for her dish of trout to be brought from the kitchen by Diana (oh, would she remember the fried parsley garnish?), Eva gave up and let the silence fall. Once or twice she glanced at Philip, but he appeared to share his daughter's economy with small-talk.

'Job going all right?' he asked, filling at least some part of the cavernous void of silence.

'Fine. Moving into derivatives, probably.'

'Good. Flat OK?'

'Yah.'

'How about you, Art? All OK?'

'Reasonable. Lousy market. Dull.'

'Bound to recover.'

'When? That's the question.'

They ate their trout in silence, Manda picking out bones with a suspicious eye. After a period of clinking and scraping Diana said, 'Well. Are you planning to show Eva round London a bit sometime? That would be fun for both of you, wouldn't it? It's the only time Londoners ever do the tourist things, they say, when there are guests. Remember when we used to go up to Tussaud's and the Planetarium and then take in a musical?'

Eva broke in to save herself, before the humiliation of Manda's response could fall upon her.

'I think Manda is a very busy worker. Perhaps I should come one day later. Now, I am very happy to look after this house and learn the English countryside. And I must go to English classes and not miss them.'

'Well, we love having you here,' said Philip,

suddenly taking on a degree more animation. 'Wonderful food. You're welcome to look after us as long as you like.'

Eva caught a glance between Manda and Art, and thought she understood it. She reddened, and ate the rest of her meal in virtual silence. After lunch, to the immense relief of all five of them, Manda made a phone call — more of a phoney call, thought Diana angrily — and returned saying that there was a problem she had to deal with in London, at her secure computer terminal, and that therefore she and Art would not after all be staying overnight.

'Pity,' said Philip insincerely. 'But work comes first.'

'Yah,' said Manda. 'I'll ring you.'

As they drove away Art said, 'What do you think, then?' And with unusual animation his beloved replied, 'I think the same as I did before. Feet under the table. Scheming little cow! But going down there made me realize there's no point. They can do what they bloody well like. If it came to it, I'd contest the will anyway.'

Art was secretly shocked, not for the first time.

'I like your mother,' he said inconsequentially. 'She's a really nice woman. And I think it's really cool of her starting a new career at her age.'

'S'pose so,' said Manda, and put her foot down, driving the smart little car up to ninety miles an hour. 'Jesus, I have to get out of here.'

Back at the Manor, comfort returned. Diana went upstairs to sort out some washing, while

Philip put on a Mozart piano sonata and threw a log on the fire. Eva washed up, then timidly came into the living-room and picked up her book from the table. Philip was there, reading in his leather chair. He glanced up and said in a voice softer and kinder than even she had ever heard him use: 'OK, Eva?'

'Yes, thank you,' she said, like an obedient child, and sat on the sofa, book in hand, staring into the fire.

'We've got a saying,' said Philip after a while. 'In politics, you hear it a lot. It goes, 'Win a few, lose a few'.'

Eva looked at him, and her face broke into a smile.

'In Poland too,' she said. Her smile turned suddenly to a stricken expression. 'Oh! I have just remembered!'

'What?' said Philip, looking over his reading-glasses with the air of some benevolent old toymaker in a fairytale.

'I forgot to give Manda the honey I brought from Poland. I forgot.'

'Good,' said Philip. 'We'll have it for breakfast. I like honey, and the silly girl's always on a diet anyway.'

The door was open, and it was a quiet passage in the music. So upstairs, folding her working shirts in the bedroom, Diana heard them laughing, and smiled. 'Win a few, lose a few,' she said to herself, and ruthlessly suppressed the pangs of guilt which always afflicted her after a visit from her distant daughter.

'I don't know where I went wrong' she said to

Lizzie on the phone the next morning. 'She's so cold and flip and never looks you in the eye! We weren't like that, were we?'

'Dunno' said Lizzie, 'Maybe our mothers thought we were.'

16

Henry answered the police sergeant's questions rapidly, staccato in his urgency. No, he had not seen Alissa and Marley since he and the boy had had supper in a restaurant on Thursday. No, he had not been near the flat last night. He had arrived this morning as usual to collect the boy and his overnight things for their weekend access visit. Last night he had been out for a drink with a friend from work, then gone home, watched television for a couple of hours, and slept. No, he had no partner living with him. There were no witnesses to his being asleep. Did the sergeant, for Christ's sake, think that he would break into his ex-girlfriend's house and stab her, leaving his child alone with the bleeding body? And then blandly turn up looking for the boy in the morning?

It was only when he was asked the identity of his work friend that the atmosphere in the interview room began to ease. 'Two Counties? Are you — you're *that* Henry!'

'Yes,' he said. 'I want to see my son now. Please! I've got access, it's my weekend, it's me he should legally be with at this moment. And I need to know where Ali is, I want to see her too. Which hospital?'

A constable came in with a note, which the interrogator read briefly, before nodding affirmatively. The questions went on, but the urgency had gone out of them. Presumably, thought Henry, a successful radio disc jockey might conceivably get off his head on drugs and jealousy, stab his ex-mistress at 2 a.m. and leave his small child to find the bleeding horror alone, but it must seem a little less likely than that a failed minicab driver would do the same. More to lose when you're middle-class. He fumed, but struggled to control himself. What he did not know was that the police had a far better reason to lose interest in him. The note said that Donny had been picked up by a patrol car near the canal, with blood on his jeans and traces of illegal substances on his person.

At last the policeman said politely: 'Thank you. You can go now. We know where to contact you.'

'Not good enough!' said Henry, and stood up, towering over his tormentor. 'I want my son!' He was tall and broad-shouldered; the white officer was a country boy from Norfolk, and had not yet learned to measure degrees of threat in a black face. He pushed his panic-button, and it was ten minutes more before the misunderstanding was sorted out and Henry given the name of the hospital ward where Ali lay, and a phone number for the Social Services official responsible for his son.

Marley came first. The next highest priority, Henry thought as he punched the buttons on his phone, was telling Ali that their son was all right. He had no confidence that Social Services would remember to do that of their own accord. He felt, at that moment, no resentment towards Ali

191

for her choice of lover, but an overwhelming tearful gratitude that she had taken the blow, and not the boy. After some enquiries made in carefully clipped, patrician tones down the phone he discovered that Marley had been taken to a foster home only two streets away. He ran all the way there, to be met by a harassed, bespectacled social worker who looked at him in horror, asked him for ID, rang the police station again, and eventually ushered him in.

The child himself provided all the ID they could have wanted. He was sitting forlorn on a plastic-covered sofa in an overheated room, eating cereal rather messily from a bowl, still in his Spiderman pyjamas.

'Dad!' he cried, dropping the bowl. He darted across the floor to fling his arms round Henry's legs. 'You're so *late! Late, late, late!*'

Henry picked him up, feeling the soft strong little arms around his neck like a blessing, and buried his face for a moment in the warm cotton. Without putting him down, he turned to the social worker.

'Presumably the flat's out of bounds?'

'Yes, I would think so,' said the woman.

'Right,' said Henry to his son. 'We're off home. But first we're going shopping for some brand new clothes.'

'Cool,' said the child. 'And trainers?' His feet, Henry saw, were encased in a pair of too-large slippers, presumably from the foster parent's emergency store.

'Yup. Trainers. Everything. It's a game. They play it a lot in Hollywood, I gather. You go out in your pyjamas and buy everything you need, starting with pants and ending with anoraks. You're supposed to go out stark naked, but they don't allow that in England.'

The child giggled, and scanning his face Henry found no sign that he understood about Ali.

'Wait till Mum sees my new kit!' he yelled. 'Come on, come on, come on!'

Two hours later, fully dressed complete with the odd price-tag, Marley demolished a burger, sucked his way through a chocolate milkshake and said to his father in a confidential tone: 'I had to go to the other lady's house because I had a bad dream.'

Henry, worn out by emotion and shopping, looked away for a moment and wiped his eyes with a paper napkin, which left a streak of ketchup across his forehead. The boy crowed. Telling Marley to sit where he was and not move, and adjuring both the waitress and a tired-looking woman at the neighbouring table to keep an eye on him, he went to the Gents to wipe it off. Afterwards, taking up a position where he could watch his son carefully through the glass doors, he took the opportunity to ring the hospital. After the usual delays and a brief sharp conversation with the policeman who was apparently guarding the victim of crime, he got a ward sister.

'How is she?'

'She's out of ITU now. Out of danger. But she lost a lot of blood and it could be a while before she's fit to go home. There may be another operation. The police are going to talk to her, but not yet.'

'Can I speak to her?'

'She's sleeping.'

'Will you tell her that Marley — her son — is OK and that he's with his dad? And tell her that everything's fine, he's not upset, he can stay with me as long as he needs, and I'll bring him in to see her when she's fit. Tell her not to worry.'

He loped back into the restaurant to find his son drawing patterns on the tabletop with spilled milk shake, unconcerned.

'Don't keep *hugging* me in *front* of strange people,' said Marley, irritated.

★ ★ ★

On Sunday, after a long lie in and breakfast at Starbucks, Henry took Marley back to his flat, gave him a video and retired into the bedroom to make a quiet phone call to the hospital.

'You can speak to Alissa now,' said the sister brightly. 'We're feeling a lot more like ourselves this morning.'

'Hi,' he said when her voice came on the line. 'Marley's fine. He's with me.'

'Did he see?' asked Ali, croaking slightly.

'Don't think so. He's not talked about it. Said he had a nightmare.'

'It was Donny. I've told the police.'

'They'd better lock him up in something bloody secure or I'll kill him.'

'He was high as a kite. I did chew him up a bit

earlier. But I never thought he'd kick the door in.'

'Neighbour says it wasn't him, he brought a bigger bloke along to do that bit. Look, shall I bring Marley to see you?'

'Yes, please. Please.' She was almost crying now, he could hear it; compassion and dismay fought within him, Ali never cried.

'Well, be prepared for a shock,' he said as lightly as he could. 'He's chosen a really vile new anorak and a Davy Crockett hat from the Disney Shop. Sorry about that.'

'What'll you do about work?' asked Ali. 'It's Monday tomorrow. He only goes to nursery at the school on Thursdays and Fridays.'

'I'll take him in. He likes the studio. Roger and Diana will keep him amused. Then I'll do my next day's preparation and interview stuff overnight at the flat while he's asleep. We can totter on for a few days. Don't worry. Get better.'

'OK,' said her voice, growing weaker. 'I'm going to sleep now. Come this afternoon.'

When they arrived, she was lying flat amid all the propped-up patients in the ward, her skin unhealthily light, attached to a drip. Henry had prepared the boy carefully for all this, but himself felt a shock he could barely disguise. He had told Marley to be quiet and gentle as his mother was poorly, and the child duly crept towards her, on exaggerated tiptoe.

'Hello, Mum. You all righ-eeet?' he said, in a whisper so piercing that other visitors turned, amused, towards the spry little figure in the lime-green anorak.

'Oh, beloved boy!' Ali reached out to him, and Henry prevented him from scrambling through the drip-lines. The mother hugged him as best she could, pulling him against the hard iron side of the bed, and said: 'Will you be a good boy, for Daddy?'

'Yup. When are you coming home? I left my tractor.'

'Daddy could get the tractor, perhaps.' Henry remembered how the toy had lain on its side in the poor wrecked little room, near the dark stain, and was filled with deep, sad pity for them all. Here was this young woman, weakened by the knife of her idiot boyfriend. Here was he himself, a failure at keeping the family together. And here, above all, was the child they had made between them in a passionate night five years ago. He was blithe, hopeful, impervious to the various wickednesses and inadequacies of the adults in his world. Marley did not understand, yet he lay helplessly open to the darkest and most grievous wounds of all.

'Mummy's a bit tired,' Henry said gently. 'Shall we let her have a sleep now?'

'What made Mummy ill?' asked Marley as they went down in the lift. 'Was it Donny shouting?'

'Sort of,' said Henry.

'I hate Donny,' said the boy. 'He ought to go to prison.'

'Probably he will,' said Henry. 'But we don't have to worry about him any more.'

'Will they make him kind, in prison?'

'I hope so.'

196

But when Marley had gone to bed, under his familiar cartoon duvet in Henry's spare room, the father sat up until the small hours with the door open, listening to his child's breathing. For once, Henry Windsor had no smart answers. He felt bleaker than at any time in his thirty-two years of life. Once, the little boy muttered in a dream, 'Wan' my Mum!' and, half-asleep in his chair, Henry murmured, 'Me and all!'

The next morning, over a breakfast of potato waffles from the toaster, he said to Marley: 'The hospital says Mummy's got to have a rest today because she's having some special things done to make her better quickly. Shall we go for a drive to the country?'

'OK,' said Marley. 'Will there be sheep? Will they tell us stuff?'

'We could look for some,' said his father. 'We could hunt them down and question them closely.'

'Can we see a big old house?' They had been to Woburn Abbey once, and the child had never forgotten it.

'Better than that,' said Henry. 'I hope we'll have our lunch at a big old house.'

For at seven o'clock on Sunday morning, in breach of all precedent and etiquette, after ringing the hospital for news he had rung Diana Hunton-Hall in tears.

★ ★ ★

'Who was that on the phone in the middle of the night?' asked Philip, buttering his toast and

197

looking around for something to spread on it. 'Bloody funny time to ring. Reminds me of that idiot — ' He named a former ministerial colleague who had, years before, had the habit of ringing early in the morning to share policy ideas which had come to him in the night. Eva, noticing his search, silently passed him the brown crock into which she had decanted the Polish honey.

'It was a friend from work,' said Diana cautiously. 'You met him. Henry Windsor. He came to dinner the night Eva arrived.'

'What the hell's he want?' said Philip, though with less irritation than he would have shown a month before at such tidings. 'You don't work Sundays.'

'He's in a bit of trouble.' Diana took advantage of his obvious pleasure in the smooth golden honey under his knife. 'He's got his four-year-old son for the weekend, and the mother's been in — an accident. The kid needs distracting so I asked them both here to lunch. They can walk up and see the black-faced sheep on the other side of the stream, and pick some blackberries, perhaps.'

'The blackberries are going soft' said Eva. 'The winter is coming, I think.'

'Well, they might find a couple. It's always a thrill for children being allowed to eat stuff off bushes. I hope that's all right by you, Philip?'

He bit into his toast, chewed briefly and replied, in what she realized were literally honeyed tones: 'No problem. If Eva can organize the kitchen at such short notice.'

'I will make little *klopsy* — with the minced meat — small children like these. And bake some bread buns so it makes like burgers,' said Eva enthusiastically. 'Little children love this. But real tomato sauce, so it is healthier. Is this child black, also?'

'Well, obviously,' said Diana. She glanced at Philip, but he was spreading more honey on his toast with dreamy pleasure, and plainly not listening to either of them.

When Henry and the child arrived, she was shocked by the pinched, exhausted expression on the young father's face. Marley, showing neither strain nor inhibition, bounced into the hall and said: 'Wow! Is this a hundred years old?'

'Three hundred, perhaps more,' said Diana. 'When they built this house, there were no cars or aeroplanes or electricity or gas or telly or cinemas or even — um — cameras.'

'Wicked,' said Marley. 'Are there sheep?'

'Sheep just over the stream,' said Diana. 'Do you want to wait till after lunch?'

'No,' said the little boy firmly. 'Sheep, then lunch.'

'I will get everything ready,' said Eva serenely. 'You go and see the sheep, and bring me some few blackberries to finish the pudding.'

'I'd like a walk,' said Henry. His eyes locked on Diana with an intensity she did not notice in her domestic fluster. 'Is that OK? Will you show us the sheep place?'

'Yes,' said Diana. 'Got stout shoes on? Good. Marley, if you don't want to get those trainers dirty, you'll have to piggyback over the stream.'

They left the house through the kitchen, Diana pulling on her Wellington boots while the child jigged impatiently, and the adults set off at a fast walk to keep up with the little boy as he ran down the wooded track towards the stream.

'Does your husband mind?' began Henry. 'I feel bad, inviting us like this, but I was going mad.'

'He's in his study. Won't appear till lunch is on the table. He's in a good mood anyway, what with Eva's cooking and the house being tidy. But look, while Marley's up ahead, tell me more about this awful thing?'

Henry told her, in a few low rapid sentences, about the previous day's shocks and the phone call in the early morning which told him that Ali's condition had worsened slightly, necessitating another transfusion and a return to the ITU ward.

'Is Marley upset?'

'I've tried to minimize it. He saw Ali in hospital, got a hug. He slept through it all, thank God, because he'd been out till half-past nine with me at a burger restaurant and had a rather large sip of my beer. He knows something to do with Donny made her sick, and that Donny's out of the frame now.'

'Out of the frame?'

'They arrested him, apparently. But the good thing is, Marley's used to having whole weekends with me anyway, so it probably won't hit him till tomorrow morning when he doesn't go home.' He paused, and his steps faltered. They were clear of the trees now. Ahead of them the little boy pranced across the damp grass, pointing at the sheep beyond the little stream. 'Oh, shit, Diana — I'm so scared.'

She put a hand on his shaking arm as they walked on.

'Hey, hey, steady. It's all right.' Miraculously, as it seemed to her, he steadied.

'Thanks. For having us today. I took him shopping yesterday but today just stretched ahead, I was in a kind of panic . . . he's mine, but he's hers too, and I don't see how I could make it up to him if she, if she . . . '

Diana was quiet for a moment, but left her hand on his arm.

'Is it that bad?'

'Don't know. Yesterday she looked OK, pale but OK. But now they've put her back in intensive care and we aren't allowed to see her. Shit, Diana. I did this! If I'd stayed with Ali . . . '

'Who left who?' Idiotically, she found herself wondering if that should be 'whom'.

'Well, fact is, she threw me out. But I went, OK? Why didn't I fight it?'

'You can't always.'

'When there's a kid, you ought to. But my parents, my adoptive parents, they never, ever fought. I didn't know how things worked in fighty partnerships. No idea. I thought that if people said stuff to each other like we said, that was the end of it every time.'

'They were old,' said Diana. 'Your parents. You said they were nearly fifty when they adopted you.'

'Yeah.' He sounded surprised, as if it had

never occurred to him before that this could make a difference. 'I suppose marriages sort of get more solid, as time goes on. Less volatile.'

They were nearly at the stream. Diana, preferring not to enter into a conversation about long marriages, called ahead to the child to wait.

'You'll have to carry him over on the stepping stones, those look like new trainers.'

Henry ran forward and gathered the boy in his arms. She watched them cross together, then carefully negotiated the stones herself. Sheep, black-faced and inquisitive, surrounded them, nudging for tit-bits. The farmer kept them as a pet flock without a sheepdog, and moved them around by coaxing and treats. Marley, delighted with his new friends, looked from one adult to the other with a bright transfigured face, then baa-ed back to the crowding ewes, reaching out to touch their tight wool, staring in wonderment into their dim, beady little eyes. All the way back to the Manor, he chattered about sheep and wool and when the baby lambs would come. Diana told him sheep-lore, or all of it that she could remember from her childhood, and Henry began once again to joke and laugh with them. When they arrived, Eva was at the kitchen door, smiling, wiping her hands on a teatowel. It looked for all the world, thought Diana amusedly, as if the Pole were the cosy old mother, welcoming back a young couple and their child.

17

Marley came into work on Monday, Tuesday and Wednesday. Henry arrived with him each morning at 8.30 equipped with crayons, drawing paper and a computer game which in the event the child hardly touched, so interested was he in drawing pictures of all the studio equipment and flirting with the admiring staff.

'So-oh gorgeous!' said sentimental Sally Beazeley, who did the breakfast show just before Henry. 'Couldn't you just eat him? That grin!' Marley preferred Roger, who gave him shy fleeting smiles and showed him how to tear up old scripts into paper dolls. He never got the knack, and his corner of the operations room became a mouse's nest of shredded paper. Suzie, the receptionist who had replaced Diana, often brought in her tiny, elderly Shi-Tzu dog to sleep under the desk, so when he tired of drawing and tearing in the studio, Marley went to Suzie and spent fruitless half-hours trying to teach the somnolent dog to shake hands. Steve, who had looked worried at the idea of Henry's child wandering round the station all morning, was completely won round and began talking about his commitment to 'family values'. This was fortunate, because by the end of Wednesday morning the saintly behaviour of Marley was beginning to show cracks.

'I'm bored,' he said to Diana, threateningly, as

he stood on the chair beside her at the console through which she watched, and briefed, Henry. 'I wanna see my mum.'

'Tomorrow,' said Diana. The news from the hospital was better; Ali was stable, though weak.

'Tomorrow is a long, long, long boring long time to wait. Now! Or I want to go and see James Bond.'

'You're too young for James Bond, aren't you?'

'Get a *video*,' said the child scornfully. 'C'mon, let me do talkback.'

In a rash moment on the first day, Diana had shown him the talkback button which fed to Henry's headphones.

'All right. During the last record you can say hello to Daddy.'

'Awesome.' He climbed, unselfconscious in their new acquaintance, on to Diana's knee and poised his small finger over the key. When Henry came out at the end of his show, he saw them there with Marley's dark arm thrown round her soft white neck for balance, their faces close together, and was overwhelmed by emotion and treacherous desire. Marley, without leaving his perch on Diana's knee, looked up at his father and said firmly: 'We're going to rent a James Bond video today.'

'Oh, are you now? Diana, what's this?'

'I didn't actually say yes, but he's very masterful.'

'Well, why not? Diana, when are you off?'

'Two-thirty. I'm covering the newsroom for Joe instead of a lunch break.'

'Awesome, as Marley would say. Shall we do

this James Bond thing? Rent the one with the moon-rocket, maybe? It is raining, after all. We could order pizzas and have a really slummy afternoon.'

Suddenly, Diana wanted nothing more than to drop her plans — household shopping, Philip's dry-cleaning, a call on Lizzie — and join this clandestine afternoon. It was unscheduled, it was absurd, it was a waste of time, but the friendship which had grown between the three of them in this strange week seemed so vivid a thing in the foreground of her life that the other parts of it, even Lizzie, seemed to be fading to distant, irrelevant sepia tones.

'Twist my arm,' she said, and reached across Marley as he slid from her lap, to pick up her files. 'It's years since I saw a Bond film. I go back to Sean Connery.'

Even as she said it, the sad thought pierced her, tinged with guilt: I shouldn't have said that. It'll remind him how old I am. She could still feel the child's warm careless arm around her neck, his breath on her cheek. She and Lizzie were not the kind of friends who hugged one another. Manda was not that kind of daughter, either. Philip and she rarely touched, these days, for all their vast shared bed. Accordingly the contact with the child, and her arm on Henry's as they walked across the damp field towards the sheep, had stirred her more than was comfortable. This was, she thought, a bad thing. Middle-aged women who remembered Sean Connery as Bond should not be open to absurd excitements of this kind. They should peck their husbands on the cheek and wait patiently for grandchildren. Or else have cats. Perhaps she should buy a cat.

Later, at the flat, on the far side of much whooping and gasping at Mr Bond's escapes, Marley fell asleep on the sofa between them and Henry reached across and took her hand.

Startled, she tugged at it, but he held on.

'Thank you for this week,' he began. 'You've been a real mate.' Uncertain whether to be reassured or disappointed by his use of words, Diana let her hand lie in his, enjoying the dry strong warmth of that captivity. It was good to have mates, friends to eat pizza with, at her age. She was lucky. She fixed her eye on the boxes of gnawed pizza-crust on the floor, tokens of a strange and happily feckless world.

'But there's something else,' said Henry after a moment. 'It's only right to tell you straight out. I love you.'

The pizza boxes blurred and swam before her eyes. People didn't say that anymore, thought Diana dizzily. Only the other week Lizzie Morgan had been expatiating, from her vicarious experience of adult children, on this very subject. 'They don't do the I-L-Y bit,' she said. 'It's more sort of 'Do you wanna hang out?' or 'Should we, like, get engaged?' The old formulae are all gone. I blame Charles and Di, with that 'whatever love means' schtick.'

'Did you hear me?' said Henry, whose eyes were fixed on her across the sleeping child. 'I love you. You're the most wonderful woman I've ever known. I love you.'

206

'I'm really fond of you — ' began Diana, but his eyes were too much for her. She dropped her gaze, and held his hand, speechless. Too much was coursing through her, too much life and impossible desire. She thought she would faint. How Victorian! said the small, rational part of her. Oh, Mr Windsor, this is so sudden! But the great dizzy shining happiness was too much. Only the sleeping weight of the child against her shoulder made her struggle to control her trembling.

Henry, seeing her condition, gently replaced her hand in her lap, stood up and carried Marley to the bedroom, where he flopped like a big doll on to the cartoon duvet and put his thumb into his mouth. Closing the door, Henry returned and held out both hands towards his guest. Diana, robot-like, lifted hers to meet them, and found herself pulled to her feet. With his arms encircling her gently but firmly she looked up into his face.

'It can't be real,' she said weakly. 'I'm married. I'm older than you. Years and years older. It's just reaction, after the terrible thing with Ali.'

'No,' said Henry. 'No. Why else do you think I rang you on Sunday morning?'

'Because,' said Diana desperately, 'I was an older woman, and you suddenly had a small child and an invalid and a crisis on your hands, and that's what older women are good at. I was honoured that you thought of me as a friend who could be called on.'

Henry held her, feeling the beating of her heart. Then he swiftly bent his head and kissed her. Diana stood passive, then suddenly, with a sob, pressed her face against his warm neck and let her arms go round his waist. Henry looked down at the fair soft hair, tousled from Marley's attentions as he bounced on the back of the sofa during James Bond's escapes, and thought his heart would burst.

'See?' he said, trying to sound like his normal lightly mocking self. 'You feel the same way. I *knew*.'

'When did you know?' said Diana, still muffled by his chest.

'Well, I didn't actually. I hoped. I knew I loved you since — oh, a long time. Weeks.'

'It's ridiculous. This can't be.' She pushed herself away firmly, with both hands on his chest, but the sensation of touching him was too strong for her, and she left her hands there, feeling hard muscle through his soft sweater. Henry's big, beautiful eyes were on her: she had not noticed before how like Marley's they were.

'I know you have to say all that,' he said. 'I respect marriage, I really do. But it was only fair to tell you.'

'Why?' Diana managed to pull her hands away and step back, her voice high and accusing. 'I was fine. I was thinking of you as the son I never had. Marley was like a grandchild. I was fine.'

She began to cry, not gracefully but with hard tearing sobs. There was nothing to blow her nose on: she reached for one of the Pizza Hut napkins, with a blob of cheese adhering unattractively to its corner. When she had regained control of herself, she looked again at

Henry and saw that he was standing stock-still, watching her, with an expression of sorrow on his face.

'I had to tell you,' he said. 'It felt like a gift. Please take it as just a gift. Thank you for everything you've done, and everything that you are. Precious.'

Replaying this much later in her mind, Diana saw that it had been chivalrous: a speech designed to feel like a conclusion, a cue for her to say something graceful, smile at the moment of folly, and go home to Philip. Why, then, did she do the opposite: run to him, turn up her face again, and let their embraces shade into incoherent babblings and impossible promises? Together, they sank on to the sofa; together they remained for the best part of an hour, alternately silent and garrulous, wrapped in happiness.

★ ★ ★

'Come to bed,' said Henry, later. She looked at her watch: it was seven o'clock. 'Tell them you're covering a late shift in the newsroom,' he said.

'I can't,' said Diana.

'Can't come to bed?'

'I don't know. No, it's not that. Amazingly, it's not that,' she said. 'Yesterday I'd have said I couldn't possibly, but now I see that I could. I probably will. Soon. What I mean is that I can't ring up and lie to Philip.'

Henry nodded. 'Yeah, I'm sorry. I see that.'

Diana lay against him, warm and secure, hating to put an end to this time. Whatever the future held, she thought, this afternoon would never come again. After a few more minutes of shared silence she said, 'I'd better go home. Supper's at eight. I suppose he'll assume I'm at Lizzie's or at work.'

'OK,' said Henry. 'But remember . . . ' He looked around, then stood up and, leading her by the hand, took her to the low table where Marley's Coke can still stood. Dropping her hand, he picked it up and wrenched off the ring-pull with some difficulty, then ceremoniously took her hand again and tried to put it on her finger. It did not fit; he tried the tip of the little finger, and left it there.

'Oh, that is so corny!' she said, but her voice wobbled treacherously.

'Take it. Something to remind you where you belong now,' said Henry. 'So you don't forget.'

'Do you honestly think I will?'

'No. But I have fears.'

'Me too.'

They kissed, and parted at the door. Out on the street, Diana felt naked, marked, vulnerable as never before; she dived into her little car and sat trembling for five minutes before she dared to start the engine. Henry, watching from his window, saw this and summoned all his self-control to prevent himself from running down the steps and drawing her back to him. When she drove off he stayed still, his hand on the curtain, looking at the spot where the car had stood. At last he turned away, gave a prodigious yawn, and after a brief moment tucking up Marley, went to his own bed. It was not yet eight o'clock, but television, reading, or solitary drinking all seemed impossible. What he needed now, if he could not have her near him, was warmth and darkness and the freedom of solitude and a long blissful waking dream.

At the Manor, Eva had roasted a chicken and polished the dining-room table until the silver candlesticks shone doubly in their deep reflections. Philip was in good spirits.

'Hard day?' he said, without much interest.

'Yes,' said Diana. And, without conviction, 'Good to be home.'

18

Henry thought he would not sleep, but after only a few minutes he slipped helplessly into a deep, dreamless state from which he awoke with a start only when Marley cried out in confusion in the small hours. Staggering from his bed, the father calmed the boy, ascertained that what he most wanted was a pee, followed by 'proper pyjamas', and tucked him up again, this time in his Spiderman suit.

Finding himself wide awake, Henry went into the tiny kitchenette beyond his living-room and flicked on the electric kettle. Back in the living-room with his mug of coffee, he tidied up the pizza boxes and looked around him, marvelling that everything was exactly the same as usual. He turned the light off, for there was pale moonlight filtering into the room and he had always loved the moon; sitting down, he picked up the television remote control, and put it down again. This was no time for distractions. He had done something the night before, something momentous and unplanned. He was not a stupid kid, to fall into situations the way he had with Ali and the girlfriends before and since. Diana Hunton-Hall was a grown-up, a woman of maturity and substance and seriousness. He must match her, if he wanted her.

He wanted her. Closing his eyes, he felt her shape against him, smelt her clean fair hair, and was overwhelmed with pity for her trembling, and love for her courage. He had been mildly annoyed, on the night of the dinner party, by Marianne's heavy drunken hints that he was some kind of toyboy, some middle-aged fling of Diana's. Had he loved her already then? He frowned. Hard to tell. Once you loved someone, you believed that you always had done. He had liked her, enjoyed her company, felt comfortable asking her advice: but surely that meant that he hadn't been in love? Being in love, in his experience, meant obsession, pursuit, passion, rows, moments of hate, clashing reconciliations, intensity.

This was not the same. The intensity was there, but it burned with a clear steady flame, a reliable lantern and not a hellish, deceptive flicker. It was like coming home. He thought that he had always been looking for a woman like Diana, and marvelled at his blindness in never knowing this before, and in wasting so much time on lesser passions. Now he was home. He loved her, she loved him, and the rest was a matter of detail.

Opening his eyes, he shook his head a little and tried to focus on that detail. For Philip Hunton-Hall he had no feeling at all. The dinner party had made it clear enough what sort of man this was: a petulant failed politician, arrogant without reason, secure in his wealth, careless of his wife. He had watched the two of them that evening, and felt pity for Diana's bright, obvious attempts to keep the man sweet. In the following weeks — while his own love grew — he had

213

watched her to try and detect any sign that she was happy, fulfilled, contented in this marriage. He had found none. Perhaps, he thought with sudden wonder, that had fed his own passion? Had it grown through knowing that this marvellous ripe woman was not loved, not made love to, not worshipped as she had a natural right to be? She was being wasted, squandered on a cold old man: her perfect kindness, good humour, gentle wit and instinct to love and support, all denigrated and wasted. Only he saw these things. She was his secret. And he alone needed her. With her, all his own doubts and self-loathings and regrets could be contained and neutralized. With her lay all his happiness.

Would he, though, make her happy? In his exalted state, it was unbearable to think of her unhappy, humiliated, the butt of gossip and contempt. He had no illusions about white Britain or the provincial affluent society in which the Hunton-Halls moved. Oh, they liked him well enough on the radio: he amused them, had quite a following among the well-heeled matrons as well as the teenagers. But for the former MP's wife to take up with a younger black man — a single parent, too — well, he knew what they would assume. This was not New York or even London. It would not matter that he was educated and successful, suave and confident. What would count was that he was younger, black, and a disc jockey. And, moreover, that he had fathered a small son on a spitfire black girl who ended up stabbed in a council flat by her unemployed minicab-driver boyfriend.

Sitting there in the pale moonlight in his living-room, he laid it all out as brutally as he could; perhaps more brutally than he needed to. They would think he was a lowlife. Correspondingly, they would think she was a menopausal nymphomaniac, a blowsy creature like her friend Marianne, going desperately for one last fling with a bit of Rastafarian rough. It would be hard, doubly hard in this small town. She had suggested he work for the BBC in London. Maybe he should apply, and take her with him swiftly and suddenly, leaving them all to think whatever they liked. But there was Marley to consider, and moreover any presenting job he got would bring him personal publicity, and inevitably bring rude and unwanted press attention down on her. For the first time, Henry wished he had chosen an anonymous trade. If he was an accountant nobody would care that he had run off with a Tory ex-MP's wife. But they would be together; that was the main thing.

He sat for a long while, thinking. Doubt crept in with the greyness of dawn: by the time Marley woke and needed to be taken to the primary school nursery session, it had become clear to Henry that, however much he loved her, his love could bring Diana little but humiliation and disaster.

★ ★ ★

Diana's night was not much better. She lay awake on her side of the great bed, listening to Philip's quiet breathing. Cautiously, once she

215

was sure he was asleep, she raised herself on one elbow and looked at him for a long time.

His head was turned towards her; silver hair a little tousled, giving him an unwontedly vulnerable appearance. His features, though, were as stern as ever: too refined to be craggy, but hard as the snow-sharp edge of an Alpine range in the moonlight. Did he love her, would he miss her? No and yes. Diana had rarely allowed herself to analyse the state of their marriage, preferring to preoccupy herself with the state of Philip's feelings. 'It's hard for him,' had been her mantra, openly to Lizzie and privately to herself. She had married an aspiring politician — goodness, how wild and dizzy was her adoration then! — and fought elections alongside him, making every shabby compromise of her own taste and views as it became necessary. She had raised a glass to his successes, and known when to be silent about his failures. She had been bored by it all, long before he lost office in the Fanfair Finance scandal, but had never dared to ask herself whether she was also bored with being his wife. Lizzie had asked her once, point-blank, around the time that the Morgans first moved to the constituency.

'Are you OK, you and Philip? Political wifehood is a strain, they say?'

But Diana had answered heartily and without daring to think: 'Oh, we're fine. We rub along. I know the score and he's very considerate.'

'Considerate?'

'Well, about me staying down in the constituency with Manda when he has to stay

216

over in Dolphin Square. And I know what you're thinking, Lizzie, and no he is *not* having an affair with some secretary. Not Philip.'

Lizzie had looked at her sideways, with an unfathomable expression, and desisted from her questions. Replaying the conversation now in the moonlit bedroom, Diana understood why. A husband being 'considerate' and 'not having an affair' were not, to Lizzie, sufficient qualifications for a happy marriage. But then, Lizzie had never understood how much Diana had loved Philip when she was twenty-one. He had been a god to her, an ideal, her lord and master: handsome, brilliant, condescending. His lovemaking itself had been something miraculous — not in its actuality, but in the very fact that he stooped to attend to her at all. She had abased herself before his maleness willingly and joyfully, granted him everything when and if he asked for it, never making moves towards him herself in case he was tired, or preoccupied, or simply not attracted to her that day.

Later, after childbirth and the burdens of running a home, she had wished sometimes that this pattern was not set: she would, she thought dismally, really have liked an occasional cuddle that led nowhere, an easy friendly physical relationship of the kind that Lizzie and Andy Morgan seemed to have. But one couldn't cuddle Philip. So, when his interest in her sexual favours waned, they barely had occasion to touch at all.

She could have reached out now, in the night, and stroked his pale hair, or traced the patrician

217

lines of his face, silver in the moonlight like a head on a Roman coin. But she had never done such a thing, and it would wake him and alarm him. She gazed on. Soon, perhaps, she would be unfaithful to this man. Unfaithful to her vows, to her beliefs, to her long-ago girlish ideal of perpetual devotion. Looking at him, sleeping like a stone knight on a tomb, this seemed preposterous. It could not happen. It would not happen. The warm, heart-beating, momentous evening with Henry would stand alone, like a marvellous song or sunset never to be repeated but always remembered. Unhappy but resigned, she fell asleep; when she woke once more, briefly, the moonlight had gone and everything was dark. She could not see Philip at all.

★ ★ ★

Thus both lovers had decided rationally by morning that it would not do. But meeting at nine o'clock, while Roger kicked and thumped at the coffee-machine outside in the corridor, they looked at one another for a moment across the music record sheets and were lost again.

'Ali's mum has come down from Birmingham,' said Henry. 'She's picking Marley up from nursery and taking him to the hospital, then out for a couple of hours in the playground to tire him out, she says. She'll bring him to the flat about half-past four and get the train home.'

'I'm working till one-thirty,' said Diana.

'Good,' said Henry, and although Roger came in at that moment balancing three polystyrene

218

cups and spilling hot coffee down his sleeve, it was already settled between them that Diana's years of fidelity were over. Henry, fluffing his way distractedly through the programme, merely thought that it would never end and his violent heartbeat never quieten.

Diana, older and more cautious, said to herself, 'It has to be. I can't think clearly at all now because of it. Over on the far side, when it's over and done with, I'll be able to think.'

19

Eva had a letter. It arrived after breakfast, and went with the rest of the post to the dresser in the kitchen. Philip always had the most letters, while Diana had mail-order catalogues and occasional notes and postcards from friends. Eva's stood out among these: it was a small, squareish envelope of cheap coarse grey paper with a row of Polish stamps and several black postmarks almost obscuring the first two lines of the address. Philip found it when he came in to collect his bundle of post, looked at it for a moment and then went in search of Eva. It was the first letter she had had at the Manor, and it gave him a slight shock to realize that he did not actually know her surname until he saw it on the envelope.

She had finished tidying up and was at the table in her room, frowning over the notes from her first week's lessons at the college in town. She had at last managed to enrol on an afternoon course — two till five, three days a week — and her attendance there was made surprisingly easy by Marianne. Fired by the idea of education, the latter had imprudently enrolled on a course in Spanish in the next classroom.

'Then I can drive you,' she said happily. 'Diana's shifts are so awkward, and the bus is rubbish even if you bike into the village.'

Eva was overwhelmed by the ease and

kindness of the arrangement.

'You are too good,' she said. 'Are you sure you want to speak Spanish?'

'*Hola! Si, si!*' said Marianne, who had lately heard through the school grapevine that her husband's young girlfriend was 'cutting up rough' and giving him a bad time. Her spirits had risen at the news, and she was spending long sessions on her exercise bike, having facials twice a week, and preparing to give him a tough welcome when, as seemed inevitable, he came 'crawling back' from his adventure. Learning Spanish was part of the strategy. She had an idea that she might manage to be absent on a mysterious little trip to Seville when he eventually came back, and planned to maintain an aloof, teasing mystery about what she did there: possibly, she confided to Eva, she might even carry out this manoeuvre wearing a black lace mantilla: 'If you don't think that's a bit over the top?'

Eva thought the whole idea alarming and crazy, but was too polite to say so. But Marianne was in high spirits about her plan. '*Che sera sera!* Oops, that's Italian, isn't it? Which lot say *Signor* and which say *Señor*? I never know.'

'*Señor* is Spanish,' said Eva. 'I know this from working there. If you are sure, it is very kind to drive me. But always I must be back in time to cook for Mr and Mrs Hunton-Hall.'

'Don't you call them Philip and Diana yet?' asked Marianne, curiously.

'It would not be respectful, perhaps,' replied the Pole austerely.

Now, she jumped to her feet at Philip's knock, and stood respectfully enough by her table, the grammar book open in her hand.

'Letter,' he said. 'For you. From home, by the look of it.'

The girl went so pale that he instinctively took a step forward lest she should fall. She held out her hand, though, and said, 'Thank you,' in a faint voice. Then, looking down at the letter, she gave a weak smile and said, 'It is from my father. That is good. I have been worried.'

Philip retreated, but the memory of her sudden pallor and scrupulous politeness touched him. Poor kid. A long way from home, this bright brave spirit: she had a passionate ear for music and language which reminded him of himself, in his far-off schooldays before politics took him. He went back to the study and sat alone, thinking of the past.

There had been a boy at school, dark and thin and tousled and intense like Eva: he was a German Jewish refugee called Waldstein, sent on some misguidedly well-meant scholarship to board far from home amid pink, xenophobic 1950s school-boys. Most had laughed at him and made crude war-comic jokes, shouting '*Donner und Blitzen!*' and '*Schweinhund!*' One dark winter Saturday afternoon Philip had found Waldstein alone, reading a limp leatherbound book of poetry behind the vaulting-horse in the gym. This spot was a favourite haven of the bullied, being close enough to the PE sergeant's flat to make attack unlikely. It was warm, too, and you could rest your back against the smooth old slope of the wooden box as if it were a friendly tree. The book was Goethe, the poem he glimpsed on the page was 'Kennst du das land . . . .' The young German had looked up at him with real fear, his eyes still blurred with tears. Philip was never an especially kind boy, and being sent away to prep school ten years earlier, at six years old, had not encouraged a habit of sensitivity. He backed wordlessly away from the tears and left the boy alone. But next day, moved by an emotion he could not name, he brought to the same spot a copy of the Coleridge translation of the poem. He said it now, aloud to the study wallpaper:

'Know'st thou the land where the pale
    citrons grow,
The golden fruits in darker foliage glow?
Soft blows the wind that breathes from that
    blue sky!
Still stands the myrtle and the laurel high!
Know'st thou it well, that land, beloved
    Friend?
Thither with thee, O, thither, would I
    wend!'

Waldstein was not there when Philip brought the paper down. He left it behind the vaulting horse but it was still there, fluttering grimily around, when the Monday gym class came in. A whisper went round that the German boy had broken down on Sunday morning, refused to leave his bed, 'blubbed like a kid' and been sent to the Sanatorium prior to being despatched

223

back home 'to Krautland'. Philip never saw him again. Now, forty years later in his elegant country gentleman's study, he hoped, with a jolt of unexpected force, that things had gone better for the boy in later life. He also hoped, in the same moment, that the letter from her homeland brought comfort to the young woman upstairs.

Philip sniffed, angry with himself for the wave of sentiment overtaking him. The changes in his head and heart these past weeks were bewildering, as well as elevating. He wished, uncharacteristically, that he had someone to discuss them with.

Upstairs in the bedroom, Eva was finding in her letter only mixed comfort. Her father was well. Max was well. They missed her, but hoped her travels were worth the 'expense and disruption'. He was 'a little disappointed that she was working as a domestic' given her level of education, and hoped that she would soon finish her studies of English 'with a suitable diploma' and return to a serious career. Her friend Matziek had been in some trouble with the police, but nobody was clear what about — probably something and nothing. Tadeusz Grocholski was thought to be engaged, so his mother said when she came into the library, and he was doing well in his job. Her father sent his blessing for her safety and speedy return, and Max — in a scrawl at the bottom — hoped she was having fun.

She folded the letter and stood for a while by the window, looking at the river, the sheep on their pasture beyond, and the brown winter fields. She had longed for news from home and here it was: not exciting, not thrilling, not even particularly reassuring. It was — she remembered a word the advanced English class had encountered in a text yesterday — 'banal'. Yes, banal. Flat, pointless. Worse, it made her life here banal too. A domestic! Yes, she was a domestic. Paid for household duties. The life at the Manor which in early-September had seemed like a blessed reprieve from wandering was now belittled, ordinary, perhaps a little humiliating. Marianne was kind and fun to be with — mostly — but she was old and quite silly; Diana was not silly, but she was an older woman, and seemed to expect very little in the way of conversation or stimulus in her own home. Diana's important life, Eva divined, was now led at the radio station.

Philip, of course, she revered: recklessly investing him with all the poetry and wisdom of his library and his music. As for other company, the village people were polite enough and a little curious about her status, but otherwise there were few new faces. It had been nice when the young black man came with his little son; it had varied the routine and wiped away much of the unease left by the visit of Manda and Art.

But it had to be admitted that her life here was not the adventurous, raffish, travelling freedom she had imagined during those café sessions with Matziek and Adam and the gang. She was living like a middle-aged housemaid who happened to have a studying hobby. She was not even an au pair, helping to bring up children like Hania in the Netherlands. Hania had said in one of her letters to Poland that she found the work hard and sometimes dull, but that it gave her pleasure to know that a family of little Dutch children were learning Polish songs and stories. 'You see, I build us an empire. An empire of the imagination.' Eva was not even doing that much, although the little black English boy now knew that *klopsy* tasted better than McDonaldburgers.

Moments of depression always drove Eva outdoors; Philip heard her step on the stairway and leaned back from his study desk to call to her before she could reach the back door.

'Everything OK? Not bad news?'

'Thank you, no. But — '

To her horror, she was weeping. His moment of unexpected kindness had opened the flood-gates and Eva began to cry like a child, sniffing and dashing her arm across her eyes, turning her head away to rest her brow on the panelling. Philip was on his feet and out into the hallway in a moment.

'My dear child, what is the matter? Something in your letter?'

'No — no — they are well. It is me. Myself. I am disappointing.'

He misunderstood her. 'Disappointed? Why? Don't do that. Here's a handkerchief.' It was cool, heavy white cotton, with his initials in the corner.

He led her to the stairway and Eva plumped down on the bottom step, still childish, and sniffed loudly. Embarrassment at weeping into his lovely handkerchief fought with a new, reckless spirit. Why not tell him? Why not give a straight answer? Why keep smiling and lying? Feelings were as real as anything else, and you should tell the truth about real things.

'I will tell you,' she said with a final sniff. 'I came travelling to learn about the world. About West Europe, and the great culture which we were cut away from for such a long time with the communists. I went to Italy and Spain and France, but if you have no money it is hard to see things, except churches and statues, or even to hear music. I thought it would be a great education, like a university of the world. Instead I am here, cooking food and talking with Marianne about her husband and silly ideas about black veils. I should be grateful. I am grateful, you are all very kind in England. But I am very disappointing. To my family, and to myself. I am — what do you say? — *tchorz* — a coward!'

Philip bit his lower lip. With her dark tousled hair she looked so much like Waldstein, terrified and defiant in the corner of the winter gymnasium, that the past and present blurred before him. But he could do better now. After a moment he said, 'No. You're not a coward. Most people don't even see what it is they aren't achieving. You do. I honour that.'

'I think I must go home,' said Eva despondently. 'I have seen the ba-ba-banality of my life.'

Now Philip laughed; really laughed, so that she looked up and gave a small damp smile.

'Is that not the right word?'

'It's a tremendous word. D'you know, I have seen the banality of my life too. What we two need is an outing.'

'Outing?'

'Yes,' he said. 'In the post this morning came two tickets for the Royal Opera. *La Traviata.* Monday. I have a friend on the Board who knows I love Verdi. And I promise you, this really is part of the great European cultural adventure. You can come with me. It won't be even the smallest bit banal.'

'But Mrs — but Diana?' said Eva, shocked. 'She should come instead?'

'She can't stand opera,' said Philip baldly. 'Used to come when I was doing corporate hospitality, that sort of thing, but she nearly always fell asleep. Sometimes she snored. Said she couldn't believe how slow they all were to sort out their problems, and that the whole thing was just ridiculous.'

'The Royal Opera!' said Eva, wonderingly. 'Does the Queen go there?'

'As seldom as she can manage, I think,' said Philip. 'I believe her tastes are rather closer to my wife's, where opera is concerned. Monday. We'll both go. Diana will be delighted to be let off.'

Eva gave a great, shuddering sigh. 'Oh!' she said mournfully. 'I have only these jeans and some other jeans and one very old skirt. Like a backpacker. Is the Royal Opera a place where ladies must be smart?'

'Diana will lend you something,' said Philip. 'Don't think about clothes, they're — um — banal. Think about the music. We've got the

228

whole opera on CD, and Kobbe's *Opera Book*. You can learn a bit about it over the weekend. Come to think of it, I think I've got a translation of the Dumas, the story it came from. *La Dame aux Camellias*. Let's see . . . '

Exhilarated and surprised by himself, he began scanning the bookshelves that lined the hall. Eva trailed after him, fascinated.

'We have a grand opera house in Wroclaw,' she said, 'but it is closed, nobody knows how long.'

'Here you are!' said Philip, triumphantly pulling out *The Lady of the Camellias*. 'Go away and read that. Then we'll discuss what Verdi's librettist did to it.'

Once, long ago in his studious schooldays, he had thought of becoming a teacher. It was, he always used to say in jocular company, only the thought of the pupils that put him off. But in these past weeks the heady sensation of having one pupil, sharp and willing and receptive, had worked the old magic on him: here was power, here was connection, here was the electric charge of intellectual life. Eva smiled at him, her cheeks still damp: he smiled back.

★   ★   ★

In Henry's untidy living-room, Diana stood for a moment irresolute. He had stepped into the hallway to answer the phone in case it was the hospital; she was alone, mildly dismayed by the daylight matter-of-factness of her surroundings. She knew why she had come here in these stolen afternoon hours; Henry had held her close in the lobby and murmured, 'Are you sure?' and she had nodded, wordless, into his chest. It was, she thought, usually at this point in fiction that the older woman became anxious about her sagging body, ashamed to show it to the younger man without the cover of darkness or candlelight. The idea was so coy and crude that it repelled her even as it flickered through her mind. If he loved her, he must love the reality of her. If he could not, better to endure a brief stinging humiliation and walk away.

When he came back, less than a minute later, she was standing naked in the centre of the room.

'I love you,' she said. 'This is it. This is me. No secrets.'

It took him a moment, but when he stepped forward and took her in his arms there were tears in his eyes, and Diana had to kiss them away and lead him, helpless with love, into the bedroom beyond.

20

Diana was wrong: it was no clearer on the other side. Lying in the crook of Henry's arm as he slept, she could see no further ahead into the dark and dangerous forest of their passion.

She felt no guilt, although she tried very hard to do so. Years had passed since Philip wanted her in this way, and she now understood that he had never really wanted her in the way a man should want a woman, wholehearted and wholebodied, without modesty or shame or self-consciousness. At first Henry had not been able to love her. Overwhelmed by her gesture he had lain helpless in her arms while she soothed and gentled him. Later, though, he brought her to an understanding of the act, and a joy in it, which she had never known. Then it was her turn to weep.

And now they were bound together. Age, class, race, marriage vows, Marley and Ali, Philip and Manda, reputation and caution, all were blown away by the great wind of this love. It could not end, it would not end, it had to run its course whatever that might be. Staring at the white ceiling, Diana blinked rapidly and tried to push aside her burning joy and envisage the practical future. Her resolve not to lie to Philip was still strong, but blurred by a sense that it would, in any case, be impossible to tell him the truth about herself and Henry because it was a truth

231

he was incapable of understanding. It was not an 'affair' or a 'fling' or a sordid sexual infidelity. It was love of an order Philip had never known or wanted. It could not be explained to him. So, she thought a little drowsily, not telling him did not count as lying.

Suddenly, with a jolt, she was fully awake again. What terrible sophistry was this? What pretentious rubbish? Of course there was a truth that he could understand and had a right to know. Especially now. If she had not slept with Henry, then loving Henry could have remained her secret. But she had, and the physical contract made with Henry this afternoon cut across an older, tamer, duller but essentially similar contract with Philip. He had a right to know.

Henry stirred.

'OK?' he said, turning his head towards her. She reached up and smoothed his tousled locks.

'Very OK. I was just thinking about what to do. What to say.'

'Simple. Say you're mine now. We gotta tell the whole world.'

'Do we have to? Now? It's so — private, so safe between us.'

'You know we have to.'

'What do we say?'

'Marry me,' said Henry. 'Then we can say you're marrying me.' She looked at him, wondering if he was still half asleep, but his big eyes were wide open.

'What?'

'Marry me. Divorce him. Marry me. Happy ever after.'

'Henry, no!'

He sat up sharply.

'What do you mean, no? It was different. *This* was different. You know that. You're the only woman I'll ever want again. You're the star, you're my life now. You and Marley; but Marley will grow up and go his own way in fifteen years or so, and you and I will never be apart again.'

Diana hugged him close, but an edge of dismay touched her, withering the glory of the last two hours. It was still mid-afternoon, she was still married to a proud and chippy man, and moreover she was still forty-four years old.

'You're too young,' she said quietly. 'I probably couldn't give you children, you know. Possibly, but not likely at my age.'

'I've already got a child. He's great. I don't want loads more children, I want you.'

'You say that now . . . '

'I say that always.'

Diana sat up, trying to regain control of the moment, but he pulled her down into his arms and she had no power, or will, to resist.

★ ★ ★

In the event, she did not tell Philip immediately. She was prevented by the very appearance of the Manor, the genteel orderliness of her accustomed home with Eva smiling and glowing over a magnificent supper and Philip chatting to her about opera.

'Thank God for that,' she said lightly when they told her the plan about *La Traviata*. 'I'm off

233

the hook, then. Who were the tickets from?'

'Alastair. He doesn't forget, unlike some of them,' said Philip, and it occurred to Diana that only weeks ago such a remark would have been made in tones fit to curdle the milk. But now it was light and resigned and almost jocular. She marvelled, and gave silent thanks.

'Anyway, you'll need some tidy clothes,' she said to Eva. 'There are some old things of Manda's. We should have thought of that before.'

Eva stiffened. Philip, who by now understood her rather better than his wife did, saw her face and said smoothly: 'Oh, I don't think she's Manda's style. Haven't you got an evening skirt and some tops? You're not that different except in height, I wouldn't think.'

Eva relaxed, free from the humiliating prospect of wearing a scornful Manda's cast-offs.

'There's the damask skirt,' mused Diana, glad of an opportunity to discuss something so innocuous. 'I was a good bit smaller round the waist when I used to wear that, but I never threw it out because the fabric's so beautiful. We could take it up at the hem, it's got that lovely velvet border. And I've got heaps of black tops. Some of them stretchy, so you wouldn't drown in them. What size shoes do you take?'

'I have big peasant feet,' said Eva cheerfully. 'My mother always said this. My grandfather's big feet: size forty-two European.'

'Well, I'm a seven,' said Diana. 'That's a piece of luck. I thought it might be a problem, me being taller.'

That night, the Act I love duet of Violetta and

Alfredo poured through the house, extolling the coupling of joy and pain. Eva curled on the sofa, frowning her way through an unnecessarily opaque Edwardian translation of Dumas' *Lady of the Camellias*. Philip sat listening, his head thrown back, a half-smile playing on his lips, rapt and apparently happy. Diana, after pretending to listen for a while, pleaded a headache and went early to bed.

★   ★   ★

Meeting her lover the next morning at work was neither as hard, nor as joyful, as she had expected. Henry greeted her with a warm but slightly distracted smile at 8.30, and Marley was not with him.

'Oh, of course, it's his nursery morning at the school,' said Diana, a little flustered, struggling to find her casually friendly professional tone again.

'Yeah, but I didn't have to drop him,' said Henry, who was finding the same difficulty, and glad of a topic. 'Ali's mother stayed.'

'With you? At the flat?' Diana felt a ridiculous sense of territory invaded.

'Mmm. I had to — er — make up the bed for her,' said Henry sheepishly. 'Couldn't put her on the sofa. She wanted to stay around and see Ali again in the morning. To be honest, I think she's likely to stay a few more nights. Solves the Marley problem, anyway.'

'Ali's OK, isn't she?'

He nodded, but bit his lip. 'Yeah, but it turns

out it was a near thing. After we left the other night she haemhorraged, and apparently there's a limit to how far you can go before it's too late. Her mum is convinced that the hospital was slow off the mark because she's black.'

'I don't actually believe that,' said Diana flatly. 'I saw the nurses cooing over Marley. No way would they want to let his mother go. Not everything's about race. Smelly old white tramps are more likely to be neglected than pretty young mothers of any colour, if you ask me.'

'It wasn't me saying it,' said Henry. 'It was Ali's mother.'

They looked at one another with sudden incredulity, and both laughed at once. This was the kind of mild, companionable spat they had often had before as colleagues: it seemed both outlandish and wonderful that they could still argue like this after the last two days. Laughing, they set to work together on the running order while Roger, faithful to his self-appointed task, spilled his way precariously into the office with three paper cups of lukewarm coffee.

After work Henry said that he had to go and fetch Marley and the boy's grandmother, and Diana, stifling a pang of disappointment, lightly replied that anyway she had to do the shopping she had neglected in favour of James Bond. In the High Street, though, she met Andy Morgan with a large carrier bag containing a substantial sheepskin mat.

'Why aren't you headmastering? How's Lizzie?' she asked, suddenly ashamed that she had not rung her friend for three days.

'It's a training day, and I'm as trained as I'm ever likely to get,' said Andy. His face was drawn and tired. 'The Macmillan nurse suggested that Lizzie might sleep better with a sheepskin mat. She's got so thin, you see, but she still needs the hard mattress or she gets backache.'

Diana looked at him for a moment, and then said, 'It's worse, then?'

'We take each day as it comes,' said Andy bleakly. 'She'd love to see you, you know. You could take this mat home and I could look in at school for half an hour.'

Diana abandoned her shopping for the second time — Philip's dry-cleaning, she thought, would probably have settled down by now at Sketchley's, made new friends on the hangers and quite forgotten its old home — and drove to the Morgans' house. When she got to the front door, unlatched as usual, she opened it on a pandemonium of noise. It was the sound of her teens: Meat Loaf howling 'Bat Out of Hell' with 1970s motorbike sound effects. She found Lizzie on the sofa, conducting the music with a rolled-up magazine.

'What's going on here? Reverting to type?' she asked lightly. Lizzie was wearing a black baseball cap of her son's with the legend 'If you're not living on the edge you're taking up too much space.' The invalid nodded, and faded the music just enough to make herself heard.

'I am getting in touch with my inner hooligan, before it's too late,' she said. 'You may as well know. I haven't got long. No — ' She waved away Diana's protestations of sympathy and grief. 'It's definite now. Months, at best. Andy knows, the big kids know, and Freddie knows. I wish I could have seen him through his A-levels, but he's got Andy and the others and we've all talked it through. My affairs have been in order ever since the last bad bit, the funeral music's chosen, so all I have to do now is roll downhill to perdition, as slowly as possible, with Meat Loaf and Ozzy Osbourne at my side.'

It was clearly a prepared speech but, astonishingly, she looked almost happy. Diana said so, and Lizzie smiled and said more naturally: 'It's a relief. Honestly. Knowing there's no more bloody treatment, no more chirpy nurses, just pain relief when I need it and no regrets anywhere. None. Everything's been said and done that needs to be done. I've had Andy, Joe, Marianne, Freddie, you' — she put a thin hand on Diana's — 'a few good friends, a lot of laughs, and on top of it all I happen to believe in Heaven.'

Diana controlled her own impulse to tears but said gently, 'Is it always as good as that? Do you keep this up twenty-four seven?'

'No. Obviously.' Lizzie grimaced, then looked up at her, clear-eyed and honest. 'But it isn't an act, Diana. This is the real me: the scared one is the aberration. I've done OK. In forty-five years I've had a better time than a lot of people manage in twice the life. And I truly, honestly think the family is going to cope, and that is a quadruple blessing. Come on, smile. And tell us the gossip. Fact is, I'm still alive.'

Diana hesitated. Her own dilemmas had

receded, yet it seemed a betrayal of her friend to hold back now from telling her that the whole core and balance of her own world had shifted in the past two days.

'OK,' she said, stalling for time. 'Gossip. Marianne Hamilton's Tony is apparently splitting up with that schoolgirl he went off with.'

'Old news,' said Lizzie smartly. 'Andy told me. However, the other bit of news is that Tony told Andy he wants his job back, but not his wife.'

'What?'

'Even from my sofa of pain, I have better gossip than you. He wants to come back and teach RE — imagine! He could do whole periods on the Prodigal Son and the Woman Taken In Adultery without even a lesson plan. But he is not coming back to Marianne. Says his marriage had been a lie for years. What a walking cliché that man is.'

'Oh, poor Madge!'

'She'll find a hunky Spaniard. How's your au pair, talking of language classes?'

'Happy. Mainly because Philip's taking her to the Royal Opera House to enlarge her vision of European high culture.'

'Good luck to her. And now' — Lizzie narrowed her eyes, shadowed by the forbidding peak of the baseball cap — 'stop wittering about Marianne, and tell me the thing you've been trying not to tell me.'

Diana dropped her eyes, and Lizzie watched her with something like satisfaction. She was right, then. Her friend's glowing vagueness meant what it looked like.

'Who is he?' she asked. 'Who?'

'Lizzie — I can't really — Philip doesn't know — '

'Someone at work, isn't it? Your eyes met over the tape recorders, or whatever they have in that place?'

Diana sat silent for a moment, then said, 'You never thought I should have married Philip, did you?'

'Of course not. Nobody should marry Philip, or not the way he was then. He was too much in love with his own career to be bothered with a wife. A robot with a perm would have done him perfectly well.'

'I sort of know that, now. But I loved him so much, I was all there for him, it hurts even to think about it.'

'Diana,' said her friend patiently, 'everyone makes mistakes. You had a daughter together, you've been his hostess, you've kept him happy, you never screamed at Mrs Thatcher or put a whoopee cushion on John Major's chair or filled Philip's red despatch boxes with syrup. You've done pretty well by him. How well has he done by you?'

'He's always been financially generous. He doesn't interfere with the way I run the house. He's faithful.'

'Does he make love to you?'

They had never been the kind of women friends who discuss sex explicitly, and Diana blushed.

'That's not everything.'

'It matters, though. Does he hug you good

morning and good night, even? Does he ruffle your hair? Diana, admit it. We can all see how it is.'

'All right, all right. No, no, no, no. We're like brother and sister. For several years now, if you must know.'

'Brother and sister. Yeah. Except that you have to jump about to keep him happy, and plot and plan to stop him grumbling, and act like a buffer between him and the slightest irritation.'

Lizzie had never talked quite as baldly as this before. Her features, sharpened by sickness, had an accusing, witch-like intensity. Seeing Diana's confusion she said more gently: 'Look, I've never really said all I thought about Philip because, what the hell? You seemed to be OK on it, it's not my kind of marriage, but what do any of us know? But it's looked pretty bloody miserable to me for the last ten years at least, and I worry. And sooner or later you were bound to find some other man to be nice to you. It only surprises me that it's taken so long. Is it that hunky manager at Two C? Steve, or Simon, or whatever he's called?'

Diana pulled gently away from Lizzie's grasp, and put both hands to her head.

'No,' she said. 'And it's not just an affair, either. He wants to marry me, and I think he's serious. But he's thirteen, maybe fourteen years younger than I am. And he's got a child by another woman who's in hospital.' She paused. 'OK, I'll tell you. It's Henry.'

There was a flicker of satisfaction in seeing that this time she really had astonished Lizzie.

241

'Bloody hell! How long's this been going on?'

'Two days. Friends for much longer. But two days ago, we were at his flat with the kid and he said . . .'

She could not go on. Even to tell Lizzie felt too much like a violation of the privacy of their contract. Her friend looked hard at her, but seemed to understand and made a small, dismissive gesture with her hand. After a moment, when neither spoke, Diana said lamely: 'And I don't know what to do. I can't leave Philip, can I?' It was the question she had needed to ask somebody ever since Henry's proposal. The relief of asking it was so overwhelming she almost thought she would be sick.

'Why not?' asked Lizzie baldly. 'Why can't you?'

'It's wrong. He's done me no harm. And he does sort of depend on me to keep him cheerful. Not so much these last few weeks, with the interest of Eva and the poetry, and he's even taken the loss of the constituency quite calmly. But I'm his sort of — keeper. He's my responsibility.'

Lizzie looked at her, incredulously.

'He's not your *child*,' she said. 'He's not some idiot baby brother. If he doesn't make you happy, or try to, you aren't tied to him till the end of your life.'

'But I'd make him unhappy,' said Diana. 'Can that ever be right?'

Lizzie closed her eyes and sighed.

'In a few months' time, I'm going to make

Andy unhappy,' she said. 'And the kids. I can't help it, I just will. And they'll get over it, and carry on. Because that's how life works.'

Diana was silent.

'Think about it,' said her friend. 'And thanks for bringing the mat, but now go home. I've got to sleep.'

21

Marley, glad to see his mother again but too young for much self-control, became noisy and demanding after twenty minutes, kicking the bedhead and fiddling with its wheels; he was visibly tiring Alissa as she lay limp and ashen in the side-ward. Henry, who had been keeping a watchful eye while he arranged the roses he and Marley had bought at the kiosk, said: 'OK, Ali? Would you like me to take him for a walk?'

'No,' she said. 'Mamma can take him. You stay a minute.'

He was uneasy with her: he missed her usual combative, sassy, defensive manner. This gentle defeated creature was not the girl he had loved, wooed, fought with, and painfully constructed a truce with for their child's sake. Her springing hair was flattened, her gestures weak and resigned, her habitual trendy green sunglasses nowhere in sight.

'OK,' he said a little reluctantly, and nodded to the grandmother who had been sitting at the end of the bed, lovingly but quietly watching the reunion of mother and child. The big, worn woman took Marley's hand firmly and said: 'Come on, my baby. We'll go to the kiosk again and see if we can find your mummy some fruit.'

'Does fruit make you be'er?' said the child.

'Yes.' They disappeared, Ali's mother saying

over her shoulder to Henry: 'Twenty minutes I can manage, before my feet go from under me.' He smiled at her, and turned back to Ali in the bed.

'She's great, your mum,' he said. 'You know she stayed at the flat?'

'Yeah. That was nice of you.'

'Best thing. Family's what Marley needs.'

'I wanted,' said Ali hurriedly, 'to talk about that. I been thinking, lying here. They won't say, but I think I nearly died.'

'You did,' said Henry, and regretted it: she looked iller than before. He added hastily, 'But there's no chance of that now. They're dead pleased.'

'When I was thinking,' said Ali, 'I realized that I've been a bitch to you.'

'No,' said Henry. 'We were both very young.'

'Not you. You were twenty-nine,' said Ali accurately. 'I was the bitch child. I said stupid things. I drove you crazy, man.'

'It's OK,' said Henry. 'It's long ago. And we got Marley, and nobody's better than Marley.'

'Yeah.' She relapsed into silence. But something still visibly troubled her, and after a while, she stretched out a thin hand towards him.

'I wanted to say' — she spoke with a quiet earnestness he had never heard — 'that maybe, for Marley, we ought to try again. I'd try not to spit like a cat, and we'd both try to get home early and be good to one another.'

He was immeasurably touched by her weakness and by the humility of her offer. He could not take his hand from her, but put the

245

other one to his brow, hiding his expression, fighting for time.

'That's a sweet thing to say, girl,' he said after a moment. 'But you're ill. You don't mean it. A lot of water's gone under the bridge.'

'Marley,' said Ali with an effort, 'needs his dad and his mum. Both. All the time.'

Thinking of the child's boisterous exhilaration swinging into petulance, Henry could only agree. Possibly her appeal might have touched something serious in him, if only she had caught him in a low moment a few weeks ago, between girlfriends and afraid of her taking Marley off to London with another pseudo-Daddy. But now it was unthinkable. He had crossed a great ocean of feeling and seen a new continent. He was bound to his son forever, but to this woman not at all.

'Ali, sweet girl, you don't mean it. Think about it. We're not alike enough. In five minutes we'd be tearing into each other like a pair of crocodiles. How good could that be for Marley? He needs calm, not fighting.'

Something was missing from his tone. For all her weakness, the young woman looked at him with clear perception, and knew that she was not hearing the most pressing reason for his refusal. After a moment she said: 'Jesus, you got another woman already? *Now?*' She knew about the last girlfriend's recent departure. He always told her these things, in case Marley should do so in a confused manner at the end of an access weekend, or ask questions needing a calm answer.

246

'No,' he began, but could not carry on. He was trapped as Diana had been: he could not lie. Ali sank back on her pillows.

'It'll be another disaster,' she said with weary spite. 'Jesus, and you're supposed to be the grown-up one.'

A burst of laughter from the nursing station and an irritable high scolding from Marley's grandmother silenced them. He was back, doing a chest-beating gorilla dance with a bunch of bananas in his hand.

'Okayee! Fruit man's here!' he said, tossing the hand of bananas on to the bed and making his mother wince.

'You stop that!' said Ali's mother, breathing heavily. 'Come on, Henry. We got to get this young man to bed.'

'Is Diana going to be there tonight?' cried the child. 'Are we going to have James Bond and pizzas and a cuddle-up?'

'Who's Diana?' asked Ali, coldly.

'She's well cool,' said Marley. 'She's got golden hair and a bright white face wiv red lipstick, and she tells Daddy what to do, down a radio button.'

'I bet she does,' said Ali sourly, and Henry felt a tremor of something like fear.

★ ★ ★

The lovers spoke briefly on the phone on Sunday: Henry did not tell Diana about Marley's remark, still less about Ali's offer; but they agreed that it was best not to try and meet before

Monday. Ali was likely to be discharged early in the week, and the flat was being cleaned and repaired at Henry's expense, so the grandmother could go home on Sunday night to Birmingham and leave the young father to mind the child at work for another couple of days. All weekend Diana avoided conversing with Philip — never a difficult task — and was grateful for the brief distraction of dressing Eva up for the opera. Childlike, the Polish girl revelled in the full sweep of the long damask skirt, and set to work skilfully to unpick the velvet border, take up a two-inch hem and replace the edging to suit her diminutive height.

'I will roll, not cut it,' she said anxiously. 'It can be taken down again afterwards.'

'Oh, for heaven's sake, don't make yourself extra work — I'm giving it to you,' said Diana. 'You'll look lovely in it. I never did. Not my colour.' And indeed the deep red figured damask, topped by a narrow black sleeveless silk T-shirt, had a gypsy glamour which brought out the girl's big eyes and the shine of her dark curling hair. Reassured that cutting the skirt was truly allowed, Eva made herself a scarf out of the rest of the red material, and lined it with some satin from a discarded curtain in the sewing basket. Then she displayed herself in full womanly elegance to Diana and Philip, before Sunday supper in the long drawing-room.

'My!' said Diana inadequately. 'You look astonishing.'

'Very nice,' said Philip, putting down his book; but he did not pick it up again until she had swirled from the room. There was a silence.

'We should have thought about her clothes sooner,' said Diana at last. 'She's been in those two pairs of jeans and thin sweaters ever since she got here.'

Philip grunted in apparent assent, and bent to his reading.

'Will you get the last train back after the opera tomorrow?' asked Diana casually.

'Of course,' said Philip, not looking at her. 'Or I might ask the driver to bring us down. Don't wait up.'

22

It was unlike any journey Eva had ever made. Philip booked seats to London in a first-class carriage, ordered her tea and scones on the way, and was met at the station by a long, sleek black hire car with a uniformed chauffeur.

'It's less expensive than people think,' he said, responding to her saucer-eyed amazement. 'And it saves having to try and park in Covent Garden.' Eva, her outfit completed by a chic 1940s velvet jacket (which had belonged to Diana's mother but no longer met across Diana's bosom), had brushed her hair back and snipped off the untidier tendrils with nail-scissors. Catching sight of herself in a restaurant's plate-glass window in Bow Street, she did not know whether to be prouder of her own appearance or of the magnificent, dinner-jacketed, silver-haired escort who so punctiliously protected her from gutters and passing cars and offered her his arm into the red-and-gold foyer. At last she was like one of the girls in Milan or Madrid: a countess or an heiress perhaps, cultured and sophisticated, escorted to the opera by her distinguished grandfather.

In the great glass atrium of the Floral Hall, bereft of her velvet jacket, she looked around shyly and felt for a moment that her arms were too bare. People were dressed in a bewildering variety of ways: slacks and sweaters, dinner-jackets, satin ruffles, fleeces, tweeds. She glanced up: her own reflection, tiny but distinct from the crowd in the red damask scarf, hung high above her on the mirrored ceiling. A sort of glass box also hung high overhead, the end of the amphitheatre bar if she had known it: but it looked as if a line of people stood suspended in the box, staring down at the milling crowds around the champagne bar. Eva felt a moment of agoraphobic panic: too big, too strange, too grand!

Philip, however, seemed not to see her confusion. He suavely brought her a drink — fizzing champagne which made her laugh and blink — and kept up a flow of comment on the production they were about to see and the politics of the opera house.

'We'll have something to eat and drink at the interval, with my friend who's on the Board,' he said. 'Better than scuffling for a meal afterwards, it's a terrible crush round here.' She nodded, anxious to be a fit companion for him, wondering what Diana would say and do. Gradually she relaxed and began chatting again about the production, asking Philip what to look out for. Soon, though, a tanned, balding young man in a loose dark suit and open silk shirt wove his way through the crowds towards them and interrupted their tête-à-tête.

'Phil-ip!' cried this elegant apparition. 'How marvellous! Must be two years!'

'This,' said Philip without enthusiasm, 'is Roger Pagden. He was one of my researchers a

251

few years back at the House, and now has a seat of his own.'

'A seat?' Eva was puzzled, but game.

'Sorry. I mean that he's an MP. A Member of Parliament in his own right.'

'That is wonderful!' cried Eva, before Philip could complete the introductions. 'You must be so proud.'

The young man smirked, then looked more closely at her.

'You're not little Amanda?' he said. 'Surely?' A glint of mischief in his eyes was met by frosty fire from Philip.

'No!' he said haughtily. 'This is a friend of Amanda's, from Poland, who's studying here. She's very kindly giving me her company tonight because you know what my wife is like about grand opera.'

'More of a Lloyd-Webber girl, I seem to remember,' said Pagden. 'How *is* Diana? Such happy times we all had down there, in your rural fastness, and such lovely breakfasts.'

Eva was not sure that she liked him: he had an aloof, faintly mocking air which she had never encountered before. When he turned his charm directly on her, however, she revised her opinion. Mr Pagden had lovely eyes, a sensitive mouth and a smile which, as her grandmother used to say, would melt the ice on a winter ditch.

' . . . but you clearly *do* like Verdi?' he was saying. 'A woman of discernment!'

Philip, a touch unwillingly, left the pair of them together while he went to the bar for more drinks. When he came back Roger Pagden was standing close to Eva, smiling down at her, crinkling his eyes as he laughed at her enthusiasm.

' — the most beautiful house, near a river like the Lady of Shalott,' she was saying animatedly. 'Do you know this poem? *On either side the river lie, long fields of barley and of rye*'!'

'You're clearly lucky in your crops,' drawled Pagden. 'When I was last at Garton Manor it was marooned in a sea of oilseed rape, and the Prime Minister couldn't stop sneezing.'

Philip was carrying only two glasses.

'Your drink,' he said to Eva, then coldly to the younger man, 'Nice to see you. Perhaps we'll run into each other in the interval.'

But Pagden did not go away. He sipped the remains of his gin and tonic, raising the glass to Eva, and continued determinedly sparkling at her. She enjoyed it: she had not been flirted with so gracefully since she left Wroclaw. The Italian pursuers had been frightening, and the Russian boys in Spain treated her as a little brother. In France, she thought ruefully, her farouche and scruffy appearance had probably put paid to any chance of male admiration. In the English village, a couple of teenage boys had shouted, 'Oi! Frodo!' which it had taken her some days (and a film advertisement in Philip's newspaper) to understand, and which had inspired her severe clipping of the tendrils of dark hair round her face.

But tonight, the polished glass on the stairway and the walls of the great atrium all told her that she was beautiful; the eyes of this Mr Pagden told her the same. She giggled a little, and blushed, and glowed with the champagne; she hardly noticed Philip's grim silence.

'You haven't seen the sights? Ah, shame! I could show you round — the London Eye on a clear day to start with, for the great overview — and you really ought to go round the Palace of Westminster. Too cold for tea on the Terrace, but perhaps we could make a date and I'd take you to the Strangers' Gallery?'

'Strangers? Is this for foreigners only?'

'No — anyone who isn't an MP is automatically categorized as a stranger. Archaic but charming. Even Philip here' — the interloper darted a sharp little glance at the older man — 'is technically a stranger, I suppose. Though he was one of us so recently . . . ah, well, that's politics.'

'I was never one of *you*,' said Philip. 'You came in as I came out.' He was feeling strange: normally he would have hated every patronizing word that Pagden uttered, maybe feeling so humiliated that he would walk away. Right now, he did not mind the Parliamentary posturing nearly so much as the spell that this offensive brat was weaving over little Eva. He clearly wanted to fascinate her, make himself sure of her allegiance and then drop her flat. That was what shits like Pagden did.

To be concerned about someone else's state of mind was such a new experience for Philip that he floundered and could not sharpen the end of his remark. 'So we were never in the House together, I mean,' he concluded lamely.

'Oh, true!' said Pagden. 'But, Eva, you must know that I sat at Philip's *feet* for *years* . . . he was always thought of as absolutely the coming man, and a job in his office was *gold dust.* People slit each other's *throats* to work for him, and as for an invitation to the sweet Manor!'

'You were very clever, then?' said Eva. 'If he invited you? Or perhaps you were just very lucky!' She was twinkling now; and Philip thought admiringly that perhaps she was not as taken by Roger Pagden as he had feared. However, he could bear the man's company no longer. He looked at his watch.

'We'd better go. We have to walk through to the other side of the Grand Tier.'

'Oooh,' said Pagden, feigning respect. 'That's put me in my place. I'm in the Amphi. Philip *is* showing you a good time.'

He bent and kissed her hand. Eva, still giggling and blushing, allowed herself to be led through sumptuous apartments to the back of the Grand Tier, and ushered to her seat. As her host showed the tickets, despite his deftness she caught sight of their price and whitened with shock. But inside the auditorium her attention was taken by the great red curtains, the gilded coat-of-arms and the Queen's initials in heavy gold thread at the corners.

'Lion and Unicorn,' she said reverently. 'The beasts of Britain. In Poland we have a great eagle.'

' "*The lion and the unicorn were fighting for the Crown*," ' said Philip lightly.

255

''*The lion chased the unicorn all round the town*'.'

Eva craned over the padded barrier before her, looking down at the warm glints of wood and brass in the orchestra pit, then up at the balconies edged with warm red shaded lamps.

'It is very beautiful,' she said. 'Royal.'

When the overture began she sat still, transported; well-instructed by Philip, she gave only brief glances at the projected surtitles, and followed the action with close attention. The idea of Violetta as a courtesan had been faintly shocking to her, conjuring up unwelcome memories of the two Bulgarian girls, Reni and Vessela, and their casual heartless hedonism. Onstage, though, the white ballgown and the vocal purity of the soprano drew her in, as they were meant to, and after a while, inexorably and irreversibly she was drawn into something closer than sympathy.

Had she, too, not had to choose between true faithful love and the adventure and excitement she craved? True, Eva had not opted to live off a rich decadent Baron (although she glanced sharply sideways at Philip and blushed in the darkness, remembering the ticket price). But she had rejected the loving and virtuous Tadeusz because staying with him would have meant staying in Wroclaw, leading a standard bland life and aspiring no higher than a cramped apartment and a job a couple of degrees better than cleaning hotel bathrooms. Yes, she saw Violetta's dilemma all right. Love was not everything. '*O, Parigi!*' sang the soprano, and

Eva understood entirely.

Then it was the interval, and Philip led her to a table where two men in dinner-jackets rose to greet him. Listening distractedly to their fast smooth conversation, fiddling with a smoked salmon sandwich and more champagne, Eva frowned over this new understanding.

'Penny for your thoughts?' said Philip, in a gap in the conversation. 'Enjoying it? I like the soprano very much. New to me. Lovely line.'

'You wait for old Germont,' said one of the dinner-jacket men. 'Wonderful. I can't hear him often enough.'

'I am enjoying it,' said Eva, seriously. 'But I think it is very sad that she will give up all her Paris life for Alfredo and still she will not find happiness in the end. Maybe she should know what her nature is and stay with her own life.'

The men looked at her curiously, as if caught unawares by the simplicity of her response to the narrative.

'Yes,' said Philip finally. 'But her nature is on the turn, see? Meeting Alfredo makes her realize she wants something she's never had.'

'I think it is also sad for Alfredo,' said Eva repressively. 'She is no good for him.'

She ate the rest of her sandwich in silence. By the second interval, on the far side of old Germont's baritone intervention and Violetta's public humiliation in the gambling scene, her mood was even darker. The tenor playing Alfredo looked more and more like Tadek. She drank more champagne, though by this time she could hardly have said whether it was to forget her own

257

doubts and troubles, or to drown Violetta's. Staggering slightly as they re-entered the Grand Tier, she was glad of Philip's arm.

The piece wound to its heartbreaking conclusion, bows were taken, and after a brief pause in the Ladies' lavatory — where her flushed cheeks and tousled hair shocked her some of the way back into sobriety — they were outside in the cold damp London air. Philip steered her skilfully past the beggars who mingled, pleading, with the well-wrapped exodus from the stalls. His car was there: he bent to say something to the driver and as Eva stood behind him, clutching her jacket round her thin shoulders, Roger Pagden shimmied up to her and said: 'Lovely to meet you. Seriously, though, if you'd like a tour of the Mother of Parliaments, I'm your man.' He pushed a slip of card into her hand; Philip straightened and turned in time to see Eva thanking him, with a polite little smile.

'Ciao, Philip!' said Pagden, and moved away. 'A bientôt, Bellissima!'

'Creep,' muttered Philip under his breath, but held the door open for Eva with a smile.

23

Inevitably, or so it seemed to both of them, Diana and Henry took advantage of the operatic outing to spend the evening together. Diana was working until seven, and when she arrived at the flat Marley was already in his pyjamas, bouncing up and down in a giant white inflatable ball made up of semi-transparent cells with a child-sized cave in the middle.

'Lookit me!' he yelled. 'Giant hamster ball, like Robbie's hamster's got!' Hurling himself against one side of the cave, he began to crawl; the great ball rolled towards Diana like a cartoon snowball, and she jumped aside as it hit the doorway and wedged itself, jerking and wobbling from the child's panting efforts, half through the doorway.

'What in *hell*,' she asked, 'is that?'

'The latest thing,' said Henry sheepishly. 'I couldn't resist it. There's an adult-sized one, too, but I didn't think two of them would fit in this room'.

'One of them doesn't,' said Diana. She eased the inflatable out of the doorway, and gave it a push so that Marley, squealing with glee, rolled back across the floor towards his father. 'It's a travelling igloo,' said his high voice from behind layers of squeaking plastic. 'I'm a rolling Eskimo.'

'See,' said Henry. 'It's educational. They were

doing stuff about the Arctic in nursery, and he was going on about penguins last week, and we just walked past the toy superstore and it called out to us by name.'

'How long does it take to blow up?'

'Half an hour of lung-busting misery,' said Henry. 'It cost nearly a hundred quid so I wasn't going to buy the bloody pump for another tenner.'

Diana smiled: it was rarely, given her daughter's current aloofness, that she let herself remember Manda's childhood moments, but the little boy's exultation in the ridiculous, habitable toy reminded her vividly of a certain wooden Wendyhouse set up in the London nursery and furnished with equal enjoyment by daughter and mother together. Even Philip, she remembered, had donated a tiny watercolour from his study to be hung on the wall. Boys, she supposed, liked something a bit more dynamic: a vehicle rather than a house. But there were already signs that this one was becoming a den.

'Can I sleep in it?' said Marley, rocking the big shape to and fro. It looked, she thought, rather like an illustration of foetal cell division in a biology textbook.

'Not sleep the night,' said Henry. 'It's plastic. There's got to be a grown-up around in case it loses its air and tangles you up.'

'Well,' said Marley, skilfully shifting his ground, 'can we take it to the swimming pool and roll it on the water?'

'Hey, that would be good,' said Henry,

diverted. 'Never occurred to me, but presumably it floats.'

'We could,' said the child, glancing at Diana, 'take it to that stream and see if I float along on the — the sultana.'

The two adults looked puzzled for a moment, then in unison said, 'Current!' and began to laugh. Marley crawled out, dark and vivid against the pale plastic, and stood with his arms folded.

'Well, I will anyway,' he said, uncertain and faintly insulted. Henry and Diana were leaning on one another now, the pent-up emotion of the past days finding an unexpected outlet in whoops and chokes of laughter.

'You shall float triumphantly on the sultana of life,' said Henry. 'Like a sultan of Arabia.'

'It's a hell-raisin' idea,' added Diana, and, 'Oh, dear, that wasn't very good.'

Marley came over to them and hugged their legs, and Diana felt immeasurably touched to be taken so indiscriminately into his hot embrace.

'Stoopid,' he said good-naturedly. 'Wait till Mum sees it.'

It took them another hour to get him off to bed, so that they could curl up on the sofa together and talk, heads together, about all that lay in their hearts until the child was fast asleep and they could go quietly into the bedroom. Diana got home at last, lips bruised and body singing, at half-past midnight. Twenty minutes later the hire car pulled up outside, sending headlight beams across the bedroom ceiling where she lay. She pulled the duvet over her head and feigned sleep.

★ ★ ★

It had not been an altogether comfortable journey home for Eva. The champagne made her a little nauseous and very drowsy, and the long car had an uncomfortable swaying motion. Philip fell silent after a few moments' desultory talk about the opera, and she fought sleep for a while as the warm, quietly humming saloon swiftly made its way out through the suburbs north of London. Eventually she gave in, and let the waves of drowsiness close over her. When she woke the car was speeding along a clear road, and the crescent moon was high in the cold autumn sky above the bordering trees. Half-tipsy, still half-asleep, she realized that she had slumped or curled towards her companion. Her head was on Philip's shoulder, her breast warm against his arm.

His hand, moreover, was on her thigh. Eva jumped, but Philip did not respond. Her eyes were still half-closed and she realized that he probably thought she was twitching in her sleep. The hand did not move.

It was a warm, firm hand; the cashmere of his coat beneath her cheek was expensively soft, and the closeness of his arm reminded her of feeling the strength and comfort of her father when she was small. It was so long since anybody had touched her in affection that Eva, still fuddled by sleep, was reluctant to move. The hand, she told herself, was only on her leg to steady it; she herself, after all, had her left arm trapped close to his side. With the cold melodious death of Verdi's Violetta still in her mind, her sleepy logic told her that this was natural: nothing more than animal warmth, shared between living creatures in the winter darkness without calculation or impropriety. She might be his daughter, or granddaughter. Yet a small, treacherous part of her liked the hand on her leg for other reasons entirely. Rather than confront this, she willed herself back to sleep.

Philip, looking out of the car window at the bright sliver of moon, hardly dared to breathe lest he disturb her. A piercing joy filled him: bred of the night, the music, the soft casual warmth of the girl, the smell of her skin and the tousled dark head on his shoulder. '*Lay your sleeping head, my love, human on my faithless arm . . .*' Lines went through his head, incomplete and confused: '*in my arms till break of day, let the living creature lie*'. Speeding through this darkness, with the night around them and the spell of the music over them still, there was no right or wrong. He had been unhappy for so long that the purity of the moment's pleasure dazzled him. Life, he thought hazily, still flowed onwards, a majestic shining torrent. He had stood for too long on the hard and stony bank, and now it was time to give himself back to its rush and gladness.

The driver knew the way to Garton Manor; he had brought Philip home often enough before, as he sat working on government or business papers in the back or sitting apart from a weary Diana. He did not need to ask for directions, so Eva slept on with Philip's hand on her warm young thigh until the car pulled up gently in front of the moonlit house. Then the girl sat up, stretched, and looked uncertainly at him.

His face was in shadow but he smiled briefly at her and said, 'Home!' Then he signed the driver's document, got out, and offered a hand to help her out of the car. It pulled away quickly and left them standing under the front porch together, Eva shivering slightly. Without thought or self-consciousness, surprising himself, Philip took her in his arms and kissed her full on the mouth, gently at first and then with passion.

At that moment, breaking away more in confusion than outrage, Eva realized how much she had missed Tadeusz Grocholski, and how sad she was to have lost him forever. She muttered something inarticulate, thanking her host for the evening, and fled into the house and up the stairs to bed.

In the morning, Philip was gone. He had, said Diana vaguely, left a message saying that he had to make a short-notice trip into Europe to sort out one of his business ventures. Eva, who had come downstairs with trepidation and a considerable hangover, could only gape stupidly for a moment, and then sit down suddenly, overcome with relief. Nothing needed to happen yet. That was a blessing. Her dreams had been tangled and troubling, with a message in them somewhere. She needed some time alone to interpret them. She was glad to hear that Diana would be 'working pretty late' that night and needing no supper.

★ ★ ★

It was agreed, in the following weeks of reports and official investigation, that Donald Louis King should never have been given bail. There was plenty of hard forensic evidence against him. He had carried a large knife and used it, and his mental stability was well known to be impaired at times by his wide acquaintance among suppliers of crack cocaine. However, after a court decision backed by a restless desire on the part of the police to see exactly where he went and who he went to see, he walked out of the cells unbeknownst to his victim while she was still in hospital.

He did not, however, last long in the outside world. Furious, humiliated, unable as he put it 'to get his head round anything', Donny stole a Volkswagen Passat in the early hours of Tuesday morning, just as Eva and Philip were getting home from Covent Garden. He drove it very fast out of town, down the wrong side of the dual carriageway, plunging on to the hard shoulder to avoid oncoming cars. Two police patrol cars, alerted by swerving and terrified motorists, gave chase. When he heard their sirens Donny swung off the main road and raced through the lanes, adrenalin coursing through his thin young body, steering with two fingers, still able to rejoice confusedly in his considerable skill behind the wheel.

The Passat, however, was no match for its pursuers. They grew closer; the young man's sense of invulnerability leached out of him, to be replaced by a terrible black despair. His last thought was that it was a woman who had brought him to this pass, and that women were nothing but trouble and shit. Then the lane bent sharply to the left, a tall tree reared ahead of him and his days on earth were ended. The police car skidded and dented its passenger door on another tree; a young constable on his first night patrol had his arm broken.

The local newspaper made much of the event, citing the risks of the drug trade even in this comparatively affluent rural backwater. Donny's picture was printed, and a photograph of the injured policeman hugging his dog with his good arm. It took several days, however, for the busy local newsdesks to track down the victim whose stabbing had caused the original arrest. When they finally found Ali it was late on Wednesday.

The girl reporter — even younger than Ali herself, and dewily sympathetic — broke the news over the phone and made an appointment to come round and do a feature interview. 'If it goes national,' she said sweetly, 'you'll get paid good money.'

Diana and Henry, close though they were to the Two Counties Radio newsroom, were far too preoccupied with one another all week to work out that the Donald Louis King killed in the stolen car was Donny the aspiring minicab driver. They never made the connection. And Ali, still bruised from her rejection by Henry, was in no mood to make conversation when she returned on Wednesday to her flat behind its mended door and took over custody of Marley.

'You're not worried? You're OK?' Henry said when he took his son to her. 'You could still come to my flat, you know.'

'Piss off. I'm not worried. Why should I be?' retorted Ali, her hand on the door. 'Leave me alone. You've got Marley on Friday, there's nothing else for you here.'

'Ali, I'm sorry. I didn't mean it all to end in such a mess. You're amazing, the way you cope with all the shit.'

Ali gave him a hard, unfriendly stare.

'I said, piss off to your blonde bitch. Leave me alone.'

24

During the two days after her ride home from the opera, Eva wandered around the house in a daze. Diana, although rarely at home and more preoccupied with her own dilemma than with anybody else's feelings, asked whether she was all right: Eva replied vaguely that she had many things to think about. Marianne turned up on Wednesday to drive her to the college, but even with her Eva did not chatter or laugh. On the way she sat silent; getting back into the car she bit her lip and stared out of the window.

'I am starting to hate Spanish,' said Marianne with a touch of petulance, narrowly missing a white van in the college car park. 'I never thought there'd be so much grammar in it. I associate grammar with tiresome people like the Germans and French.'

'There is always grammar,' said Eva absently, still staring out of the window. Then, with more force: 'There have to be rules, I think.'

'But as long as people know what you *mean*,' began Marianne. Eva, however, turned towards her and said with sudden vehemence, as if the idea came at the end of another train of thought entirely: 'Meaning is like feeling. You cannot just follow your feelings. You need to obey rules if life is to be — orderly and kind.'

'Well, I'd not argue with that,' said Marianne. 'My husband broke the rules and look what happened. Still, he'll be back.'

'He is coming back? That is good!' Eva was trying to be polite and concerned now: she realized she had been distant with the kind Marianne, and blamed herself.

'Well, I've not actually heard anything from him,' conceded the other woman. 'Too ashamed. He'll come round soon enough. But the good thing is, the girl's vamoosed. Good riddance.'

Eva did not understand 'vamoose' but got the sense. 'Oh,' she said. 'She has left him?'

'Young girls,' said Marianne with great self-satisfaction, 'have no staying power. Certainly not when they're with a man of his age. '*Say it early, say it late: Spring and autumn should not mate*'.'

'Love can happen to anybody,' said Eva, 'at any age. I believe this. Sometimes it follows rules, but they are different rules from the ordinary ones.'

'Oh, it can *happen*,' said Marianne. 'But can it last?'

Eva, suddenly and without warning, burst into tears. Marianne glanced at her in consternation, then pulled over to the wide grass verge and turned off the engine.

'You've not been right all day,' she said firmly. 'Come on, tell Marianne. I may be a silly old trout who likes a drink and couldn't hold on to a husband, but I'm not stupid.' Her fleshy arm went around Eva's shoulders; her perfume was cloying but sweet, her bosom soft. Eva buried her face in Marianne's neck and wept like a child. Then, piece by piece, she recounted all

269

her doubts and troubles without reserve or guile.

★　★　★

After Henry had taken Marley back to the council flat, with a considerable bribe in the way of computer games not to inflict the big white plastic igloo on a convalescent mother, he met Diana in a coffee-shop on the square by arrangement. As soon as they had sat down he said, without preamble, 'Ali knows about us. Marley told her.'

Diana tried to sip at her coffee with nonchalance, but her hand was shaking.

'Oh.'

'It was bound to happen.'

'Yes.'

'I think we should bring it into the open.'

'Tell Philip?'

'Well, obviously. And then tell work. Everywhere. Then we can get on with our life. Together.'

Diana looked at him: young, fit, confident, his red shirt open to show the thin gold chain he always wore around his neck. She glanced down at herself: a sensible quilted waistcoat, striped shirt, well-cut but distinctly matronly grey trousers, polished leather slip-on shoes rather than the trainers of his generation. The whole thing suddenly seemed to her quite impossible and inappropriate. She looked like — well, not his mother, not quite, but perhaps his teacher. Or his social worker. How could she tell Philip,

270

and their acquaintances, and a curious world, that she and this magnificent wild-haired youth constituted 'an item'? They would look at her in the way they looked at ageing Western women who picked up Masai beach-boys in Kenya and sold their tawdry 'love' stories to the tabloid press.

'It's too soon,' she said feebly.

Henry reached over and took her hand. His touch steadied her, and her perspective returned. This was not a toyboy absurdity. This was Henry, and he loved her, and she knew the innermost places of his heart just as he knew hers.

'Ali,' he said, 'will eventually tell someone. She will. I know her, she'll get in a temper and blurt it all out. Philip would prefer to hear it from you.'

'It's too cruel,' she said. 'He's had so much to face lately. With losing the seat, I mean.'

'Do you love me?'

'You know I do.'

'Do I love you?'

'I believe you do. Yes. You do.'

'Does Philip love you?'

She pulled her hand away, and fished for a tissue to blow her nose most unromantically.

'I don't know,' she said. 'He doesn't make love, he doesn't say he loves me, but we're used to each other. It's a marriage. We made a child together, and a home. I look after him.'

'But,' said Henry, 'you said things have been pleasanter and home better since Eva came to cook for you. That proves that the looking-after is something you don't have to do personally.'

'He's older than me. I'd feel such a heel, walking out on him with a younger man.'

'He's rich. He'll sort himself out. Oh, Diana, come on. This isn't like you. You're brave and honest and good. This isn't the way you do things.'

'Give me a couple more days.'

He had to be satisfied with that.

★ ★ ★

In the car, Marianne looked round for a handkerchief to dry Eva's tears after the flood of confidences, but could only find a rather expensive silk scarf. She handed her that, and said: 'So he's gone away?'

'I am afraid,' said Eva, 'that it is because of me.'

'Could be. Could be business. Could be plain embarrassment. But I think you might be making too much of it. Was he drunk? Honestly, dear, men kiss all sorts of people when they're drunk. I should know.'

'I do not think Mr Hunton-Hall gets drunk like that,' the young woman said primly.

'Well,' conceded Marianne, 'I do admit I've never actually seen him out of control. Bit of a dry stick, I always thought. But you say he groped you in the car?'

'I think,' said Eva with the grandiose naïveté of youth, 'that he may be in love with me.'

Marianne pressed her lips together. 'Spring and autumn,' she said. 'Nothing but trouble. But if he thought he was in love, why didn't he stay

272

on and keep up the siege?'

'I think he has a great conscience,' said Eva, 'and a powerful moral strength. He has gone away so he cannot kiss me again. He will be hoping I am gone away when he gets back. It is like a — a tragedy of love.'

Marianne found this hard to respond to. The child was, she thought, a desperate romantic, and frankly putting far too high a value on a middle-aged man's heavy pass in a taxi. However, she had to concede that Philip Hunton-Hall was not the usual class of lunging buffoon who made a fool of himself over an au pair girl. He was — she looked for a word and suddenly found it — a more *refined* type. Highly strung, maybe. She herself disliked him for all the times he had shuddered delicately at her exuberance, but Tony had once observed that Philip was a 'rare spirit' and not a typical politician at all underneath all that Tory grandee veneer.

Maybe the girl was right, and he had fallen heavily for her. If so, there was nothing but trouble ahead. He couldn't stay away for long. She wondered whether to talk to Diana about it: a wife could often steer her man off the rocks. Then she surprised herself by wondering whether Diana would actually care all that much. They never seemed particularly devoted, as a couple.

Eva had composed herself now. 'I am sorry,' she said. 'It is not your problem.'

'Of course it is, dear, I'm fond of you. But this boyfriend of yours — Tadek — are you sure

273

he's given up on you?'

'He is engaged. I think it is to my friend Halina. She has loved him for a long time.'

'Well, suppose you wrote to him? People do change their minds.'

'Impossible,' said Eva. His final 'See you by Fredro' still rang in her ears. 'Anyhow, I think it is better to move on. I understand now that, truly, he was not the right husband for me to have. When I have learned English better I will get a job and an apartment-room in Warsawa. I only cried about Tadek because it reminded me — because Philip reminded me — '

She was brimming again, and Marianne finished her sentence. 'Reminded you what it's like to be held,' she said. 'Yes, I see that.'

'I have lost Tadek,' said Eva bleakly. 'Yet I am thinking all day about Mr Hunton-Hall.'

Marianne stared at her for a moment, and then said in quite a different voice: 'Oh, no. No don't say that.'

'It is possible,' came the faint but grand reply from behind the silk scarf, 'to give your love to two men in a life, yes?'

Marianne stared at her for a moment, then started the car.

'Maybe I'm not the person you should be asking,' she said. 'I gave mine to one man, such as it was, and a fat lot of good it's done me.'

★ ★ ★

A thousand miles away, Philip was at the end of a second long and busy day. His journey, begun

274

at dawn on the morning after the opera, had taken him first to London where he called an unscheduled meeting with two of his partners in the Polish project and delivered them an ultimatum which startled them very much. He tracked down the third partner by mid-afternoon, and gave the same message; to his surprise and slightly shamefaced pleasure, this time it was met with considerable enthusiasm.

'I wasn't happy myself,' said Lord Arvonleigh, looking at him curiously. 'It felt bloody mean, considering. But this idea makes it feel much better. You're giving away a hell of a lot of private equity, though. Did you have trouble with the bank?'

'They had trouble with me,' said Philip, and grinned like a schoolboy. That night he caught a plane to Warsaw and summoned up more meetings for Wednesday. Through it all he was exhilarated and energized, not at all like a disappointed old man who has made a fool of himself with a young woman. When he had put the last brick of his new edifice in place, he shook off his local colleagues, packed up in his hotel, and for the first time in two busy days, hesitated.

He could fly home — there were always first-class seats — but that would mean facing Diana and young Eva late in the evening, or appearing to surprise them at breakfast. Instead, he booked another night in the hotel, ate red soup and dumplings — how that reminded him of Eva! — in a pavement café and walked for hours through the evening streets, trying to read the faces of passers-by. It was growing cold, and the beggars on the pavement bothered him; he gave away his last zlotys and booked an early cab to the airport on his credit card. That night he slept sweetly, dreaming of boyhood, the high soaring chapel roof and the thunder of the organ.

★ ★ ★

The journalist arrived to see Ali armed with a plastic toy helicopter and a bag of sweets for Marley. 'Because he's had such a worrying time, poor baby' she said. She had learned this technique from an older, expertly manipulative woman reporter. It misfired slightly this time because Ali, not apparently being quite the feckless underclass mother the reporter had assumed she was, immediately confiscated the chocolates and said he could have two each evening, no more.

The helicopter, however, was a success. Its twang and whirr punctuated the subsequent interview, and were clearly audible on the cassette tape which the reporter listened back to later, in the office, with chuckles of glee.

'You must have had a terrible time,' it began, in the reporter's breathless girly voice. 'Are you feeling OK now?'

'Getting that way,' said Ali curtly. She wished she had not agreed to talk to the press, but the prospect of money had thrown her off-balance for a moment. Also, she needed to talk to somebody now that Mamma had gone back to

Birmingham to tend her ailing father. 'I'm not going to say that I'm glad Donny died, though. So don't bother asking.'

'Well, you were *close*,' said the girl. 'And, of course, he's little Marley's father . . . '

It was, she thought later, an exceptionally lucky hit. Ali began to talk properly at that point, more anxious to convey information than to conceal it. She made the point most forcefully that Marley was no relation whatever of Donny's, and that she herself knew better than to get pregnant by a lowlife like that; reinforcing this, she said at some length that Marley's father had a very good job and saw plenty of his child. Artfully provoked, she then identified the father, which caused the first surge of glee in the reporter's heart. For she knew about Henry: had interviewed him, indeed, when he won his Sony Award. That was the first, and least, of the unexpected treats in this interview. Later, preening herself in the office, the reporter reflected that a lesser journalist would have been content with just that one story — 'Radio star is father of car-chase Donny's stab victim's child', or whatever. She, however, had probed on, just in case there was more.

'Are you still on good terms, then? That's very civilized,' she said. And then, as if on an impulse, 'He hasn't married, has he?'

'No,' said Ali, but something in her eyes prompted the reporter's next question.

'Got a girlfriend, has he?'

'Yeah.'

'Well, they do go off with younger girls when they get responsibilities . . . ' said the reporter, pencil poised.

And Ali — tired, depressed, nervous and missing her mother — told her that he had bloody well gone off with *an older woman*, like that bloody Prince Charles. Then she revealed who the older woman was, the receptionist bitch at the radio station who was married to the old MP.

'I'll need to check it out,' said the reporter to the editor. 'But, hey, if it does stand up!'

'You know the rules,' said the editor. 'You're on staff. You can offer it to the nationals for the day we print it, and not before.'

'When's that going to be?'

'If you can get a quote off Mrs Hunton-Hall, plus the DJ, then we'll run it on Saturday. Give you time to write it properly. Talk to Dave if you need help.'

25

'Philip's back,' said Diana to Henry on Friday morning. 'Turned up mid-afternoon, very cheerful.'

'So you told him?' said Henry.

'Stop harassing me,' said Diana. It was the sharpest tone she had used to him all week. 'I'm all over the place. I'm not behaving like myself, and Philip isn't behaving like Philip, and everything feels weird.'

'So anyway, you won't be having supper at the flat tonight?' Henry said. Their voices were low; Roger was just outside the door, arguing with the manager.

'Eva's cooking something special,' said Diana despairingly. 'She seems to have cheered up a bit, too. She and Philip were chatting away for hours last night. I went up to bed early with a migraine.'

'You'll go on having migraines until you tell him,' said Henry inexorably. 'They're brought on by lying about important things.'

'Stop being so psychobabbly,' said his lover, annoyed. 'It wasn't a real migraine anyway.'

★ ★ ★

'Come for a walk,' said Philip to Eva. He was in the kitchen with her, drying up the breakfast things. She hated using the dishwasher for mere

279

toast-plates. 'It's a lovely day. Come and walk by the river.'

'I should clean the house' said Eva.

'It's my house,' said Philip. 'For the moment, anyway. And I say it doesn't need cleaning.' He dropped a kiss on the top of her head, light-hearted and fatherly, and she turned to wind her arms around him, astonishing herself at how right and habitual this novel activity already seemed.

'You really don't mind?' she asked.

'About the house?'

'No. About how I cannot love you? Properly? Not yet?'

'That's not the bit that matters,' said Philip. 'If I were twenty-eight instead of fifty-eight, it probably would be. But for now — no, I don't mind. Marvell was wrong. No winged chariots anywhere near. Happiness doesn't gallop. It lies still and stretches in the sun. A hundred years have passed since yesterday.'

'A thousand,' said Eva. 'It is the same for me.'

Hand in hand, they stepped out of the kitchen, not bothering with boots, letting the sparkling grass soak their shoes and socks. They walked past the barn, silent and content, and embraced again under its shadow.

'I'm an old man,' said Philip after a while. 'An old, failed politician who's never made anything but money.'

'Not to me. Not failed to me,' said Eva.

Philip looked down at her, tenderness in every line of his marble face.

'You have saved me,' he said. 'Even if you

walked out on me right this minute, I am saved. Even before last night, I was saved.'

'I will never walk away,' said Eva seriously.

'You might. There are younger men.'

'Tadek was young. But I have understood now that he was wrong for me. He wanted me to be his wife, but not to be myself.'

'There's a proverb,' said Philip, smoothing her hair. 'You like proverbs, don't you?'

'We used many at school, for learning English,' said Eva. 'A bird in the hand, a silver lining. What is yours?'

He took her hand again and swung it, pulling her along as he strode towards the shining stream, and almost sang as she panted to keep up: 'Better to be an old man's darling than a young man's slave.'

*   *   *

Diana was taking back the last of the programme CDs and preparing for a lunchtime newsroom shift when Steve popped out of his manager's office, looking worried. He generally looked worried, so she thought little of it, but when he saw her he looked so miserable that she stopped even before he called her over.

'There's a phone call for you' he said. 'It's from the *Evening Star*, I'm afraid.'

'Oh, God,' said Diana. And, hardly realizing she spoke aloud, 'What's Philip been up to now?' Her memories of press phone calls were all entangled with old party scandals, and in particular with the infamous winter of the

Fanfair Finance allegations.

Steve looked even more miserable. 'It's not him,' he said. 'I'm afraid it's you. And — um — Henry. But I think Henry's gone?'

'He's collecting Marley,' said Diana automatically. 'Ali's going to a hospital appointment.' Then the full impact of what he had said hit her, and she had to lean against the wall for a moment, her hand against the midriff of a large framed photograph of Henry in a Hawaiian shirt. When she followed the manager's gaze and realized what she was doing, she snatched the hand away and pushed her hair back distractedly.

'Do I *have* to speak to them?' she said helplessly.

'They say they're quite confident,' he replied. 'I think they'll run some form of the story anyway. You could just deny it, I suppose.' He did not sound convinced, and was avoiding her eye. 'Probably your best option.'

'Steve,' said Diana desperately, 'Henry and I are not just some fling.'

'Oh, God,' he said. 'I was so hoping you weren't going to say that.'

Terrified, her heart in her throat, Diana went to his office and picked up the phone from where it lay on the desk, its coiled cable as menacing as a rattlesnake. The next day, in the local and national papers, her quote came out as: 'I don't discuss my personal life in public but my husband and I have a very strong and trusting relationship.' She had no way of knowing whether that was what she'd really said or not. The whole call was a terrifying blur of shame.

282

It hardly mattered what she said, in any case, because the girl reporter had just caught up with Henry at Ali's flat, where he provided the superior, headline quote by unhesitatingly saying, 'Diana Hunton-Hall is a wonderful and beautiful woman and I am proud to say that she is the love of my life and always will be.'

That left only Philip: but they did not manage to get hold of him on the phone that Friday at all, for the very good reason that he had taken it off the hook while he and Eva, infinitely close, sat entwined all afternoon on the drawing-room sofa with their beloved Chopin weaving butterfly patterns around them.

★　★　★

One other thing happened during that afternoon. Anthony Hamilton came home, found Marianne watching a Bette Davis film on television with a box of chocolates, and entirely spoiled her day by telling her that despite the defection of his schoolgirl mistress, he wanted a divorce as soon as possible.

'It wasn't ever about her,' he said, imprudently. 'It was about us.'

She did not take it well. After berating him as a dirty old man and regretting — in considerable detail — every year of their thirty-two-year marriage, she followed him into the bedroom where he was trying to pack, and began throwing his clothes out of the window and ripping his trousers apart at the crotch.

Diana got home, afraid and ashamed as she had not been since she was discovered in childhood misdemeanours. It was discovery, she thought, and the prospect of a public shaming that bred guilt. If one could sin one's splendid sins unseen, remorse would be a rare thing indeed. Only media, spiteful intrusive media, delivered the modern punishment of the wicked.

She had managed to speak to Henry briefly on his mobile, only to be told that he had not attempted the slightest obfuscation or ambiguity, but proclaimed his new love from the rooftops. She was angry with him, confused, frightened and simultaneously appalled at her own cowardice. Imagining the moment when she told Philip, she had pictured herself in control of the scene, setting the stage and delivering a considered preamble, careful not to hurt his feelings, skating over the question of actual infidelity, but noble in the defence of her own right to love and be loved.

The thought that the journalists might have got at him already and put the matter quite another way was a torment to her. She had to stop her car in the woodland at the end of the long drive and breathe deeply and slowly for a few minutes to calm herself.

But inside the Manor all was quiet, with Eva cooking chicken pieces — and meeting Diana with an odd start of confusion — and Philip sitting as usual in his study, running through some business contracts. He greeted her in his normal way, and went back to the paperwork. Diana almost ran upstairs, took sanctuary in the shower, and changed into a plain, indeed rather dowdy, blue knitted jersey dress left over from her time as an MP's wife. It was the sort of dress, she used to say to Lizzie, that one wore when setting out for Sunday church in a barrage of flashbulbs, on the day one's husband was pictured snorting cocaine off a couple of prostitutes. The memory of this joke crossed her mind as she put it on, and made her wince. She was the adulteress now, the target for paparazzi and sneerers.

Over dinner the three of them talked desultorily about the opera and the weather and the latest news on possible war with Iraq. Only at the end of the meal, when they were all drinking coffee in the long sitting-room, did Philip do something strange. He nodded to Eva, who smiled fleetingly, said good-night to Diana, and vanished.

'She's off early,' said Diana.

'I told her I needed to talk to you,' said Philip. 'Privately.'

Diana braced herself. This was it, then. How typical of Philip to play a part — cold and correct — all through a normal evening and only then accost her. Deceitful, frigid man.

She stopped herself. No. Philip was Philip. Perhaps it was even quite kind of him not to make a scene in front of a relative stranger. She composed her face to an expression of polite, but not alarmed, interest.

'Diana,' he said, 'you know that things

between us haven't been so good in recent years.'

It was not the opening she had expected. She blinked.

'Umm . . . well . . . ' she stalled for time. 'You've had a lot of troubles, what with Edmund and the constituency — '

'To hell with them,' said her husband. 'What I mean is that you and I have had very little real communication.'

'I've tried,' said Diana, rather sulkily. Then, in a rush, 'Look, you might as well come right out with it. I presume those reptiles rang you up. And, yes, it's all true. What can I say? It's true. I didn't go looking for it and I couldn't help it. You think I haven't tried, but I have! You're not an easy man, you know.'

She stopped to catch her breath on a treacherous sob, and saw him frowning at her in puzzlement.

'I don't know what on earth you're talking about,' he said. 'What I was getting round to saying is that, with regret, and with all possible respect and gratitude for our past life together, I would like to ask you for a separation leading to divorce. You'll be well looked after financially, of course. But I don't think we should go on pretending that we've got a marriage. It demeans both of us.'

'You want a divorce?' said Diana. 'Why?'

'I've fallen in love,' said Philip simply. 'I don't expect you to understand it or excuse me. I don't even know if the love will come to anything. I feel that it may not. But now that I know what that kind of love is, and how far it has

286

the power to take me, spiritually and morally and in every way — ' His voice, in turn, almost broke: Diana had never heard anything remotely like it. 'Now that I understand that love, I have to be free to follow it. I really am sorry. You'll be looked after as well as it's in my power to do.'

He had not made such a long speech to her for years — unless, she thought wildly, you counted ill-tempered rants about the Prime Minister, which tended to run to several minutes in length. But they were never really addressed to her. This time his eyes were on her, awaiting a response.

'I don't know what to say,' she said feebly.

'I'm sorry. It's a shock. I thought the same about marriage as you: till death us do part, for better, for worse. I suppose I was reconciled to the — the pointless dead flatness of it all. But it's been getting worse for too long now. I've understood things better. We might both be happier if we called it a day, and looked for our own futures.'

Diana found it very hard to explain to herself, or later on to Henry, why she did not come clean at that moment. Even more unaccountable was the question she did not ask, and which only occurred to her an hour later, lying in bed gripped by genuine astonishment and a counterfeit migraine.

'With whom,' she enquired of the empty darkness on Philip's side of the bed, 'do you think you are in love?'

She hoped, although with a pang of shame at the feeling, that it was not Marianne Hamilton.

26

Diana woke with a start from a confused dream of the past. She had been at the school gate, in London, explaining to her daughter about the move to the constituency. Manda had been stamping and crying that it wasn't fair — this, in fact, was as much a memory as a dream. But in the dream Diana kept saying to her, 'We have to go there, we have to put down roots,' and Manda had shouted back, 'What's the point of roots? It's just burying your feet so you can't move!'

She tried to be sure whether this remark, too, was a memory; eventually she decided that it probably was. It sounded like Manda: until she became a laconic, beautiful adolescent she used to have a childishly picturesque turn of phrase. But what Diana could not understand was her own distress, the sense of horror that attached itself to the memory of the dream. Something was teasing nastily at the corner of her consciousness: this often happened to her after bad dreams, and since childhood she had learned that the only way to banish it was to examine and confront it, visualizing it as clearly as possible. She closed her eyes and tried to conjure up the nightmare: after a few moments she could only say for certain that it was white, and tangled, and dead.

Fleetingly she thought of Lizzie: was it an idea of a cancer she was looking at? Then it came to her, with Manda's angry voice overlaying the image again. It was a root. A set of roots, tugged from the soil and dying in the light. Tears squeezed between her eyelids, and trickled down her cheeks to settle annoyingly in her ears. Uprooting, that was it. Philip, without seeming to feel the slightest warmth of sympathy towards her, was putting an end to nearly twenty-five years of marriage, throwing her out like an unsatisfactory pot-plant. What had he said about love? . . . *now that I know what it is, and how far it has the power to take me, spiritually and morally and in every way . . . I have to be free . . .*

And what about her, then? Had she not often had good reason to want freedom, through the long hard years of dancing to his tune, padding him against the cruel shocks of politics, plotting how to cheer him up? What about her 'spiritual and moral' growth and liberty? He had confined her, stamped out her individuality, used her, and now he was throwing her aside. The bastard — the bastard! She tried to think of Henry, but his image had become blurred and indistinct.

She looked over to Philip's side of the vast bed, and saw to her sudden shock that he was not there. Where, then? There were three other free bedrooms, all habitually kept made up, which he could have gone to. It was cold, and she hesitated for a moment, but the childish rage which gripped her was strong enough to propel her out of bed and into her dressing-gown. Knotting the belt, she stumbled across the room — her legs were stiff, these days, after sleep, which seemed a frightening harbinger of age.

Looking down the corridor, she hesitated; no lights showed beneath any of the doors. She padded past Eva's room, and stopped outside the one with the quaint arched doorway where Marianne had slept on the night of the dinner-party. Turning the handle gently, she saw that her instinct had been right. The curtains were not drawn, and in the moonlight glimmer from the window she could see a shape in the bed, and Philip's mop of silver hair. It was, she thought dismally, the first time in their marriage that either of them had deliberately chosen to sleep in another room. She knew that other couples did it after a row had erupted, or even when one had a bad cold and the other was less than sympathetic. She and Philip, however, had merely opted for the ultra-wide bed. Perhaps this in itself was a sign of the flat passionlessness between them: they could not even be bothered to quarrel, or to notice whether the other was sharing the same bed.

She had come for a purpose and decided to fulfil it, although the dignity of moonlight and the peacefulness of his sleeping face made her hesitate for a moment.

'Who is it?' she said, her voice sounding louder than it was in the sleeping house. 'Who?'

He did not stir. She went to the bed and stood over him, pink and angry in her fleecy dressing-gown.

'Philip! Wake up. It's only fair to tell me. Who is this woman?'

He groaned and woke, staring at her with deep blue eyes.

'What?'

'You said last night that you had fallen in love. Who with?'

'Jesus, Diana, it's three o'clock in the morning!'

'Who the *fuck* is she?' Even as she spoke, Diana realized that she did not really want to know. Once she knew, this passion of his — moral, spiritual, whatever the hell he called it, but enough of a passion to burn up decades of marriage like tissues thrown on the fire — would be attached to a real woman. A rival woman. She would know the identity of someone who, unlike her, had unlocked what lay deep within Philip and caused him to talk and act in ways she had never seen. Furious, almost weeping, she repeated the question whose answer would do her such inevitable harm.

'Who — is — she?'

Philip sat up, and smoothed his hair.

'Eva,' he said.

Diana screamed, and choked on the scream.

'She's a *child*. What are you, a *pervert*?'

'She is twenty-two,' said Philip gravely. 'Don't think that this hasn't bothered me, because it has. It does. That's why — '

She cut across him. 'You're making it up, aren't you? To wind me up. You just want to hurt me because, because — because you've messed up your career and — anyway, you're making it up! She wouldn't look at an — an old *fart* like you!'

'No,' said Philip, sadly. 'I'm not making it up.'
She could not bear the pity in his eyes, and
backed away, almost snarling.

'Then why aren't you curled up in bed right
now with your pubescent bloody little darling?'

'Don't be crass,' said her husband. 'It isn't like
that. Eva wouldn't dream of doing that, not yet.
I'm still married, after all. Our courtship is very
new. She's a serious young woman.'

'You're telling me you haven't — ?'

'Certainly not. In fact, it may be that we don't
ever take it in that direction, but in others. I
know I'm too old for her. She says not, but we
both have to give it a lot of thought.'

'What directions? What the hell are you talking
about? Are you senile? Are you or are you not
having an affair with the bloody au pair girl?'

'Maybe,' said Philip, 'it will be what you call
an affair. But for the moment, it is a most joyful
and loving friendship. Eva is going to work with
me as a translator in a charitable foundation I
am setting up with our Warsaw partnership. My
financial partners and I have decided we need to
inject some non-profit-making capital into
Eastern Europe, and kick-start a housing
association movement in the more problematic
areas of the big cities.'

'I thought you were just doing an ordinary
property speculation,' said Diana, so thrown by
this change of tack that she had to shake her
head violently as if to clear physical cobwebs
from around it.

'I was,' said Philip. 'I changed my mind. I
don't want to exploit the rising countries in the

East. I want to help. I want to make a difference. The Adam Mickiewicz Housing Trust will do just that.'

'So you're not having an affair? You're not in love?' She knew she sounded stupid, repeating a question he had answered.

'No, I am not having an affair. But, yes, I am in love.'

'I don't see the connection with your Warsaw deal.'

'To me, it makes perfect sense. Diana, let's both go back to sleep. I'm sorry about all this, I told you that last night. We can go over it in the morning. Go back to bed.'

She had reached the door before he said, in a low warning voice,

'And don't think of going to wake Eva, if you haven't already with all this shouting. None of this is her fault at all. If you start going for her, I won't be able to forgive you.'

Diana went back to her marital bed, and lay there until dawn alone and awake. Two doors down, her dreams only suffering the vaguest of influence from the raised voices, Eva heard doors slamming and woke properly for an instant. But, exhausted by happiness and wonder, she was asleep again in moments.

27

Philip got up early; he had promised Eva that he would tell his wife everything first, before she needed to face her. Eva had protested, saying, 'I must be with you,' but he overrode this, telling her to stay in bed the next day until he woke her with a cup of tea. He had decided to tell Diana the news in small easily digestible increments, if at all possible: unaccustomed to emotional calculation, he had assumed that it would be. Now, with a faint pricking of shame, he realized that this idea had never been feasible. Her nocturnal ambush had put paid to his strategy. When he heard her moving around downstairs, earlier than usual on a Saturday, he knew he must see her and complete the picture. Pulling on a pair of flannel trousers, shirt and sweater, he abandoned his usual morning shower and hurried down. Diana was sitting at the kitchen table, boot-faced, sipping at a cup of scalding tea as if she wanted to get it over with as soon as possible.

'Oh, you're up,' she said coldly. 'I'm going out.'

'We have things to discuss,' said Philip. 'I want to make this as smooth as possible for you.'

'So kind,' she said sharply. She glanced at the clock: the newspapers were due any minute. It was highly unlikely that Philip's broadsheets of choice, *The Times* and *Telegraph*, would have the story; but the tabloid whose reporter had rung the radio station would catch his eye eventually. She knew what she ought to do. She should tell him everything, now, while he was still feeling guilty himself.

Two feelings warred against this course of action, though. One was a sense that he bloody well deserved a shock, having given her one; and the other was pure embarrassment. She, after all, had slept with Henry more than once. Philip, if he was to be believed, was technically faithful and had merely laid his knightly sword and shield at the foot of Eva ('Holy little slut!' said a cruel small voice within her) and planned to waft off with her and do good works in the Warsaw slums. If anyone was on the moral high ground this morning, it was Philip.

Diana could not remember ever feeling so miserable. She was shocked, wrong-footed, put down, shamed and rejected all at once. She bore both the guilt and embarrassment of the secret adulteress and the outrage and resentment of the innocent injured wife. It was insupportable. Tears welled in her eyes, and Philip took a hesitant step towards her.

'I'm so sorry,' he said, groping for unaccustomed words. 'I told you everything the wrong way. Please, please don't think it's because of you. It's all been my fault, my years of obsession with bloody politics, my failure to understand you or to look outward at the rest of the human race . . . ' Even as he spoke, he realized that without Eva, without all he had learnt from her in these short weeks, he would not have been able even to begin framing such an apology. He felt like a baby learning to walk: unsteady, exhilarated, unpredictable.

Diana jumped up. 'I'm off,' she said abruptly. 'Got to see Lizzie.'

'Is she worse?' asked Philip, attempting solicitude.

'Fat lot you care,' said his wife, and snatching her car keys off the hook, marched out into the muddy winter morning.

Philip sighed, made two cups of tea, and went upstairs to sit on Eva's bed.

★   ★   ★

Ten minutes later, Diana walked into the newsagent's in the village and before she even saw the headline, knew that hope was vain. The story had indeed broken. Three sets of neighbourly eyes rested on her momentarily then slid away; she knew that look of old, from Philip's travails with the press. Behind the counter Mr Armitage handed her the paper and took her money with a crooked attempt at his normal smile, then hurried into the back room in reply to a clearly imaginary call from his wife.

She retreated into the car with the paper, but after a first glance put it down and drove out of the village street, to park up a field track beyond prying eyes. It was worse, far worse, than she could ever have thought. Philip's whole history was there, with pictures of him with two Prime Ministers and a shot of the jailed director of Fanfair Finance, and the famous snatched photograph of Philip trying to hide his face in his raincoat as he left 10, Downing Street after his sacking as a minister.

Henry's history — wildly embroidered — was also fully laid out: found under a tree in Windsor Great Park, adopted, spotted in a 'notorious gangsta rap club' (she knew it was no such thing, but a rather decorous South London youth club disco), snapped up in his mid-twenties by the local radio group of which Two Counties was the star. There was a shot of him interviewing the new MP who had deposed Philip ('lots to talk about' sniggered the caption 'since both were taking over from Hunton-Hall in their own way'). There was a picture of him looking about twenty, with his shirt hanging open to reveal a bare muscular chest with HEZ picked out on it in stick-on sequins and a regrettable gold medallion. There was a highly flattering picture of Alissa, holding Marley, and reams of lurid material about the stabbing, Donny's drug habit and untimely death.

The main picture of Diana was particularly unfortunate. Taken just before Philip's election defeat in 2001, it showed her in a mumsy suit with a silly little peplum waist which she had always hated, sporting a rather stiff perm instead of her current tousled blonde crop, and looking sideways at Philip in the immemorial manner of devoted political wives. 'The look of love,' said the caption, 'in happier times.' Unkindly, next to this terrible picture, the layout designer had dropped in a quote from Henry saying 'Diana is a beautiful woman'.

Altogether, the reports ran to four full pages. When she had read them all Diana took a deep breath, ran her hand through her hair, and reached unsteadily for her mobile.

'Henry?' she croaked. 'Have you seen it?'

'Not yet,' said a blithe young voice. 'Got to pick up Marley. You coming over?'

'You haven't even *looked?*' said Diana incredulously.

'Well, you know the sort of crap they write in advance, really, don't you?' said Henry, still sounding unworried. 'I'll catch up with it later. Don't worry, beautiful. Honestly. It's a nine-day wonder.'

'I had a shock when I got home last night,' said Diana, close to tears. 'Philip's asked for a divorce.'

'Well, that's fabulous. He isn't going to slow things down, then? Brilliant.'

'No,' said Diana, staring at her misted windscreen and breathing hard. 'He asked for the divorce before I told him about us. I mean, I haven't even told him yet. He'll probably hear about the newspaper report first. He wants a divorce because he's in love with the Polish girl. The housekeeper. Manda's penfriend.'

This time there was a brief silence. Then, 'Wow!' said Henry respectfully. 'You mean Eva? Nice girl, made us those spicy burger things? Marley's still barracking for me or Ali to get the recipe.'

'Did you hear what I said?' she squeaked. 'He's in love with her! Artful little minx!'

'Chill,' said the faint, still cool and amused

298

voice. 'That's good! Weird, coincidence, but good. Think about it — everyone happy! No guilt! You're free! C'mon, baby, celebrate!'

She rang off; and then, because she had never put down a phone on him in the whole brief history of their love, rang straight back again, but his mobile must have gone out of range. Pushing away the veil of tears with her sleeve, she drove on; and twenty minutes later, heard Lizzie Morgan say much the same as Henry had done. She was lying on the sofa wrapped up in a bright blue fun-fur blanket with a pattern of polar bears on it, her teenage son and daughter sprawled on the floor beside her. They stayed in the room while Diana broke her news, and she did not like to banish them; Marie and Freddie, she thought, had the right to spend every minute they wanted beside their fading mother.

Neither showed any sign of tactfully removing themselves. While she told Lizzie about the scenes of the night before they listened with politely veiled interest, though Freddie was fiddling with a computer game at the same time. When it became apparent that her own lover was Henry from 2C Radio, Marie's face betrayed incredulous amusement, but with natural good manners she immediately concealed it.

'I think it could be for the best,' said Lizzie at last. 'You and Henry don't have to go through all that guilt stuff about whether to leave Philip. Couldn't have come out better, really.'

'Then why do I feel so terrible?' asked Diana bleakly.

'Shock?'

'Maybe. It's just that Philip's so different. Sort of alive, and feeling, and thinking about other people. She's done something for him in what — four weeks? — which I couldn't achieve in two decades'.

'Well, Henry did something for you in a week that Philip never managed in two decades,' pointed out Lizzie, reasonably. 'Fair's fair.'

'Yes, but — the waste!' wailed Diana. 'Our whole lives!'

'Come on,' said Lizzie. 'That's life for you. Sometimes the good bits come at the end, sometimes at the beginning, sometimes it's all good but it just stops all the same. Learn to roll with it.'

'But I don't know that I want to,' sobbed Diana. 'At the moment, I just — I just want everything back the way it was.'

'Before Henry? Before you fell in love? Oh, get a grip,' began Lizzie, her thin dry voice showing irritation; but at this point Marie got up, stretched gracefully, and announced her intention of going to the kitchen to make some coffee for anyone who wanted it.

'I'll have my herbal stuff,' said Lizzie. 'Now look, Diana — '

A moment later, though, and before Lizzie could complete her scolding, Marie came back with the news that Marianne Hamilton was in the kitchen, crying on Andy and shouting something about religious education, hypocrites and sacking the bastard, all of which meant that she couldn't get at the kettle.

'Oh, I am going to miss all this,' said Lizzie

300

with a sigh. 'Do you think you're allowed violent emotional scenes in Heaven? Do you suppose there's a Flaming Row Channel which you can tune into on Heaven TV, like a sort of permanent run of *Footballers' Wives?*'

'I can't face Marianne,' said Diana. 'Oh, Lizzie, I'm so sorry — I shouldn't be burdening you with all this and I ought to stay to help with poor Madge, but I can't — '

'Get out the front door then, quick,' said Marie, jerking her head towards a heavy tread in the hall. 'She's on the way through. I just saw Dad escaping down the garden path.'

★ ★ ★

At Garton Manor, Philip and Eva ate toast together in the kitchen, and talked about their plans.

'It is sad that you must sell the Manor,' said Eva. 'It is so beautiful and peaceful.'

'Our lives here haven't been beautiful or peaceful,' said Philip, a little sadly. 'Better to give someone else a try with it.'

'I feel it is because of me, my fault, that you must do this.' Eva put her hand on his.

'No. But it's up to Diana anyway,' said Philip. 'She should have the house. It's worth about half my remaining capital, not counting the pension fund which she also gets half of. So she'll probably want to sell rather than pay the upkeep. There won't be as much else to play around with as there might have been because of what's been committed to the Trust. But I can afford a small

301

flat in London or a little house outside. If that's what you want. We ought to be near London for the airports, and to keep an eye on the partnership.'

'I cannot get accustomed to thinking that it is 'we', you and me,' said Eva. 'It is too soon, and too confusing. I think we must stay separate, independent. It does not stop our loving.'

'The other alternative is to live in Poland and come over for business meetings,' said Philip. 'Live close to the project. That might suit rather well.'

'You would live in Poland?' said Eva incredulously. 'Leave England?'

'Yes,' said Philip thoughtfully. 'I think I would. I might rather like it. I could learn the language. It's time I learnt something new, from the beginning. Keeps your brain alive when you get older. And this is such a bad-tempered, cross little old country these days. If I had my books and my music, and you nearby . . . '

'No,' said Eva. 'To move like that is too much. You would be sad. I know what it is like to miss your homeland.'

'Yes, but I'm older than you. I've got more of my homeland wired into my bones and blood. Poor child, you uprooted yourself before you'd had time to flower. You've been lonely here, haven't you?'

'But I am young, I can change.'

'I can change too. I have changed.'

'No, you must live mostly in England,' said Eva firmly. 'You must live here, and I will live often here while this strange love is alive.'

302

'Fair enough. I do know that it might not be forever.'

'I want to love you forever.'

'Sweet.'

They held hands across the table, smiling into one another's eyes. Eva frowned, after a moment, and said, 'I have to write to my father about all this. He will not be happy.'

'Why?'

'You are married. We are a Catholic family'

'You said you didn't go to church?'

'That's true. I don't like priests now. They always talk about politics and government things, never about the spirit. And my father is angry about them not fighting the communists hard enough. But he likes the Pope. And we are still Catholic. Marriage is very serious.'

'Would you like me to come over and see him?'

Eva considered, then said a brief, 'No.' Then, flushing slightly, she said: 'Anyway, nothing is needed because we are not married and we are not making love.'

'I would like to marry you. And make love to you. You know that. But only if you were sure. I am so old!'

'I would like to marry you. But I don't know if it's right. I think I would feel too sad and guilty about Mrs Hunton-Hall.'

Philip picked up her hand and kissed it. 'Me too,' he said. 'I haven't been much of a husband for the last twenty years. I'm amazed I have the effrontery even to suggest that you — '

The doorbell rang. Surprised, he got up and

wandered towards the front door, relaxed, still smiling.

'Mr Hunton-Hall, sorry to trouble you,' said the man on the doorstep, and stepped smartly sideways: from behind him, coming out of the laurel bushes, two photographers fired off motor-drive volleys, their flashes surreal against the grey morning. 'We're just doing a bit of a follow-up on this morning's story.'

Eva appeared behind Philip, and because he seemed to be trembling from the surprise, laid a loving hand on his shoulder and stood close. The motor-drives whirred and rattled once more.

★ ★ ★

The habit of dignified affront was not easy to abandon after half a lifetime. When Philip had been made to understand what the reporters were there for, he sat for a while staring down at the headlines in the paper, struggling with his emotions. Eva was beside him, calm but a little confused; her presence alone made him guard his tongue and his temper. The reporters, a middle-aged man and a young sharp-featured woman, sat passive and watchful: he had, in the end, let two of them in to sit at the kitchen table simply because he needed to see the newspaper they brought with them.

'Well,' he said eventually, 'I think I'll reserve my position. I haven't had an opportunity to discuss this with my wife.'

'Is she living here?' asked the male reporter.

'Was she here last night?' asked the woman.

'Of course,' said Philip. 'She lives here. I told you, I have to discuss this with her before I say anything to you. You'd better go.'

'And this young lady? I noticed she was comforting you at the door — your daughter?'

They knew she was not: Manda's white-blonde coolness featured often enough in the society pages.

'I am Eva Borkowska from Wroclaw,' said Eva. 'I am staying here to learn English.'

'Pretty thoroughly, by the look of it,' said the man, and Philip rose to his feet, white with anger.

'I told you, get out!'

'*In his £40,000 state of the art kitchen,*' wrote the woman reporter in her head, '*comforted by a mystery East European brunette of very tender years indeed, Philip Hunton-Hall seemed less than anxious to bring home his erring wife. Sauce for the goose, as they say in the countryside, is sauce for the gander. And rural entanglements don't come much saucier . . .*'

It was as if he saw the words running through a bubble over her head, like a surtitle at the opera.

'Out!' said Philip. 'Now!'

'We'll leave you the newspaper,' said the man kindly. 'For reference.'

28

The launch of the Adam Mickiewicz Housing
Trust was a low-key affair; two broadsheet
newspapers turned up, one tabloid, an internationalist magazine, a reporter from Radio 4 and
a BBC World Service producer who was making
a programme about the initiative. A well-known
actor of Polish ancestry recited part of the
Mackenzie translation of 'Pan Tadeusz' while the
journalists, a little bemused, riffled in their press
releases to find out the relevance of ' . . . *vari-
painted cornfields like a quilt, The silver of the
rye, the wheatfields' gilt*' to an urban regenera-
tion and social housing scheme in Warsaw. When
he came to an end, sonorously hymning ' . . . *a
grassy band Of green, whereon the silent pear
trees stand*', they shifted in their seats and
started on the questions. Philip answered them
with patience.

'Where's the money coming from?'

'The first three million from a private
donation. After that we have some venture
capital at a very good rate, and we're hoping for
input from US charities.'

'Who was the private donor?'

'That's not being made public.'

'Any truth in the rumour that you are in fact
the private donor?'

'No comment.'

'Mr Hunton-Hall,' said the tabloid reporter,

'in reports of your proposed divorce it was suggested that you had disposed of a large part of your private fortune just before your marriage failed, and that this had seriously disadvantaged your wife of many years. May I ask if there's any connection here?'

'You may ask all you like. But none of that is any business of the media.'

'Your daughter Amanda has given an interview . . .'

'I'm well aware of that. No comment. My daughter's views are all her own.'

The reporter continued as if he had not spoken ' . . . an interview in which she said, and I'm quoting here, that you've 'gone senile over some Polish girl and given away' her inheritance.'

'I'm sure she said no such thing,' said Philip smoothly. 'Newspaper quotes can be dreadfully misleading, as you no doubt know. The main point we are trying to get across today is that although what this Trust is able to do is only a drop in the ocean, I hope it will be a start. In a situation where there is a widespread problem of low-quality crumbling communist-built housing in Eastern European cities, and on the eve of at least one historic ally joining the European Union, it befits us to set up partnerships to kick-start a building programme in the interests of harmonizing standards of living.'

'Why not build housing for people in Britain?' asked the internationalist magazine. 'Charity begins at home, and all that?' The other journalists looked at him gratefully: they knew he was only asking the question in order to get a strong answer, but none of the rest would have liked to be the mouthpiece of such a sentiment.

'While I would never belittle the distress caused by this government's failure to tackle homelessness — ' began Philip.

'And your Conservative government's equal failure!' snapped the left-wing broadsheet crossly.

' — I feel that we should acknowledge the great inequalities between those countries lucky enough to entertain democracy and a dynamic market economy this past half-century, and those which were trapped in a retrogressive, stagnant communist rut. We are all Europeans. Our cultural inheritance is a common jewel, and to me, if I may speak personally, a lifelong inspiration. The music of Chopin and Kodaly, the plays of Vaclav Havel, the poetry of Mickiewicz . . . '

The reporters scribbled dutifully. It was quite a good story. Millionaire ex-MP Devotes Fortune to Polish Charity. Eighties Fat-Cat Turns Philanthropist. Family Rift Over Charity Handover. 'Address inequalities of Iron Curtain legacy,' Says Tory Grandee. 'Cultural Debt to Lost Europeans'.

It would do. It would make a talking-point. 'A bit like that educational philanthropist bloke who pays for bright slum kids to go to posh schools,' said the Radio 4 man, as the gaggle of reporters filed out. 'Anyway, I can't see the catch, and the Polish Ambassador looked pretty pleased. They're using local staff to administer it, it's not some bureaucratic job-creation scheme like the EU stuff.'

'That quote from the daughter . . . there was something about a Polish girl in the red-tops a couple of months back,' mused the senior broadsheet man. 'Can't quite remember it now. When his wife ran off with that rap DJ or whatever. P'raps there's a romantic angle?'

'I dunno,' said the other. 'He's a dry old stick. Bit of a bore, really. Not his style.'

★ ★ ★

Diana looked around her at the long empty living-room. It was, if possible, even more beautiful without the furniture: its proportions perfect, the frosty landscape framed in the windows more poignant. Behind her, the last tea-chests were being carried across the hall by aproned removal men. The sale had happened far too quickly for her comfort, but Philip, ever solicitous albeit at a distance, had warned her that property prices were likely to drop sharply in the New Year, and that the offer of £850,000 she had received in the first week of advertising was one she would do well to accept. It seemed he was right as usual about financial matters, for the newspapers had now begun to say the same thing almost every week.

She wandered into the empty, dusty hallway. The kitchen door was ajar, and she could hear a clink of mugs: wandering through, she found Marianne making tea.

'Good, you kept the kettle out,' she said thankfully. 'Clever.'

Marianne handed her a mug, and called out to the removers that there were three mugs for them on the table.

'Come into the garden,' she said. 'Don't look around too much. Doesn't do to get mawkish.'

'I'm fine. I don't know what I'd have done without you, these past few weeks.'

'Nonsense! It's kept me sane. I'm really sorry about the state I got in after Tony came back that day.'

'Well, I'm sorry about your car.'

'I was drunk. I shouldn't have been anywhere near a car. It's lucky I managed to write it off before I got to the end of Lizzie's drive. I tell you, I'm never going to touch another drop. Probably.'

Holding their warm mugs the two women wandered down the path, towards the little gate that led to the field, the stream, and the pasture where the black-faced sheep wandered disconsolately around in search of wisps from the morning's dump of hay. Diana gazed at the sheep for a minute, her eyes filling with tears.

'Well, thanks anyway,' she said. 'I'm glad you came to stay. It was all such a muddle for a while.'

'I think Philip behaved despicably,' said Marianne. 'Going off like that, with that Polish slut!'

'No,' said Diana sadly, 'not a slut. They're still not living together, you know. I don't think they even sleep together. Certainly they didn't at first. It's a sort of old-fashioned courtship. I don't begin to understand it. But then, I don't

310

begin to understand Philip.'

'Brains in their trousers, all of them,' muttered Marianne, and Diana let it go, because she had grown fond of the kind tipsy bumbling woman who had been at her side during these weeks. Lizzie understood the complexities of her failed marriage better, but Lizzie was weak now and preferred to talk affectionately over old times, student days, and all their children's babyhoods. Diana's last gift to her friend, she thought bleakly, was keeping quiet about her present unhappiness.

'Well, thanks anyway, Madge. For everything. Are you going to sell up too, once I've got myself out of your hair?'

'No,' said Marianne. 'I like my house. Tony's in that flat in town — did I tell you he's over an Indian takeaway? Couldn't happen to a nicer creep. The money's tight, but I think I'll have some lodgers. We're near enough to the university campus to have students. A bit of young life would be fun.' She slid her eyes sideways and asked, hesitantly: 'Talking of young life, how's Manda getting on with it all?'

'I think,' said Amanda's mother sadly, 'that she shot her bolt with that interview in the *Mirror*. No word from her since. Art did ring, to sort of apologize, but I told him it was Philip they should apologize to. She's been more than generously provided for, and she had no right to say those things. I suppose she'll come round. I wrote to her.'

'She'll come round,' said Marianne, kindly.

Diana stood, looking down the field, and

311

sipped at her tea. She felt empty. This was it, then: this was what came of headlong self-abnegating love at twenty-one, years of bright anxious faithfulness, and a second headlong love at forty-four. You thought you were defying everything, changing the face of your world, cracking the stale earth open with the fire of your passion to form a new marvellous virgin continent. But the land crumbled beneath your feet and, rootless, you succumbed to a wave of killing cowardice. Panic, shame, confusion, but above all cowardice. She replayed, for the hundredth time, the last scenes with Henry before she resigned from her job and withdrew into the Manor with Marianne.

'*You see where it's brought us? You see how impossible it always was?*'

'*I don't see that at all. Diana, sweet one, it's fine. Chill!*'

'*You see how people look at me? You see what they think? Even the bloody Guardian's having a go now.*'

'*Who cares?*'

'*I care. You'd care, if you cared about me. The only chance is for us just to go — London, anywhere. Now.*'

'*Sweetheart, I have to work. I haven't got a job in London. Nor have you. There's Marley to think about. And pay for. Come on, we can tough it out.*'

They could have done, she thought now. If she had had the courage to hold her head high, stay at work, step out openly with Henry and spit at the press, they would still be together. Instead

312

she had fled, hidden at home on the pretext of selling the house, and put up barriers against him, as well as the world. He had rung her, several times.

Diana, it's me. Don't hang up.

Diana, what's happening? This isn't like you. I love you. Come home.

Diana, this is doing my head in. Let me come round, just to talk.

The calls had stopped, two weeks into the siege, just as she was about to concede defeat and open her arms to him again. Just as she was about to forgive him. In the pain and confusion of that time she had genuinely convinced herself there was something in Henry to forgive: insensitivity, flippancy, insouciance about her losses. Now, after weeks of silent aridity during which she could not even bear to switch on the radio lest she hear his voice, she saw that in reality poor Henry had been as mature and reasonable and kind as any woman could possibly expect. But he had given up on her: who wouldn't?

Finishing their tea, the two women turned back to the gutted house, and gathered the kettle and mugs into the plastic box Marianne had organized for this purpose. Diana glanced round the lovely kitchen for the last time.

'I never really cooked here, those last few weeks,' she said. 'Only Eva did. Wonderful things. Spicy, mincey, cabbagey Polish things. It was like a sort of magic, wafting round us. I think it turned all our heads.'

'Come on,' said Marianne. 'Let's go. We'll pick

up a video and a Chinese, and make a night of it. It's been hard work, all this packing.'

The furniture was going into store, with most of Diana's possessions. With a large suitcase and a hatbox full of oddments, she was to stay for a while at Marianne's while she considered what to do. Unspoken between the friends was the understanding that the probable trigger for her leaving the area would be the death of Lizzie. The two women climbed into the car, Diana in the driving seat. As she was letting off the handbrake, her mobile bleeped.

'Oh, read it, would you?' she said, slipping into gear. 'It'll be the confirmation from the storage company.'

Marianne jabbed the 'yes' button on the phone, and peered longsightedly at the display.

'It's not,' she said. 'It's personal.'

Diana stepped on the brake, the car skidding slightly on the muddy gravel.

'Manda?' she said

'No.' Marianne handed the phone to its owner, her plucked eyebrows raised.

COME HOME, it said. WE GOT THE BIG HAMSTER BALL SO WE CAN ALL FIT INSIDE NOW. I BUST THE SMALL ONE. MARLEY.

29

'Maybe we needed that space,' said Diana to Henry. They were sitting in the children's playground on a misty spring afternoon, watching Marley swinging by his knees from a wooden frame shaped like a galleon. 'Maybe we needed that really bad month.'

'I didn't,' said Henry. 'I nearly bloody topped myself.'

'Was the text message really from Marley? I never dared ask.'

'No. I'm that kind of dishonest, exploitative parent,' said Henry smugly. 'But he did say, when I bought the big rolly-ball, that we could all fit in it. So I thought, one last throw of the dice . . . '

'I behaved very badly. I think I'd have rung you within another couple of weeks to eat dirt.'

'We've been through all this. Shush.' He looked at her, thinking how much more he loved her for her time of weakness, and how satisfyingly it evened them out in terms of maturity. These things should not be a competition, thought Henry, but all the same it helped.

'It was Philip, you see,' said Diana. 'It unhinged me a bit.'

'Did you see him on Newsnight that time? Bloody impressive, I thought.'

'Yes. He never used to be that good on TV

when he was in Parliament, but I was rather moved.'

'Found something to believe in, I suppose. Is he still with the girl?'

'It's all pretty mysterious. He flies out to Poland a lot. I think she's based there, doing research in her home town for the next building project or something.'

'But they're an item?'

'Henry,' said Diana fondly, 'you have got to learn that not everything in life is that clear.'

* * *

In the great square of Rynek, the strollers were out again in the first warm days of spring, and the awnings ready for hardy outdoor diners. The city stretched, and yawned, and enjoyed the first blush of sunshine on her tall Flemish gables and warm pink plasterwork. She was Vratsao, Wratislavia, Breslau, Wroclaw; she had seen armies come and go, languages change, sieges and betrayals, emperors and kings and commissars and priests and a Führer. She had endured floods and starvation and bombs and destruction and rebuilding, and shrugged off every insolence. She always knew that the ant-like people who made her would be back, in some guise or another, to recreate what others had destroyed. Everything had happened to her already, so there was little to fear.

Eva Danuta Krystyna Borkowska, citizeness of Wroclaw, all the more Polish for having seen the lands beyond the city's horizon, walked swiftly through the square towards the small office which linked her by fax and internet to the world. In a frame on her desk there, the words of the national poet and namesake of the Trust were inscribed not in Polish but in English, and not formally but in the neat italic handwriting taught to upper-class Englishmen at school half a century before:

Then shoulder to shoulder! Let us engirdle the little circle of the earth with the chains that bind us to each other. To one end let us aim our thoughts, and to one end let us aim our souls. Hail, dawn of liberty, behind thee is the redeeming sun!

'It loses in the translation,' Philip had said apologetically.

'I don't think so,' said Eva. 'I think it gains.'

THE END